BLOODLUST BITES

BOOKS BY LUANNE BENNETT

The Charley Underwood series
Bloodlust Blues

The Fitheach Trilogy
The Amulet Thief
The Blood Thief
The Destiny Thief

The Katie Bishop Series
Crossroads of Bones
Blackthorn Grove
Shifter's Moon
Dark Nightingale
Bayou Kings
Conjure Queen
Dirt Witch
Daddy Darkest

House of Winterborne Series
Dark Legacy
Savage Sons
King's Reckoning

The Chronicles of Jesse Ames
Red Widow

Gods & Savages

Open Season

BLOODLUST BITES

LUANNE BENNETT

SECOND SKY

Published by Second Sky in 2024

An imprint of Storyfire Ltd.
Carmelite House
50 Victoria Embankment
London EC4Y 0DZ
United Kingdom

www.secondskybooks.com

Copyright © Luanne Bennett, 2024

Luanne Bennett has asserted her right to be identified
as the author of this work.

All rights reserved. No part of this publication may be reproduced, stored in any retrieval system, or transmitted, in any form or by any means, electronic, mechanical, photocopying, recording or otherwise, without the prior written permission of the publishers.

ISBN: 978-1-83525-874-3
eBook ISBN: 978-1-83525-873-6

This book is a work of fiction. Names, characters, businesses, organizations, places and events other than those clearly in the public domain are either the product of the author's imagination or are used fictitiously. Any resemblance to actual persons, living or dead, events or locales is entirely coincidental.

For Bobby. It went by so fast.

For Bobby. It went by so fast.

ONE

I went still when I saw the front door of the Stag ajar. I hadn't even gotten my key all the way into the lock before it started to open on its own. After stepping inside, I noticed the light on in the kitchen through the order window.

"Dog?"

His pickup wasn't out front, but sometimes Dog parked around back and came in through the alley. But it was barely seven a.m. The sun wasn't even up yet. Dog rarely got to the Stag before ten. Sometimes earlier on delivery days. I'd come in to catch up on some admin stuff, but there was no reason for him to be here yet or any of my other employees.

I walked into the hallway and pushed the kitchen door open, half expecting to see Dog walk out of the pantry. The kitchen was empty, but someone had gone through it like a hurricane. There were busted dishes everywhere, and the cabinets and the refrigerator were open. Whoever did this was looking for something, and I had a good idea of what it was.

A sound came from down the hallway. I grabbed a knife and walked back out of the kitchen, gripping it so tightly my fingers were starting to turn white. Someone was in the back room.

"I have a gun, so you better take yourself out that back door!" I yelled as I crept toward the room. "We don't keep product in the bar, so you're wasting your time." They were probably after the co-op's blood supply, which we didn't keep in the bar for good reason.

The noise went silent. My hand shook as I reached for the knob, but the door swung open before I could grab it. Standing on the other side were the two men who'd been looking for Tucker a few nights ago.

The knife slipped from my grip as one of them grabbed me by my shirt and slung me against the wall, pinning me to it by my neck with a cold hand.

A smile slid up his face. "Where is she?"

I could barely breathe, let alone speak, so he finally let up enough for me to get a word out. "I already told you. I don't know the woman you're looking for." I wasn't proud of it, but I thought I was getting pretty good at lying lately. At least at telling white lies. But when his grip tightened again, I knew he wasn't buying it.

"Our employer doesn't take kindly to liars." He patted my cheek roughly. "You don't want to find out what he does to people who lie to him, so you really should fess up now while you still can."

The other guy, the one with the jet-black hair, was leaning against the desk with a stone-cold look on his face.

I heard the sound of a gun cocking near the door. "And *you* don't want to find out what we do around here to strangers who threaten our own." Beau was standing in the doorway with a rifle in his hands. The one I kept behind the seat of my truck. He pointed the barrel at the other guy when he pushed away from the desk and walked toward him. "That's close enough!"

"Take it easy." The man held his hands up. "We're on our

ONE

I went still when I saw the front door of the Stag ajar. I hadn't even gotten my key all the way into the lock before it started to open on its own. After stepping inside, I noticed the light on in the kitchen through the order window.

"Dog?"

His pickup wasn't out front, but sometimes Dog parked around back and came in through the alley. But it was barely seven a.m. The sun wasn't even up yet. Dog rarely got to the Stag before ten. Sometimes earlier on delivery days. I'd come in to catch up on some admin stuff, but there was no reason for him to be here yet or any of my other employees.

I walked into the hallway and pushed the kitchen door open, half expecting to see Dog walk out of the pantry. The kitchen was empty, but someone had gone through it like a hurricane. There were busted dishes everywhere, and the cabinets and the refrigerator were open. Whoever did this was looking for something, and I had a good idea of what it was.

A sound came from down the hallway. I grabbed a knife and walked back out of the kitchen, gripping it so tightly my fingers were starting to turn white. Someone was in the back room.

"I have a gun, so you better take yourself out that back door!" I yelled as I crept toward the room. "We don't keep product in the bar, so you're wasting your time." They were probably after the co-op's blood supply, which we didn't keep in the bar for good reason.

The noise went silent. My hand shook as I reached for the knob, but the door swung open before I could grab it. Standing on the other side were the two men who'd been looking for Tucker a few nights ago.

The knife slipped from my grip as one of them grabbed me by my shirt and slung me against the wall, pinning me to it by my neck with a cold hand.

A smile slid up his face. "Where is she?"

I could barely breathe, let alone speak, so he finally let up enough for me to get a word out. "I already told you. I don't know the woman you're looking for." I wasn't proud of it, but I thought I was getting pretty good at lying lately. At least at telling white lies. But when his grip tightened again, I knew he wasn't buying it.

"Our employer doesn't take kindly to liars." He patted my cheek roughly. "You don't want to find out what he does to people who lie to him, so you really should fess up now while you still can."

The other guy, the one with the jet-black hair, was leaning against the desk with a stone-cold look on his face.

I heard the sound of a gun cocking near the door. "And *you* don't want to find out what we do around here to strangers who threaten our own." Beau was standing in the doorway with a rifle in his hands. The one I kept behind the seat of my truck. He pointed the barrel at the other guy when he pushed away from the desk and walked toward him. "That's close enough!"

"Take it easy." The man held his hands up. "We're on our

way out of town and just thought we'd stop by to give you a second look at that picture. See if the woman is starting to look familiar."

Beau adjusted his aim. "Oh yeah? Maybe you should have thought to stop by when the bar is open."

Before I could give Beau a look to shut him up, the stranger leaped forward and the rifle was out of Beau's hands and pointed back at him. "What the—?" He looked down at his hands in disbelief.

The man pressed the muzzle to the spot between Beau's eyes. "Hesitation will get you killed, boy. If you're going to point a gun at someone, you better have the guts to use it." A crooked grin slid up his face. "Like I do."

The guy pinning me to the wall suddenly backed off, letting go of my neck. Without pulling his eyes away from mine, he reached for the gun barrel and lowered it from Beau's face. Then he looked at his friend and flicked his head toward the door.

The other guy handed the gun back to Beau as if he'd just borrowed it for a second. "Looks like this is your lucky day." Then he followed his buddy out the door and disappeared down the hallway.

Beau stood there for a moment looking like he'd shit his pants. He nearly dropped the gun as he set it on the desk with shaking hands and went back out to the bar to make sure they were gone.

I followed him into the hallway but suddenly felt shaky myself from all the adrenaline racing through me. Like I wanted to throw up. As I braced myself against the wall, a hand gripped my shoulder from behind. I spun around, slamming my palm into Dog's chest. He flew into the back room as a jolt of energy traveled across my arm and into his.

As he hit the floor, the wolf came out. Then it disappeared, leaving an angry Dog glaring at me as he climbed to his feet.

"Christ, Charley." After catching his breath, he came back into the hallway, keeping his distance this time. "What the hell did you do that for?"

Beau reappeared and looked at the two of us. "Did I miss something?"

"Yeah. Charley just tried to fry me."

"I'm sorry," I said. "But you oughta know better by now than to sneak up on me like that." He'd come in through the alley. "What are you doing here this early?"

He nodded to a crate on the floor in the back room. "I swung by to drop off that vodka and gin you asked me to buy last night. I've got some errands to run this morning, and driving around with a case of booze in my truck is a bad idea. Wouldn't want to give Murphy a hard-on if he pulls me over."

I'd forgotten about that. My distributor had shorted the bar's alcohol delivery yesterday afternoon, and my customers liked their tonics. "Yeah, no kidding. Thanks for picking it up."

"You looked like you were about to hit the floor when I walked into the hallway, so I was trying to catch you." Then he looked at Beau. "What's your excuse for showing up so early?"

That was a good question. It was the early-bird special around here today, and miraculously nobody got killed. "Yeah. Shouldn't you be rolling out of bed in about three hours from now?"

He walked behind the bar and started looking for something, finally holding up his cell phone to kiss it. "Thank God. I thought I lost it. I was so tired last night when I got home, I didn't even realize it was missing." Then he put his hands on his hips and nodded his head. "It's a good thing I didn't come back for it last night or you'd still be fending off them thugs in the back room."

"Thugs?" Dog squinted at me. "What's he talking about?"

I released a long breath. "Remember those guys who came in here the other night flashing that picture of Tucker? They decided to come back this morning and let themselves in. They're still looking for her." I rubbed my sore neck. "I came in early to get some work done and interrupted their fact-finding mission."

Beau shook his head. "Bastards. I heard them threatening you back there when I walked in and remembered that rifle you keep in your truck."

"Why didn't you just grab Louie?" That's what he called the gun he kept under the front seat of his car, and he probably would have stood a better chance of not having it snatched out of his hands.

"It's in my nightstand." He shrugged. "You know. With all this crazy stuff going on around town lately, I sleep easier having it under my pillow at night."

One of these days he was going to shoot something he ought not be shooting.

"They threatened you?" Dog said.

"If you call slamming me against a wall a threat, then I guess so."

"And you didn't try to fry them?" He rubbed his chest and winced. "Jesus, Charley, you decked me for just touching your shoulder."

"I don't know!" I was getting frustrated. "You know I can't control it. Besides, just as things were getting hairy, they left. One minute Beau had a rifle pointed at them, and the next, they'd disarmed him and were walking out the door."

"What were they looking for at the crack of dawn?"

I shrugged. "I think they were just trying to send me a warning by busting up the place, and I happened to walk in on them before they got to the liquor bottles behind the bar." The memory of the last time someone broke in and trashed the place sent a chill through me. "By the way, they tore the kitchen up. I guess they thought they'd find Tucker stuffed in the refrigerator."

Dog glanced at the kitchen door. "This isn't funny, Charley."

"I know that." It also didn't make sense. "If they're convinced I know where Tucker is, then I'm sure they've been watching the bar. They have to know she works here by now."

Beau's brow furrowed. "So why go to all the trouble to break in here and threaten you? They could just snatch her off the street on her way to work or follow her home."

I shook my head. "I don't know. I've been asking myself that same question."

Dog had a knowing look on his face. "I do."

"What are you talking about?"

"It's the pack. Those bastards didn't smell right when they showed up here the other night, so we've been keeping an eye on Tucker ever since. I figured better safe than sorry, at least until we confirmed that they'd left town. I guess it was the right call."

It looked like leaving town wasn't their plan. "Does Tucker know she has wolves tailing her?"

"Not yet, but I think it's time we tell her."

It was time for more than that. Tucker was hiding something, and it wasn't just her ability to peek into the future at random moments in time. She had some serious explaining to do. After closing tonight, she was going to come clean if I had to force it out of her myself.

TWO

Tucker hurried down the bar with a drink in her hand. She set it in front of a customer and started back toward the register.

"Hey," the man called out to her.

She turned around with a sigh. "What?"

"I didn't order this." He tapped his finger against the side of the glass. "I ordered a beer."

Seeming to get her head together, she went back down the bar and grabbed the drink. "Sorry about that." After setting the bourbon in front of the correct customer, she walked over to the tap. She topped off his draft with several inches of unnecessary foam and started to turn around. Every eye in the place shot to the bar as the glass slipped from her grip and shattered on the floor, spraying beer everywhere.

After watching it all unfold through the order window, I shoved a broken plate into the trash can and headed for the kitchen door. "That's it. I'm not waiting until we close to talk to her. We've got enough broken glass in here, and I can't afford any more."

The woman had been a bag of nerves ever since those men first showed up a few days ago. Worse than a cat negotiating a pack of hungry pit bulls, and it was time to get the truth out of her. There was more to the story she'd told us about those men being sent here by her former boss down in Atlanta. According to her, they intended to kill her, and after what happened this morning, I was starting to believe it. But why? What exactly had she done to make someone want her dead?

"I'm sorry, Charley," she said when I walked around the bar. With a frazzled look on her face, she glanced at the mess on the floor again. "I don't know where my head is tonight."

"Same place it's been every night this week. I was going to wait until after closing, but we need to have a talk now."

We started down the hallway to the back room, but Dog opened the kitchen door and motioned us in. "I want to hear this too."

Tucker's face was all doom and gloom when we walked inside. "Are you firing me?"

My brow tightened as I glanced at Dog and then back at her. "No, I'm not firing you. And will you stop asking me that every time I say we need to have a talk." Although she was becoming an expensive project that a different boss probably would have canned by now. That was the third glass she'd dropped this week, and everyone behind the bar was getting tired of cleaning up pools of liquor and beer on the floor.

Dog crossed his arms and continued to stare at her. "Those men that came in here the other night," he began. "You can start by telling us the real reason they're looking for you."

"I already told you. They want to kill me."

That's all she would volunteer after we'd gotten rid of them the other night. Then she'd clammed up tight and hadn't said a word about it since. But after what happened this morning, that was about to change.

"They broke into the bar this morning and started tearing the place up," I said. "I walked in on them before they could do too much damage."

Her eyes flew wide. "What?" Then she started to look me over like she was expecting wounds to suddenly appear on my body.

"They didn't hurt me, but they made it very clear your ex-boss wants to get his hands on you. Why is that, Tucker?"

Her eyes focused on the floor for a moment and then slowly lifted back to mine. "You'll think I'm crazy."

"I already do, so you might as well validate my assessment of you."

She suddenly lost her timid bird demeanor and looked me square in the eye. "But I'm not crazy."

"Good, because I can't have a crazy woman tending my bar."

After settling down, she finally started the conversation. "I'm not exactly normal."

Dog snickered. "You're in Crimson. Nothing's normal around here, so out with it."

"Like I told you, I can see things."

She'd had a strange reaction the night Atticus Devereaux, my neighbor from across the street who was now sitting in a jar in Candy's back room, walked into the bar. She saw right through his facade when no one else in this town could.

"You mean you can see past glamour?" I said.

She hesitated. "It's more than that."

Before she could shut down again, I added some incentive. "Either tell us the truth, or the door is right over there." Dog glanced at me sideways. "Don't look at me like that," I said to him. "I need to know who and what is working for me. And the rest of you have a right to know too."

"I get glimpses of things that are about to happen!" she blurted out.

I eyed her curiously. "You mean you can see the future?"

"Well... kind of. Things just pop into my head sometimes. I can't control it. It just comes and goes."

I could understand that.

Beau had his head stuck through the order window. "No shit!" A moment later, he walked into the kitchen and planted his hands on his hips as he ogled her. "That little talent might come in handy."

"Who's watching the bar?" I asked him.

"Lucy just got here." He continued to stare at Tucker like he was devising ways to exploit her talents.

I gave him a look that sent him back out the kitchen door. Then I continued with the interrogation. "Get to the part about your ex-boss."

There was another brief hesitation before she started talking again. "At first he wanted to use me for my abilities."

I bet he did. She'd mentioned once before that her special talents were the reason she had to leave Atlanta. "You wouldn't be of much use to him dead, so why would he send those men to kill you?"

She nervously twisted the hem of her shirt. "I stuck my nose where it didn't belong and saw something I wasn't supposed to see." She took a deep breath and let it back out slowly before continuing. "I guess I should start by telling you my ex-boss is a bad person. Mean as a snake," she added with a flash of anger in her eyes.

"Get on with it," I said.

"One of the bartenders told me to go down to the storeroom in the basement to get more tequila." She let out a frustrated sigh. "It was his job to make sure everything was stocked properly, but like usual he didn't do a very good job of it and told me to go down there to fetch more, like I was his gofer or something. I had a good mind to tell him he could go down there and get it himself."

I barely contained an eye roll. "Would you just get to the part about what you saw."

She finally stopped rambling and got on with it. "The basement under the club was more like a dungeon. It was creepy down there. I went to grab the tequila as fast as possible so I could get back upstairs, but as I was opening the storeroom door, I heard a noise. A whimpering. It was coming from down a long hallway." She went quiet again, like she was reliving it. "I was kind of scared, but I followed the sound. It was coming from one of the rooms, so I opened the door to see what it was." She shrugged and just looked at me.

"And?" I waved my hand for her to continue.

"There was a cage in the room with a woman locked inside."

Dog squinted at her. "A cage? You mean like a jail cell?"

"No. It was like one of those big dog crates. She was crying, and her hands were tied behind her back." Tucker's eyes came back to mine. "Her fangs were wrapped around a ball gag in her mouth, and her cheeks were streaked with black mascara from all the tears streaming down her face."

"She was a vampire?" I said.

Tucker nodded. "That poor girl was pleading with her eyes for me to get her out of there, but the cage door had a lock on it. Then I heard another sound coming from somewhere else. I walked back into the hallway and heard muffled voices." She stopped for a moment and stared at the wall as if the memory still frightened her. "I was terrified, but something kept moving my legs toward another door farther down. I wanted to run from that basement, but I had to know what was beyond that door." She licked her lips before continuing. "I could hear the music coming from the club above as I crept closer to it. That room must have been right under the stage. The door was cracked open a few inches, and I only intended to peek inside and then get out of there. But then I saw all those men and women in the room circled around something."

"Are you okay?" I asked when she stopped and stared blankly at the wall again. "What was happening in that room?"

She looked back at me. "There was a cage in the middle of it like the one in the other room. My boss was standing next to it, and he was taking bids on another girl locked inside."

Dog nodded knowingly. "He's trafficking."

"Trafficking?" I said. "Why would anyone sell vampires?"

"As blood slaves?" He glared at Tucker. "Isn't that right?"

She stepped back, looking at him like he'd just slapped her. "What are you saying?"

He cocked his head slightly. "You worked in that place, you tell us."

"Well, I didn't know what was happening right under my feet, so I'd appreciate it if you'd stop looking at me like that."

He finally let up on the accusatory stare. "What happened next?"

"I tried to get the hell out of there, that's what happened." She muttered a few words under her breath. "That's when the shit hit the fan. I got so flustered, I stumbled against the door and it swung open. Everyone in the room turned and looked at me. That's when I noticed another familiar face. A senator I'd seen on TV, Miller Remington. But this time I was seeing his real face, and it wasn't human."

I put the pieces together quickly. "Well, that explains your old boss wanting you dead."

"I'm guessing the senator will be looking for you too," Dog added. "He's got a lot to lose, getting caught buying a trafficked female vampire *and* the threat of being exposed for not being human." He looked back at Tucker. "What exactly is he?"

"I'm not sure. A demon or something even worse." She let out a huff. "I'd like to see him get re-elected after his constituents find out his dirty little secret."

I asked the next question with apprehension since he had me in his sights. "Is your ex-boss a demon too?" After Atticus Devereaux, what were the odds of having two demons come after me?

She slowly shook her head. "But he might as well be."

So they wanted to exploit her talents *and* keep her quiet. "Don't let the pack let her out of their sight," I said to Dog. "At least until we can figure this out."

"No need to ask. She won't be taking a piss without a wolf watching her."

Tucker pressed her hand to her chest and gave him an adoring look. "Thank you, Dog."

"You can thank me by keeping your head low for now. In the meantime, I'll do a little digging on your ex-boss. What's his name?"

She hesitated. "Mr. K."

"Is that with a *c* or a *k*?"

"No. Like the letter K." An uneasy look crossed her face. "It's short for King. That's what he made us call him. The King."

"Your boss made you call him the King?" I snorted. "Didn't you think that was a little strange?"

"Well, yeah, but the money was good and I needed the job. If you met him, you'd know why he called himself that. The man's an egomaniac." She shrugged. "We called him Mr. K when he wasn't around."

"I'm going to need his real name," Dog said.

"I don't know his real name."

Dog stared at her for a moment. "Great."

Maybe this town wasn't the best place for her right now. "Why did you come to Crimson?" I asked. "Don't you have family you could have stayed with?"

She scoffed. "None I have a lick of desire to see. My father disappeared before I could crawl, and the rest of them just want to use me to win the lottery."

"I was wondering about that," Beau said through the order window. "Can you dig around in that crystal ball head of yours and pick the winning numbers for me?"

"Get back to work, Beau." I had to admit, I was wondering about that myself. "You can't actually see the lottery numbers, can you?"

She smiled meekly. "Like I said, it comes and goes. I can't really predict anything other than bad weather when my hair starts to frizz. As far as how I got here, I stuck my finger on the map and it landed on Crimson. I never thought they'd find me up here after all this time, though."

"How long have you been on the run?" Dog asked.

Her shoulders sagged as she exhaled dramatically. "A while. They tracked me down once in a place west of here, but I managed to get out of there right after they showed up flashing my picture around. I ended up here a couple of months ago, but I guess they found me again."

"You've been in Crimson for months?" I thought she'd only been in town for a couple of weeks.

"I stayed off the radar for a while until I thought it was safe. Until my money started running out." Her expression sank. "I'm sorry, Charley. I should have never come in here looking for a job."

Beau stuck his head through the order window again before I could give her the speech about guilt being a useless emotion. "Candy's here to see you, Charley."

"I'll be right out." I glanced at the sinkful of dirty dishes. "Why don't you help Dog in the kitchen for the rest of the night." Dog needed the help, and I didn't need those men storming the bar if they spotted her. I had a good mind to give her the week off, but I figured she was safer here than in that tiny apartment above the thrift shop, even with the wolves standing guard.

Candy was sitting by the window when I went out to the bar. I took a seat next to her. "Long time no see, stranger."

She slid her eyes to me as she sipped her drink. "I just saw you yesterday."

"But I haven't seen you today." I couldn't remember the last time I went a day without at least talking to Candy on the phone. But business had suddenly picked up, and I'd been busy fending off thugs in the back room. I hadn't even had time to eat.

She set her glass down with a sigh. "With another girl getting attacked, I just wanted to drop by to smother you with another warning to keep yourself safe out there."

"What are you talking about?" I was usually privy to such news.

She swiveled around on her stool to face me. "You mean to tell me I heard something before you did?" A chuckle slipped from her mouth as she turned back to the bar. "You must have fallen off the gossip train."

"Quit beating around the bush and just tell me."

"Another girl got herself tied up and nailed to a tree out in the woods last night, just like Patrice Henderson. They found her this afternoon."

My eyes went wide. "You're kidding me?"

"Oh, no, honey. I wouldn't kid about something like that. Some hikers up from Savannah found her just a little ways north of town."

"And?"

She shrugged. "That's all I know. I was hoping you could fill in the blanks for me."

"I haven't heard a thing. Who told you?"

"The mayor. His wife called to tell him the news, so we had to end our session before I could squeeze all the details out of him."

"You're still working with Mayor Adams?" Last time I saw him at Hecate's Cauldron, he was hollering at Candy with his pants down around his ankles. The man running the town of Crimson had serious issues.

She let out a heavy sigh. "If you knew what was going on in

that thick head of his, you'd be screaming for a recall election. The therapy I'm giving him should be tax deductible for community service."

I let out a groan and looked at the restaurant across the street. What was left of Morceau was about to be demolished. "Well, we can't blame the attack on Atticus Devereaux this time." He'd been responsible for inciting acts of violence all over town until we stopped him.

She followed my gaze. "No ma'am, we can't."

"Please tell me that bottle is still sitting on your shelf." I would have preferred to dispose of Devereaux properly instead of leaving him imprisoned in Candy's back room, but she seemed to think it was safer to let him rot there, where she could keep an eye on him.

"That devil is locked up tighter than a virgin." Her sly grin disappeared as her eyes narrowed. "If you ask me, that Ian Masterson has something to do with it."

I wasn't convinced one way or the other about Masterson having a hand in the crimes. When I'd asked him point blank if he'd attacked Patrice, he said it wasn't him. But since when did vampires of his kind tell the truth? I'd definitely call Masterson a suspect, but there were plenty of bad actors in Reaperstown.

She finished her drink and stood up. "I've got things to do, so I better get going. I don't suppose I could convince you to stay at my place until they find the killer?"

Not that again. Now I definitely wasn't telling her about what happened that morning. At least not yet.

I got up and walked her to the door. "I'll be fine. I've got Rex to protect me. Not to mention these." I held my hands up. My magic was hit or miss, but I wasn't exactly defenseless. Just ask Dog.

"Speaking of which," she said. "We need to come up with some lesson plans for you. Schedule some time with the Squad."

Just the thought of subjecting myself to the ladies' "lessons" made me shudder. "Any training I need can come straight from you."

"Charley, this is important. Putting it off is just asking for trouble. You've got things inside of you that need to be harnessed before something reckless happens. And by reckless, I mean dangerous."

"I know that. I just have other stuff to deal with right now." Like making sure those men didn't come back and bust up my bar again and finding out where Samuel had disappeared to. I hadn't seen him in a while, and I didn't like the way it made me feel. A little sick to my stomach wondering if he'd left town without even saying goodbye. "We'll do it soon. I promise."

She let out a groan and shook her head at me. "I believe you're more stubborn than your mama was, and Delia had some mule somewhere in her bloodline."

It was time to end the conversation before she had me agreeing to it. "Let me get Dog to walk you home."

She pinned me with a dry look.

"Right." Arguing with her was a lost cause. "Just text me when you get to the shop."

I stepped outside and kept my eyes on her until she walked the two blocks back to the Cauldron, dreading the visit I knew I'd be getting from Tom Murphy in the morning to warn me about the second attack. Let the hovering and smothering begin.

THREE

I slept like an insomniac fighting sleeping pills. One minute I couldn't keep my eyes open, and the next I was wide awake. Rex flying around the house all night didn't help, but every time I opened the door to let him out, he'd fly up to the ceiling fan and refuse to budge. Something had him wound up.

My legs nearly gave out under me when I swung them over the mattress and stood up. It felt like someone had slipped me a mickey as I steadied myself against the wall and made my way to the bedroom door. But I knew sleep deprivation would eventually catch up to me, like it was now. Coffee would help. I just needed to make it to the kitchen.

"What's it going to be this morning?" I asked Rex with one eye open and one shut. "Cereal or the usual?" He'd recently taken a liking to Goldfish crackers. Not the best diet for a crow, but I'd let him outside before I left for the Stag so he could wash them down with whatever crows ate in the wild.

I dropped a handful of crackers on top of the refrigerator where he was perched and grabbed my phone to check the time. It was 6:10 a.m. I'd forgotten to set the alarm on my phone.

"Hurry up and eat your breakfast, Rex. I need to get out of here."

After Patrick recovered from being possessed and returned to the co-op, we decided to keep Beau on as backup. Emergencies happened, and lately there had been a lot of them. I was meeting them both at the Stag at six thirty because Patrick wasn't available tonight. He had a date. If I didn't show up on time, Beau would never let me hear the end of it for getting him up so early, especially after he rolled out of bed before dawn yesterday to retrieve his phone. But crack-of-dawn meetings came with the territory when your partner was a vampire.

I stuffed a handful of crackers in my mouth and went to get dressed and brush my teeth. Ten minutes later, I was shooing Rex out the door and climbing into my truck. As I was backing out, I looked up at the sky and saw a few dozen crows landing in the tree above me where Rex had perched.

"That's not a good sign," I said to myself, remembering the last time that many birds descended on my house.

On the ten-minute drive into town, I couldn't stop thinking about that girl they'd found in the woods, and how similar it was to the Patrice Henderson case. A case that was still open. It was believed that a vampire had attacked her because they'd found fang marks on her body. But vampires weren't the only things with fangs in this town. And now there was a second victim. With nearly half the population of Crimson being vampires, it could have been anyone. An upstanding citizen by day and a killer by night. A real Jekyll and Hyde. What if it was one of my customers?

"Stop it," I muttered to myself as I drove into town and pulled up next to the police car parked in my spot. It was Tom Murphy.

I climbed out of my truck and resisted the urge to kick his door. I could see him through the window talking to Beau, and based on the way my bartender was gesturing at him, they seemed to be in the middle of a heated conversation. I knew Murphy would show up today to try to give me some unsolicited advice on safety, but I wasn't interested in hearing it. However, I was interested in information about the girl they found. I was also wondering why he was harassing Beau.

"You're here awfully early, Officer Murphy," I said to him when I walked inside.

"Cut the formality, Charley."

"Then quit acting like you're here on official police business." I glanced at Beau who looked a little ruffled. "What's going on here?"

Beau snorted. "Murphy saw my car parked out front and decided to come in and interrogate me. And for the record, he didn't read me my rights."

"That's because you're not under arrest," Murphy replied. "Yet."

My brazen bartender took a step closer to him. "Are you threatening me?"

Murphy got a grin on his face. "Take another step and you'll find out."

I got between them before Beau could say something that would get him thrown into the back of that patrol car parked out front.

"Just tell me what's going on?" I said.

Tom backed off and stuck his notepad into his pocket. "A girl was found in the woods yesterday afternoon. Kim Widby. She was tied to a tree with her hands nailed to the trunk. Just like Patrice Henderson." He narrowed his eyes at Beau. "You remember Patrice, don't you?" After giving Beau a few seconds to squirm, he answered my question. "I was just asking your bartender here when he last saw Kim."

"Instead of harassing Beau, why don't you just ask her?"

He took a step back because I'd managed to get in his face without even realizing it. "It's hard to question a dead person."

"Dead?" I'd just assumed she was found alive like Patrice.

"You heard me. It was the same M.O. as the Henderson case only she wasn't hanging on by a thread like Patrice was. The girl's throat was ripped open."

Beau lost his bravado, and suddenly there was fear in his eyes. "You didn't tell me she was dead."

"And you didn't tell me where you were Wednesday night," Murphy shot back.

"Aren't you missing something obvious here?" I said to Murphy. "Beau doesn't have fangs. Besides, he was working Wednesday night." I tried to remember what time he'd left because that would be Murphy's next question. "He left around eleven and went straight home, didn't you?"

Beau nodded with that fear still in his eyes.

"Did you even know the girl?" I asked him. If I recalled, she was younger than us and was a sophomore during our senior year of high school. Her family lived on a farm quite a ways out and rarely came into town.

"Uh…"

Murphy took full advantage of his tongue-tied state. "Answer the question, boy."

I grabbed Beau by the arm and steered him toward the hallway. "He's done talking to you."

"Are you the law now?" he said to me.

"I know my rights, and Beau's. If he's not under arrest, he doesn't have to answer any more of your questions."

Murphy zipped it and headed for the door. On his way out, he looked back at Beau. "We're not done with this conversation."

As soon as the patrol car pulled away, I started in with my own questions. "You didn't answer my question, Beau. Did you know her personally?"

He yanked his arm out of my grip. "What the hell are you trying to say?"

"I'm not saying anything, but you can bet your ass Murphy will be back." I stared at him for a moment trying to read his face. He looked real uncomfortable. "Why would Murphy even question you?"

He walked over to the bar and grabbed a beer from the cooler. "May I?" he asked.

"Why not. Have two." Maybe it would loosen his lips.

Taking a swig, he ran his hand over the top of his head. "I might have hooked up with her once or twice."

"Once or—? When?" Please tell me it was years ago.

He shrugged. "A month or two ago."

"You mean recently." I shook my head. "Recent enough for Murphy to connect you to her. Great."

He cocked his head. "Me and a lot of other guys. I ain't trying to slut-shame the girl, but she spent a lot of time down at the Beast."

I recalled the image of Kim Widby. "Are you telling me that shy girl who blended in with the wallpaper was hanging out with a bunch of dangerous vampires? At the Beast?" I couldn't even fathom it.

Beau huffed a laugh. "Just like Patrice Henderson. Everyone around here thought she was a shy little thing too, but she sure liked to party hard." He finished his beer and tossed the bottle in the trash. "You rule your kids with a heavy hand, they'll eventually come out swinging. At least that's what happened with Kim. She just wanted to have a little fun, like half the women in this town."

"Tell me they can't connect you to Patrice too."

"Hell no! Do I look like some fuckboy to you?"

"Uh... yeah."

Patrick walked through the front door, saving me from having to continue the conversation about Beau's love life.

I looked at the time. "You're late."

"Baby, I'm fashionably late. There's a difference."

"This is Crimson. Late is late." I beckoned them to follow me.

When we reached the back room, Beau stopped in his tracks just inside the door, like he was having a flashback of that gun pointed at his face.

"What the hell is wrong with you?" Patrick glanced down at Beau's frozen feet. "You look like you just stepped in a pile of dog shit."

I stared at Beau, warning him to keep quiet. The events of yesterday morning were on a need-to-know basis, and right now, Patrick didn't need to know anything. The sun would be coming up shortly, and we didn't have time to get into it.

Patrick took a seat in the chair behind the desk and swung his feet up on the top. "We got us a problem."

"With the donors?" I felt a headache coming on. We'd finally stabilized the supply chain, and I wasn't sure I was up for *another* problem.

He lowered his feet back down to the floor and straightened up in the chair. "Calm down, woman. We've got plenty for tomorrow, but there's some talk about competition. Someone else offering to buy vampire blood."

"Competition? You mean Masterson?" I wanted to kill that vampire. His last parting words to me were to stay on my side of the fence. I'd thought it was a truce, and he would do the same.

"It might be Masterson, but maybe not. Then again, it could just be talk. Greedy donors trying to inflate the wholesale price of blood."

Beau shook his head with a huff. "Figures. Never trust a vampire."

Patrick lowered his sunglasses. "What was that?"

"I ain't talking about you. Just... vampires in general."

Patrick cocked his head. "Boy, you better watch your mouth."

Beau was about to dig himself deeper, so I held up my hand

to end it. "Just let it go, Beau." He meant well, but sometimes garbage just spilled out of his mouth.

"No one's said anything to me directly," Patrick continued. "I just wanted to mention it so you're not blindsided if it does become a problem."

"Where are these rumors coming from?" I asked.

Seeing the concern on my face, he tried to gloss over it. "No one worth worrying about. I shouldn't even have mentioned it." He stood back up and held his hand out. "The envelope?"

I reached into the top drawer and handed him the money for the blood deliveries he was collecting tonight. "There's a little extra in there to make sure we've got it all covered. Be here a little early. We've got a lot of people showing up in the morning."

"Speaking of which." He looked at Beau.

"Oh, yeah!" Beau went over to the filing cabinet to retrieve a list. One of his new responsibilities for the co-op was to take the blood orders, which thrilled Patrick because he didn't have to do it himself anymore.

He started to read off the orders. "Millie Wilson ordered two vials. Bob—"

"Just give me the damn list." Patrick snatched it out of his hand.

"Take it easy!" Beau said. "Show some respect for your co-worker."

"Co-worker my ass." Patrick stuck the envelope and list inside his jacket. "I better get out of here before the sun comes up. Wouldn't want to be stuck here all day. I got me a hot date tonight, and I need a few hours to prepare my fine-ass self."

I heard someone walk into the bar and looked at Beau. "Did you lock the front door?"

He shook his head and pointed his thumb at Patrick. "He was the last one in."

We went back up front to tell whoever it was that we weren't open yet. Obviously.

"This early two days in a row?" I said to a man I thought was Dog. When he turned around, I realized my mistake. "Sorry, I thought you were someone else. We don't open until this evening."

He trained a pair of spectacular green eyes on me, and I felt a strange urge to step back. He was big and tall, with black hair and tribal tattoos similar to Dog's. But he definitely wasn't my cook.

"Holy mother," Patrick muttered. He took his sunglasses off to get a better look at the stranger. Then he strolled over and ran his eyes up and down the man's body. "You lost, sugar?"

I intervened before Patrick got himself stuck here for the day. "You better get going." I nodded to the window where the sun would be peeking through in a few minutes.

Ignoring me, he continued to stare. "I'm Patrick, and you are?"

The guy gave him a firm look. "Not interested."

Patrick threw his hands up. "Okay." Then he put his sunglasses back on and headed for the door. "If you ever change your mind, I come here often."

After he left, the man looked back at me, a grin slowly sliding up his very attractive face. "You don't remember me, do you?"

"Have we met?" I was pretty sure I would have remembered those eyes. And that body. Not to mention the perfectly chiseled jaw covered with a day's worth of stubble. They didn't grow a lot of men like him in Crimson.

"What did you say your name was?" Beau asked.

His eyes stayed on mine. "I didn't."

Okay.

"We're not open until this evening," I repeated. "Six o'clock, like the sign on the door says." When he just stood there looking at me, I tried a firmer tactic. "I don't mean to be rude, but you need to leave."

He strolled toward me. "Well, aren't you a little carbon copy of Delia."

Beau stepped in his path. "That's close enough. Either state your business or walk back out the door."

I could practically smell Beau rethinking his decision to cut the guy off, so I put him out of his misery and stepped out from behind him. "You knew my mother?"

"Yeah, I knew her. I remember you too." His cocky grin returned as he gave me a once-over. "But you've grown up since then." He extended his hand. "Magnus Ryan, but call me Mag. I used to live here."

"In Crimson?"

He chuckled. "In this bar."

I glanced at the back wall that used to hold hundreds of signatures before vandals recently destroyed it, recalling the name MAG boldly scrolled across the center, like colorful graffiti. "Your name used to be on that wall."

He followed my gaze and frowned. "Well, that's a damn shame. Why'd you paint over it?"

My sentiments exactly. Painting that wall after it had been desecrated wasn't just a damn shame—it was a tragedy. A deletion of history.

"That's a story I don't have time to tell. I've got work to do, so if you don't mind." I nodded to the door hoping he'd leave without incident, but instead he walked over to the bar and sat down. "Hey. Did you hear me?"

Damn right he did.

"I don't mean to be rude," he said, staring at my reflection in the mirror behind the bar, "but I've been riding all night, and I could use a drink."

I noticed a motorcycle parked out front. "It's seven thirty in the morning."

"Might as well be midnight to me."

Beau leaned closer to whisper. "Want me to call Murphy?"

"That won't be necessary," Mag said. "I'm just in town to see an old friend. One drink, and I'll be out of your hair. Promise."

I'd learned a long time ago that sometimes the easiest way to defuse a powder keg was to meet it halfway. If a drink would get him to leave without incident, so be it.

I walked behind the bar and grabbed a glass. "Fine. What can I get you?"

"Jack Daniel's. Number 7 if you've got it. Anything else if you don't."

I poured him a double and set it down in front of him. "It's on the house."

His brows hiked. "That's nice of you, darlin', but Delia wouldn't appreciate me not paying my tab." He pulled a twenty from his pocket and slid it toward me. "Keep the change."

"You knew my mother well." I prayed he wouldn't tell me he'd slept with her. He was definitely her type. A real bad boy.

"She was a good woman. I was sorry to hear about her passing." He raised his glass. "To Delia Underwood."

Before I could pry more information out of him, the front door swung open and Dog came through it. "What the hell are you doing here?"

Mag shot his drink back, but he didn't turn around. Didn't even flinch from Dog's growl. A smile appeared on his face as he set the glass down and took a steady breath. "I'm here to see you, old friend."

FOUR

Dog walked toward Mag but stopped halfway. "We're not friends."

Mag finally stood up to face him. "Is that any way to greet family?"

Family? A gasp nearly slipped from my mouth.

"We're not family either. Not anymore."

A cold grin slid up Mag's face. "Once pack, always pack. You can't take that from me."

Dog headed for the kitchen, growling over his shoulder, "What do you want, Magnus?"

"Magnus? I guess I'm still on your shit list."

Dog snickered. "You're on everyone's shit list. Charley!" he barked as he continued into the kitchen.

I followed him, catching a glimpse of Beau's uneasy face when I brushed past him. "You better make it quick," I said to Dog when I walked into the kitchen behind him. "I don't think Beau is too happy being left out there with that guy. Who is he anyway?"

He started pacing back and forth, knocking things off a rack as he brushed past it like a bull in a china shop. "How long has he been here?"

"A few minutes. He got here just before you did." My curiosity was through the roof.

He stopped pacing and gave me an incredulous look. "And why the hell did you serve him a drink?"

Before I could say another word, he grabbed his trusty meat cleaver from the cutting board and stalked toward the kitchen door.

"Dog!"

He ignored me and swung the door open so hard I thought it would break off the hinges.

I followed him back out and looked around the bar, but Mag was gone.

Beau nodded to the front door. "He just left."

I heard the bike start up. By the time we made it outside, he was circling the square. He came back around and stopped in front of the Stag. "See you soon, brother," he said to Dog before revving the engine and disappearing down the street.

When we walked back inside, I glared at Dog. "What the hell was that all about?"

He snarled and slammed the blade into the top of the bar and then wagged his finger at me. "Don't you ever let that son of a bitch in this bar again!"

I swatted his finger away. "Since when do you tell me what to do in my own bar?" I usually took Dog's advice, but not when he tried to shove it down my throat. Now he had *me* riled up.

Beau started inching toward the door. "Uh... should I leave?"

"No!" Dog and I barked in unison.

Dog settled down and yanked the cleaver out of the bar. "I'll sand the mark down later."

That bar had more gashes than a butcher block already. "Just tell me what the hell is going on."

"He's a former member of the pack," Dog began. "Got kicked out eleven, twelve years ago. He used to show up every six months and try to weasel his way back in, but I haven't seen his sorry ass in years."

"He must have done something pretty bad to get axed by the pack," I said. "Care to elaborate?"

"Not today. All you need to know is that wolf is nothing but trouble. Delia finally figured that out too."

There was the mention of my mother again. "Was there something going on between them?"

"Your mother was smarter than that, but she trusted him. Until she didn't," he added, glancing out the window. "I came in early to finish cleaning the kitchen. There's still a lot of broken glass under the shelves, and it hasn't had a good scrubbing since Mutt left." Halfway across the room, he glanced back at me. "Stay away from Mag, Charley."

"You need any help?" Beau asked.

Dog continued into the kitchen without a reply, which meant *keep your distance*. Seeing his former pack member had really set him off, but he definitely wasn't ready to talk about it.

"I'll take that as a no." Beau walked over to the window and looked out. "You think that wolf will show up here again?"

"Probably."

"Better take Dog's advice and kick him out if he does."

Mag had come off a little pushy, but he hadn't done anything offensive. People didn't always see eye to eye, and some deserved a bad reputation. But I had a golden rule to never judge someone as "bad" until they'd earned it. And people generally showed their colors pretty early on.

"Unless Dog cares to tell me the truth instead of trying to order me around, I'll give Mag the opportunity to prove him wrong. But the second that wolf walks in here and starts trouble, he's banned. That's the deal," I said for Dog's benefit since he was listening through the order window.

He just grumbled and stepped out of view. A moment later, I heard the pantry door slam shut and water running in the sink.

"I might as well get some work done since I'm here," I said to Beau on my way to the back room. "I'll see you tonight."

* * *

Despite all the noise coming from the kitchen, I managed to get more work done than I had in weeks. Work intended for yesterday morning before those guys showed up.

I stood up from the desk when I heard someone walk into the bar. It was foolish of me to think that Beau would have the sense to lock the door behind him on his way out this morning. And since it was barely noon, it definitely wasn't Lucy coming in this early.

There was no one in the room when I walked up front, but I could hear a woman's voice coming from the kitchen. She was talking to Dog. I was about to go see who it was when I heard a noise behind the bar. It sounded like an object had hit the floor. Then I heard something rustle back there.

I stepped quietly toward it, praying I didn't come face-to-face with a giant rat scurrying across the shelves. It wouldn't have been the first time. When I walked around the bar, I got startled and nearly crashed into that crate of liquor bottles Dog had picked up for me. I was staring at a mound of black hair near the floor. "Nae? What the he— What the heck are you doing here?"

A stream of giggles escaped the girl's mouth as she handed me a container of red cocktail straws she'd picked up off the floor. "Sorry, Charley. I dropped them." She laughed again, covering her mouth with her other hand. "I was looking for some candy."

Last time she was in here, I snuck her a piece of caramel from my stash under the bar. I guess she had a good memory.

Like all wolf children, she was striking. There was something about their eyes that radiated their otherworldly pedigree. A wildness that drew you in. It faded as they got older, but then again, even at their worst, most adult wolves were attractive.

Before I could ask the child what she was doing in my bar, the voices in the kitchen got louder. It must have been Coda in there, Nae's mother. She was one of the females in the pack, and she was having a heated conversation with Dog.

Nae, short for Nadeen, frowned when she heard a string of expletives come from her mother's mouth. Words no ten-year-old should be hearing.

"Let's see what we can find." I started rummaging around the shelves for something sweet. My stash of caramels was long gone, but we always had a few mints or butterscotch candies lying around somewhere. Anything to draw her attention away from the conversation in the kitchen that included several references to "that bastard."

"I found some!" Nae's green eyes lit up as she broke off a square of a chocolate bar she found in the drawer next to the register. It was Lucy's.

"Uh... I don't think you want that, Nae." Before I could snatch it out of her hand, she stuffed the entire piece in her mouth.

The excitement in her eyes went south when the bitterness of the eighty-percent dark chocolate assaulted her taste buds. She frantically looked around for somewhere to spit it out.

"The sink!" I grabbed her shoulders and turned her around. After evacuating the dark blob from her mouth with dramatic flair, she looked at me like I'd tried to poison her. "I warned you."

I handed her a glass of water to wash it down with and a handful of peanuts from a bowl under the bar. "You're not allergic to peanuts, are you?" I asked her before dropping them in her hand.

Coda walked out of the kitchen and looked around the room. "Nae!"

"She's over here," I said, walking the girl around the bar.

Coda looked at the dark brown stain on her daughter's shirt. Nae had dribbled it down the front while spitting it out. "What is that?"

"She got into some chocolate in one of the drawers," I said. "*Dark* chocolate."

"Oh..." She slowly nodded her head. "I guess that'll teach her not to take something without asking."

"Kids." I brushed it off. "Better she learns it now."

She gave her daughter a firm look. "Next time stay put when I tell you to."

"Is everything okay?" I said when Dog walked out of the kitchen behind her.

Coda's bare smile disappeared as a bitterness filled her eyes. "Everything's fine. I just wanted to face the bastard."

Who? Dog?

Nadeen shrank back against me when she heard that word come out of her mother's mouth again. I put my hand on her shoulder and glanced at Dog.

"Take Nae home," he said to Coda. "We can talk more tonight. I'll stop by after closing."

Coda gave him a warning look. I had a feeling there'd be hell to pay if he didn't show up to finish whatever conversation they'd started in the kitchen. Then she reached for Nae's hand. "Come on. Let's go. Say thank you to Charley for the candy."

The girl got a sour look on her face but found her manners a moment later. "Thank you for the peanuts, Charley, but that chocolate sucked."

"Nadeen!" Coda scolded.

I laughed. "Have mercy on her. She's ten and just had her first taste of bitter chocolate."

The girl walked toward the door with Coda, waving at me as they left.

I kept quiet as I went back behind the bar to check the supply of napkins and glasses. I was curious about the heated conversation, but it wasn't my business unless Dog decided to volunteer the information.

He eyed me for a minute or two while I fiddled around back there. "Just ask, Charley."

"Ask what?" I started to wipe down the bar without looking at him.

"What the discussion in the kitchen was about. You want to know why Mag was kicked out of the pack?" He motioned to Coda's car pulling out of the parking space in front of the bar. "That's why."

Okay, he opened the door to the conversation. "You'll have to be more specific than that."

"Nadeen is his kid." He let out a bitter laugh. "The son of a bitch just won't admit it."

"Wait. You're telling me Magnus is Nadeen's father?" I remembered his striking green eyes and black hair. I could see him fathering Nae.

"Isn't that what I just said?"

"Easy, tiger. I'm just a little surprised, that's all."

He lost the attitude and inhaled deeply. "He got Coda pregnant but denied Nae was his. Tried to say she was sleeping with every wolf in the pack."

I was slightly confused. "I thought it was forbidden?" Dog had told me that relationships within the pack weren't tolerated because it usually got messy. There were other packs in the mountains to mingle with, not to mention humans. It was no different than corporate policies forbidding employee romances in the mundane world, and it could have deadly consequences for wolves if animosity developed between pack members. It was just wise to discourage it.

"It's one of the many reasons Mag won't own up to it," Dog said. "If you ask me, Nae is better off not having that sorry excuse for a father, but he still needs to support his kid. If it wasn't for the pack, Nae and Coda would be living in the woods right now."

It still didn't explain Dog's borderline hatred for the wolf. I could see it in his eyes. And it took a lot to get yourself kicked out of the pack. Something worse than being a deadbeat dad. "Are you telling me everything?"

"Everything I have proof of."

I wanted to push him for more information, but he'd already shut down the conversation and was heading back to the kitchen. I needed to stop by the Cauldron anyway before driving back out to the house, so I dropped it.

"Just keep your distance from him, Charley." He looked back at me before disappearing into the hallway. "I mean it."

FIVE

I walked into the Cauldron just as the Squad was getting ready to leave. I hadn't seen them since the night we destroyed Atticus Devereaux's restaurant and stuck him in Candy's back room.

"Charley!" Desiree Dubois approached me with a wide smile. Then she grabbed a lock of my hair with a displeased look. "Have you ever considered a shade of red?"

Between her cherry-red hair and Candy's long mane of fire, I think this town had enough redheads. "Not really." I continued past her and smiled at the rest of the witches. "Twice in one month. You ladies are becoming regulars in town." They usually showed up once or twice a year: on Halloween and at Christmas to remind everyone that it was also Yule, the winter solstice.

"We've been discussing the latest attack," Candy said. "Someone needs to hunt that monster down, and I wouldn't count on the Crimson PD to do it. Rick Carter couldn't find a missing cat if it ran across his feet, and Tom Murphy's not much better."

"You won't get an argument from me," I said. "Murphy was

at the Stag this morning interrogating Beau about the attack. Can you believe it?"

Mia Winston gasped, her retracted upper lip exposing her large teeth. "The Henry boy?"

Candy gave the witch a dry look. "The only thing Beau Henry is guilty of is a case of raging hormones. If you had a daddy like his, you'd be feeling your oats too, as soon as you got free of that man."

Beau's father was a strict disciplinarian. Growing up, Beau didn't dare defy him.

"He isn't the brightest bulb in the bunch," Candy continued, "but he's no more of a killer than any of us." She glanced at Desiree. "Well, most of us."

Desiree recoiled. "What are you accusing me of?"

"You have been known to be heavy-handed on the arsenic in your flying ointment. As for Beau," she continued, looking back at me, "Tom's just looking for a scapegoat. The mayor is probably coming down hard on him to find the killer. It's an election year, and folks around here are getting restless."

That may be, but focusing on Beau wasn't serving anyone. It was just plain stupid.

Katherine Belltower was studying me curiously. "Have you been practicing, Charley?"

"My magic?" I shrugged. "Of course." I didn't have the nerve to tell her I'd barely had time to think about it since the last time I saw her. I'd get around to it eventually, when I didn't have a business to run and thugs breaking into my bar.

Her eyes narrowed as her lips raised into a sly smile. For a moment I thought I was busted. But then she made her way toward the door. "Come along, ladies. We have work to do."

As they were leaving, Katherine suddenly turned. A sphere of light flew from the palm of her hand and shot toward me. I nearly lost my balance as I sidestepped the magic, cringing as it flew past me and ignited into a ball of flames before slamming into the far wall.

Candy stared at the smoldering spot and then swung her head around to glare at the witch. "Was that necessary?"

"Apparently." Katherine held my gaze. "Practicing, eh? You should have been able to absorb that magic and shoot it right back at me. Don't waste our time if you're not going to take this seriously."

"All right. I'll work on it."

Desiree slowly shook her head with a tsk. "Delia would not approve." As she pulled her contemptuous eyes away from mine and turned to follow the others, her foot caught the edge of the threshold, nearly causing her to face-plant on the sidewalk. Flustered, she shot me a wicked glare. "You little..."

I bit my lower lip. "I didn't do anything."

"Careful, Charley," Candy muttered. "You don't want to be on that witch's bad side."

I couldn't help it if my magic had a mind of its own.

The room felt lighter the second they walked out the door. Like fresh air had suddenly been pumped in. "Is it my imagination, or do those women suck the oxygen right out of the room sometimes?"

"You're not imagining anything." Candy shook her head as they climbed into their ancient car and backed away from the shop. "They're a bunch of energy-sucking queens, but they know their shit, and we're going to need them if the law around here doesn't find that killer soon." She glanced at the damaged wall again and groaned. "That's what we were discussing when you got here. The ladies are going to do a little scrying to see if that vampire left a trail on the astral plane."

Astral plane?

I was curious about what that was, but I didn't have time to get into it. I had another reason for stopping by. "What do you know about a guy named Magnus Ryan? He's a wolf that got kicked out of Dog's pack."

She slid her eyes sideways to me. "I know who he is. The question is, how do you?"

"He came into the Stag this morning. Dog wasn't too happy about it and told me to stay clear of him."

"Good advice. That wolf leaves a mark everywhere he goes, and it stinks."

"Dog told me about Mag and Coda. About him not wanting to take responsibility for his daughter."

"Nothing unusual about that, honey. Men can be messy creatures who don't always pick up their trash on the way out, and I don't mean that little girl. If you ask me, he did her a favor by disappearing."

"That's what Dog said. I'm not so sure Coda feels the same way, though. She showed up at the bar looking for him, but he was already gone."

Candy sighed. "Sometimes there's no taking a man out of a woman, no matter what he does to her. But Mag isn't your typical wolf. He's made an art form out of being a rogue. Got himself a reputation with the ladies."

"A good one or a bad one?"

"Bad as it gets. Hooks them with his looks and charm. Then he leaves them broken when he gets bored. I swear that wolf puts a spell on women. I never fell for it, but he almost fooled your mama."

"Dog said they were never romantically involved."

"Oh, it was nothing like that, but not for lack of him trying. She had a soft spot for him, though. He used to sit at the bar for hours rambling about how he planned to get out of Crimson. Go to Vegas. Maybe that's where he's been all this time."

"I don't remember him ever being at the Stag, and I grew up in that place." I must have been around sixteen when he got kicked out of the pack, so why couldn't I recall his face? "I wouldn't have forgotten a wolf like him."

Her lips rose into a grin. "Like I said, your mama had a soft spot for him, but she wasn't taking any chances with her pride and joy. Mag liked to collect women, and you were a pretty young thing. When you were around the bar, Delia made sure Mag wasn't."

"Well, I wasn't stupid. She didn't need to hide me from him." It kind of annoyed me.

Candy shot me a dull look. "You were a sixteen-year-old girl with raging hormones. You've seen those eyes of his."

I certainly had. Maybe my mother was right.

"Then things started to get sticky, with the rumors about him and Coda flying around. Dog took priority, so your mama decided it was best if Mag stayed away from the Stag to avoid a war. I guess you know the rest."

Part of me was hoping Candy would enlighten me on some of Mag's redeeming qualities, but it sounded like he didn't have any. "I guess I need to figure out how to get rid of him next time he walks into the Stag, and I'm pretty sure there will be a next time."

She rubbed her fingers over the burned spot on the wall. "You won't have to."

"What are you talking about?"

"Well, damn it." She let out a sigh. "I'm going to have to paint this entire wall." Then she looked back at me. "That wolf will make his own bed. Then all you'll have to do is get out of the way and let Dog clean house. And if I know Dog, it'll be the last time Mag shows his ass in the bar."

"I just hope they don't take out a window or the wall of booze behind the bar in the process," I said. "I can't afford it right now."

She ushered me across the room and practically pushed me

out the door. "Quit worrying about things you can't control. Then go home and do your laundry or something before you have to get back to the Stag."

Was she a mind reader now? That was exactly what I needed to do.

"And lock your doors when you get inside. There's a killer on the loose. In fact, maybe you should move back in here for a while. You still have your toothbrush upstairs."

How many times was she going to ask me that? "No one's chasing me out of my house this time, so save your breath."

I climbed into my truck and headed for home. I had just enough time to throw a load of laundry into the washing machine, make myself something to eat, and possibly take a quick catnap before going back to the Stag. If that wolf decided to show up tonight, I needed to be on my toes.

The first thing I noticed when I pulled up to the garage and got out was something slumped on the porch. Something big. The closer I got to the house, the faster my heart started to race. When I realized I was looking at a person sprawled on his stomach next to my front door, I stopped, caught my breath, and then cautiously continued up the steps.

"Are you okay?" Of course he wasn't, but I couldn't think of anything else to say. After nudging him gently with my foot and getting no response, I bent down and flipped him over. I straightened back up and stumbled back against the railing when I saw all the blood. Then I recognized him.

"Keith?"

* * *

Murphy finished examining the body and stood back up. "It's Keith Barnes all right."

"You think? Jesus, Tom, of course it's Keith." I was rattled.

Finding one of your customers dead on your doorstep would rattle anyone. And Keith had been a regular for years, until he got himself locked up for assault. "Can you just get him out of here." I looked up as Rex sailed across the yard and landed in his favorite tree. If only I could get inside that bird's head and see what he'd seen.

"The coroner is on the way." Murphy opened a plastic bag to deposit a few hairs he'd picked off Keith's shirt with tweezers. "You said you just found him here when you got home?"

"No, Tom. I killed him myself in the yard and dragged him up the steps to the porch."

He cocked his head. "Are you done now?"

"Sorry." I looked down at the bloody mess around Keith's throat where it had been torn open. "Looks like someone gnawed on his neck."

Murphy nodded. "Just like the women."

"You think it's the same person?" The wounds on Keith's throat did suggest it. But he wasn't female, and he wasn't nailed to a tree, which was the killer's M.O. He'd been dumped unceremoniously in a heap on my front porch.

He nodded a few times. "Most likely. The wounds are consistent with the other victims."

"With all that damage, how can you tell?" There was blood everywhere, and his neck looked shredded to me.

He got down on his haunches and pointed to Keith's right clavicle. "You see how the bites start near the shoulder and continue along the bone?"

I bent down to get a better look. "Yeah, I see them."

"They get bigger and stop at the sternum. It's like the killer was leaving a trail of kisses, only with a set of fangs instead of lips. Then he goes in for the kill at the jugular."

His observations were impressive. Maybe Murphy wasn't such an idiot after all.

"The coroner will be able to compare the wounds and confirm it," he said as he straightened back up.

"Why are you being so generous with information?" I asked. He was usually more official. Tight-lipped so I had to pry it out of him.

"Because you need a good scare, Charley. That's the work of a serial killer. It's not safe for you to be out here on your own." He nodded to the corpse. "And that right there wasn't left on your front porch at random."

He was doing a good job of convincing me, but I wasn't about to let him know that.

"Is something unclear?" he asked, seeing my perplexed look.

"Something is very unclear. I thought Keith was still in jail. Did you finally see reason and let the poor man out?" That freedom had ironically sealed his fate.

Keith had been locked in a cell at police headquarters for weeks now, ever since he attacked one of the employees at the pharmacy. He beat the guy senseless in the alley behind the building and put him in the hospital. Everyone knew Keith had fallen victim to a vicious spell and was compelled to commit the crime, but the wheels of justice turned slowly around here.

"No ma'am. I stopped by headquarters this morning around nine a.m. and saw him in his cell with my own two eyes. So, either he escaped on his own, or he had help."

Rick Carter hung up his phone as he walked up the steps. "That was Jen. She said, other than the two of us, no one came in or out of the jail room since this morning."

"You mean the airhead you've got manning the desk over at the station?" It had been a piece of cake to manipulate her into letting me talk to Keith in his cell the day after the attack occurred.

Carter frowned at me. "That's not a very nice thing to say about the girl. She's a hard worker."

A brown-noser was more like it. I'm sure she stroked his ego on a daily basis.

"She's not a girl, Rick. She's a grown woman. Have you considered that maybe someone snuck past her and let Keith out the back door of the jail room?"

"That's impossible," Murphy said.

"Why? Because I suggested it?"

"Because there is no back door in the jail room. There's one in the front and one down the side hallway that leads to the alley, and it automatically locks from the inside. Anyone coming or going from the building would be in plain view of the reception desk. And Jen is required to lock the front door if she takes a break, if that's what you're going to ask next."

I pointed to the body. "Well, he got here somehow. If you've got a better theory, I'm all ears."

Murphy got his usual authoritative look, like he didn't appreciate my tone. "I don't need to tell you anything, Charley. We'll handle it."

The bigger question on my mind was why Keith? And why dump him on my front porch? "Why would the killer target him?"

"That's a good question. He was a regular at the Stag, so why don't you tell me?"

So now Murphy wanted me to do his job? "Like I said, it's not the killer's M.O., and he went to a lot of trouble to get to him."

"Or *she* went to a lot of trouble," Carter said.

I guess the killer could have been a woman. God knew there were plenty of them with fangs in Crimson.

"You're coming back to town with me," Murphy said. "I need to make an official report and get a few samples from you. Carter can wait for the coroner."

"You're serious?" I waited for the punchline.

"Keith Barnes was just murdered and left on your property.

This is standard procedure in a homicide investigation." Murphy walked down the steps and headed for his patrol car. "Let's go!"

It was getting late, so I cooperated for the sole purpose of getting him off my ass so I could get to the Stag by five o'clock. "I'll follow you." He looked back like he was about to argue with me. "You think I'm planning to run?"

"Don't test me, Charley." Giving me a warning glare, he continued toward his car.

I climbed in my truck and followed him back to town, getting more heated by the minute at Tom Murphy's absurd suggestion that I might be a suspect. As I drove past the Stag on the way to the police station, I caught a glimpse of Beau looking out the window. I wondered if he'd be pulled in for more questioning next.

I parked next to Murphy and got out, following him into the station. Jen was sitting behind the desk, chomping on gum as she scrolled the screen of her phone.

"I'll deal with you in a minute," Murphy said to her as he walked past the desk toward his office.

"Hey, Charley," she said as I walked past her.

"Jen." I continued into the room and waited for Murphy to get on with it.

He opened a cabinet and pulled out two plastic bags, one with a long Q-tip-looking thing inside. "I need a DNA sample from you, so open wide." He stuck the swab in my mouth and rubbed it against the inside of my cheek. After sticking it in the bag, he started scraping under my fingernails and took a few clippings.

"Is this really necessary?"

He glanced up from my hand. "You're not getting any special treatment."

"Oh, I wouldn't dream of it."

When he was done, he asked me the same questions I'd

already answered back at the house. Then he told me I was free to go. Before leaving his office, I looked back at him. "Are you familiar with a wolf named Magnus Ryan?"

His eyes flashed. "Where'd you hear that name?"

"He walked into the Stag this morning. I know all about him and thought you might want to check him out." I didn't have a clue if Mag was involved in the murders, but given his reputation and sudden appearance back in Crimson, I figured he was as much a suspect as anyone. It might also get Murphy off Beau's ass if he had someone else to focus on. Then again, if Mag was a rogue with women as Candy had said, maybe he did need to be questioned. He could have been living around these parts for months before walking into the Stag this morning.

"Did he mention where he's staying?"

"No, but he'll show up in town again. I'd bet my bar on it."

Murphy took a deep breath and seemed to be considering what I'd planted in his head. "You can go now."

On my way out, I stopped at the desk. "Keith didn't have any visitors today?"

Jen looked up from her phone. "I don't think I should be talking to you about this."

"You're right." I hooked my thumb over my shoulder. "I'll just let Tom know you wouldn't tell me anything."

Her chomping jaw went still as she glanced at his office door. "Tom's asking?"

"Yeah, he's busy writing up a report and asked me to come out here."

"I already told Rick over the phone that no one's been back there since they left the station this morning." She thought about it again and squinted at me. "But there was a guy in here asking for directions."

"Oh yeah? What did he look like?"

She got a blank stare on her face. "Well, that's funny."

There was nothing funny about any of this. "What's funny?"

"I can't remember." Her brows pulled together. "I think he had dark hair, but—"

"Jen!" Murphy bellowed from his office. "Get in here!"

That was my cue to leave. "I better get going." I hurried toward the door before Murphy came out and caught me questioning her, leaving her sitting behind the front desk with a confused look on her face.

SIX

"I can't believe someone would kill Keith." Beau looked shell-shocked. "I mean, he got on my nerves sometimes, but he wasn't a bad guy."

I'd pulled him into the kitchen with me and Dog to deliver the news. "He had his faults," I said, "but he didn't deserve this." Keith had been a regular customer at the Stag for years. And yeah, he could be a pain in the ass, but I was going to miss him sitting at the bar.

"It's so random," Beau continued. "The poor guy was probably just in the wrong place at the wrong time."

I shook my head. "This wasn't random. As of this morning, Keith was still in jail."

Dog stopped prepping the potatoes. "He wasn't out?"

"Nope. Murphy saw him in his cell this morning around nine a.m. Then he miraculously ended up dead on my front porch several hours later. How's that for a mystery?"

"I don't like it."

"I'm right there with you, Dog. Someone just sent me a deadly message. And to make matters worse, it looked just like the handiwork of whoever is killing women around here. Keith's throat was torn open."

Beau cocked his head. "But he was a guy. The killer's only been targeting women. Could have been anyone with fangs who killed him. A vampire, a wolf."

Dog shot him a glare. "Not one of mine."

"Take it easy," Beau said, stepping back. "I didn't say it was."

"Murphy's convinced it's the same killer, and I'm inclined to agree. He pointed out some striking resemblances to the wounds on the other victims, and it was pretty compelling. Now I just need to figure out why the killer left that body on *my* doorstep."

Dog wiped his hands on a towel and slapped it on the cutting board. "That's it. You're not staying out there alone."

"Of course not," I said. "I know damn well the pack will be hovering over my house." Between me and Tucker, they'd be spread pretty thin for the foreseeable future. "And let's not forget I've got a few tricks up my own sleeve."

A short laugh escaped Dog's mouth. "You mean your little adrenaline rushes? I can guarantee you the killer won't put his attack on hold while you figure out how to zap him with your beginner's magic."

"Very funny."

"It wasn't meant as a joke, Charley."

"Look, Dog. I'm done sleeping in other people's spare bedrooms, but I'll compromise with you. If it makes you feel better, you can have the pack watch the house at night. If it is a vampire, that's the only time I'll be vulnerable." Although that body was left on my porch in broad daylight, so there was a possibility it was something else with fangs. Regardless, a daytime attack was unlikely.

Dog nodded firmly. "Deal."

The conversation with Jen back at the station was bothering

me. "There's something else. It might be nothing, but I'm grasping at straws trying to make sense of how Keith got out of that jail cell."

"What?" Beau said. "That Keith pulled a Houdini?"

"I was leaving the station after being questioned, and I asked Jen if anyone had been in there that morning other than Carter or Murphy. She said a man came in looking for directions. Then she got this weird look on her face and said she couldn't remember what he looked like."

Beau scratched the back of his neck. "That's strange. You think the killer glamoured her and sprang Keith from his cell?"

"I guess it's possible." I hadn't noticed any cameras in the jail room when I went to see Keith right after he'd been arrested, so there was no way to find out.

Dog was eyeing me. "Murphy took you down to headquarters?"

"He all but called me a suspect. Then he took some DNA samples."

His eyes flashed as if the wolf wanted to come out. "I bet the son of a bitch enjoyed that. Did he check your mouth for a set of fangs too?"

"He enjoyed it all right. I'm sure he'll be knocking on Beau's door with a DNA sample kit next."

Beau's eyes went wide. "Me?"

"Don't act so surprised. He already tried to interrogate you about Kim Widby's murder. Just don't tell him anything. And if he tries to arrest you, you definitely need to keep your mouth shut."

"Then tell him you want a lawyer," Dog added.

Poor Beau. He looked like he wanted to piss his pants.

The front door opened, and the familiar sound of curses came spilling out of Lucy's mouth. "Where the hell is everyone?"

Beau and I walked out front and saw her standing behind the bar with her back turned to us. "You're late?" I said.

"My car wouldn't start. I had to get a jump."

Her car was acting up a lot lately. "Come on, Lucy. Can't you be more creative than that? It's the second time this week."

She turned around and gave me a dose of attitude. "Big. Damn. Deal."

There was a bruise covering her right eye. "What happened to you?"

"Nothing."

"That ain't nothing," Beau said, walking over to get a closer look at it. "What'd you do? Run into someone's fist?"

"Get away from me!" She grabbed a couple of bowls and filled them with peanuts. "I got into a fight with Wes."

Dog came out of the kitchen to see what all the fuss was about. "Your brother did that to you?"

"He came home drunk at two a.m. and started acting like a fool. He turned the TV volume all the way up and dropped a whole gallon of milk on the kitchen floor. The idiot," she grumbled. "Then he started punching the wall, so I climbed out of bed and hit him over the head with an empty beer bottle." She shrugged. "I don't think he meant to hit me back, but I got in the way when he turned around swinging."

Dog sighed. "One of you is going to have to move out of that house before you kill each other."

If you ever yearned for a whole new family, all you had to do was take a look at the Wyatts to make you appreciate the one you had. I kind of felt sorry for Lucy for having been dealt that hand.

"I can't have you working the bar with a bruise covering half your face." She'd have every customer in the place ribbing her about it. Then she'd end up going off on one of them, and we'd have a free-for-all on our hands.

"Are you giving me the night off with pay? Because if you aren't, I'm staying."

I went into the hallway to make a quick call and then came back over to the bar. "Come on. We need to fix this."

Reluctantly, she came around the bar but stopped when I headed for the front door. "Where are we going?"

"To the Cauldron."

Lucy finally followed me out the door, and I put up with her bitching for a block before stopping to look at her. "Will you shut it! I swear to God. You're your own worst enemy."

"Fine, but she better not try to feed me any funny stuff. And none of that crystal-waving nonsense either."

Candy didn't do crystals. She sold them to tourists, but that was the extent of it.

When we walked into the shop, Candy was waiting for us, armed and ready to take on that shiner. She patted the stool next to the counter and opened her vintage makeup case. It was more like a suitcase. "Take a seat, baby. We'll get you all fixed up."

Lucy shot me a hostile glare. "Are you kidding me?"

"There's nothing funny about that bruise," I said. "Sit down."

Candy took a therapeutic breath before diving in. Then she reached for Lucy's chin and raised it up to examine the damage. "Well, that is a doozy. Who'd you piss off?"

"Her brother did it to her," I said.

She grabbed a compact with three different shades of concealer, dabbing a little of each around Lucy's eye to find the right shade. "I hope you gave him a little love right back."

"Don't encourage her, Candy."

"Why? If a man puts his hands on you, you better beat his ass. If you don't, he'll just keep doing it." She glanced up at me. "Got to let him know he can't use you as a punching bag."

"He was drunk." Lucy shrugged. "And I hit him first."

Candy continued to dab makeup around the bruise with a sponge and stepped back to look at her handiwork. "I guess that was your first mistake. You can't reason with a drunk."

"I was just pissed off. He's been going to some bar every night this week and coming home hammered. Wes ain't no Boy Scout, but he's never been a mean drunk either. At least not to me."

Wes and Richie Wyatt were major assholes who messed with their little sister relentlessly, but I had to admit, she'd never once walked into the Stag with a bruise like that. "What bar was he at?"

She hesitated and then mumbled something I couldn't make out.

"What did you say?"

"I said he went to the Beast!" She practically growled it out. "Are you happy now? My brother is a card-carrying degenerate."

I could have told her that. But she was clearly distressed, so I thought it best not to add insult to injury.

Candy patted some face powder over the concealer. "We all need to feel our oats now and then, but that place is only good for two things: to get bitten by a vampire or laid by one."

Nice, Candy.

Lucy reared back and gave her an incredulous look. "Are you implying that my brother is screwing vampires?"

Candy squinted at her handiwork, not the least bit concerned that the Stag's resident Tasmanian devil was inches away from her face. "Either that or he's partaking in illegal drugs."

That was something else the Beast was known for.

"It's nothing like that," Lucy said. "After he sobered up this morning, I asked him what the hell he was doing at a club like the Beast. He said they've got girls down there."

I snorted. "Well, yeah. Vampires. And women looking to meet vampires."

"That's not what I'm talking about. Wes said they have dancers now. You know. Strippers." She glanced at Candy. "No offense."

Candy motioned to the pole in the corner. "Do I look like I offend easily?"

"I just don't want you to think I'm a bigot or anything."

She smirked. "Oh, I would never think that about a Wyatt."

Lucy's brow furrowed. "What's that supposed to mean?"

Trying to change the subject before my bartender showed her ass, I grabbed a mirror next to the makeup case and handed it to her. "Have a look."

Candy crossed her arms. "Now people won't think you went three rounds with a kangaroo."

Lucy examined her eye for a moment. "You can't even see it now. You should be a makeup artist."

"That's not the first shiner I've fixed up," Candy said, packing up her makeup case. "Back in my dancing days, a lot of the girls requested my services."

I checked the time. "We better get going." Tucker wasn't coming in until seven, and that was just to help Dog in the kitchen where I was keeping her for a while. That meant Beau was alone behind the bar on a Friday night.

"Lucy can go on ahead of you," Candy said to me. "We need to have a talk."

No one in this town could keep their mouth shut for more than five minutes, so she probably already heard about Keith.

"Tell Dog I'll be back in a few minutes," I said to Lucy.

When she wouldn't budge, Candy gave her some incentive. "Why don't you run along before I break out the candles and incense."

That got her off the stool. After she walked out the door, I cut to the chase. "Keith Barnes was murdered. Whoever did it dumped his body at my door this afternoon." She didn't even flinch, which confirmed my suspicions. "Who's been running their mouth?"

"Mayor Adams. We were in the middle of a session when he got the call from Carter." She let out a steady breath. "Bodies are dropping like flies around here."

"For the life of me, I can't understand why the killer would leave Keith's body on my front porch?"

"Oh, I don't know. Foreplay?" Her eyes filled with worry. "Maybe you're next, which is why I'm moving in with you." She gripped her sapphire amulet tightly. "I'd like to see the bastard try something with the two of us taking him on."

"You're not moving in, Candy. Dog already told me the pack will be watching the place. And do I need to remind you that a vampire can't enter my house without an invitation?"

She knew better than to push it. "All right. But let's just hope the killer is a vampire and not something else with fangs. Good luck keeping a werewolf out."

The only kind of wolves around here were shifters. The next closest wolves were north of Crimson, but the pack would have smelled them if they'd blown into town. A werewolf on the other hand...

Candy gave me a weak smile. "I know you don't believe it was Ian Masterson who attacked Patrice Henderson, but I don't trust that vampire. Even if he's not the killer, he could still be involved somehow."

"Then maybe I should have another talk with him."

She looked at me like I had a screw loose. "Do I need to take your temperature?"

"Don't worry. I'm not going anywhere near him without the pack with me." The truth was, I wasn't nearly as afraid of Ian Masterson as I was before we made a truce, but I wasn't a fool either.

"Well, at least you have some sense." She glanced out the window. "You better get back to the Stag. Dusk is setting in."

I hated that we all had to worry about that. I missed the days when I could walk around at night and not have to worry about a vampire I happened to pass on the street. Now we had elements out there giving half the citizens of Crimson a bad name.

As I headed toward the bar, I wondered if Candy was right. Was I next in line? A breeze blew down the street, and I picked up the pace as an unsettling feeling came over me. The feeling that I was being watched.

* * *

The night was busier than usual, even for a Friday, and I'd jumped in to help behind the bar so Tucker could stay put in the kitchen. At least for the time being.

It was almost closing time when I spotted the black SUV pull up in front of the bar. Those guys from Atlanta were bold, I'd give them that.

Beau spotted them too. "What do we do?"

"Don't panic, and get Lucy out of here." The last thing I needed was for her to start running her mouth if they looked at her wrong and have a repeat of yesterday morning.

"Charley—"

"Just do it." I glanced at the rifle on the shelf under the bar. I figured I'd keep it around for a few days for this very reason, and now I was glad I did. I just prayed I didn't have to use it.

As Beau and Lucy walked into the hallway, I went over to the order window. "We've got company," I said to Dog. "Make sure Tucker stays in the kitchen. In fact, lock her in the pantry."

He followed my gaze out the window. "Fuck. Let me handle them."

I shook my head. "No. I'll get rid of them." We still had a

bar full of people, including a lot of vampires. Granted, most of those vampires were more lovers than fighters, but they still had fangs. I just hoped those guys weren't brazen enough to pull another stunt. "Just make sure the pack is on their toes tonight." I let out a nervous chuckle. "I'll holler if I need help."

Tucker walked up behind him. "What's going on?"

Dog stopped her from looking through the order window as the two men got out of the SUV and approached the door. "Your friends are back."

Her eyes expanded as a gasp slipped from her mouth. Then she did as Dog instructed and hid in the back of the kitchen.

They scanned the room as they walked inside. The one with the black hair came toward the bar while his colleague stayed near the door. The asshole had the nerve to crook his finger at me, but I wasn't moving out of reach of that gun. When I refused to budge, he strolled over, muscling his way between a couple of patrons to get right up to me.

"You can ask me again," I said, trying to appear confident while my hands trembled, "but the answer is still the same. I haven't seen the woman you're looking for."

One of my regulars, a vampire, was listening to the exchange. He must have smelled my fear because he looked at the guy and smiled, revealing his fangs. "Is there a problem, Charley?"

"No problem, Dave. Everything's just fine."

The man stared at me for a moment, and then his eyes wandered to the order window. I held my breath as he locked eyes with Dog, the tension between them palpable. When he reached into his jacket, I went for the gun. A moment later I was looking down the barrel at him.

Chaos erupted in the room as people scrambled, most of them running for the door.

"I wouldn't do that if I were you," I said when the thug's hand disappeared deeper into his jacket. "Take your hand out."

Dog was out of the kitchen and standing by the bar a second later. "You heard the woman." A growl came from his throat.

The guy pulled a business card from his pocket, holding it between his middle and index fingers as he threw his hands up. "Take it easy. We just stopped by on our way out of town to give you this." He set it down on the bar. "In case you tossed the last one we gave you."

It was that same glossy black business card they'd presented the first time they'd showed up here. "I won't be needing it."

His brows arched. "If you change your mind, our employer will be generous with a reward. Very generous."

Dog growled again, this time flashing his wolf eyes. "It's time for you to leave."

Never lowering the gun, I seconded that. "I'd do as he said, if I were you."

He backed up toward the door and looked at his buddy. Then they left and got back in the SUV, circling the square toward the town exit.

Beau came out of the kitchen a moment later. "Are they gone?"

"They're gone," Tucker said, walking up behind him. "If they knew I was back there, they wouldn't have thought twice about coming into the kitchen after me."

"Doesn't mean they won't be back," Dog said. "Atlanta is just ninety minutes south of here." He grabbed the gun that was still wedged in my hands by a death grip and handed it to Beau. "Get this thing out of the bar."

While Beau went to stash it in my truck, I made an announcement to the few stragglers in the place. "We're closing early, folks." As they were leaving, I gave Dog a weary glance. "Can you guys close up without me?"

"You okay?"

My adrenaline was still in my throat. "I'm fine. I just need to take care of some business in the back." The business of steadying my shaking legs.

As soon as I got to the back room and sat down at the desk, I heard scratching. I got back up when a faint meow came from the other side of the door.

"Hey, Sebastian," I said as I cracked it open to let the cat in. But he just leaned into the doorframe and rubbed his scent all over it with his cheek. "Are you coming in or not?"

He looked up at me and meowed again before running down the steps and stopping near the dumpster.

"Forget it, cat. I'm not coming out there." Nothing good ever came from that dumpster, especially at night.

He disappeared into the darkness, meowing with more urgency. When I stepped outside, I couldn't see him anymore. "Sebastian?"

Another urgent meow.

"Damn cat," I muttered, walking down the steps into the alley. "Where are you?" I went toward the spot where he'd disappeared, giving that metal box a wide berth, and saw the tip of his tail sticking out from the shadow of the building. As I was reaching for him, a figure stepped out.

"Jesus, Samuel!" I backed up but relaxed when I realized I wasn't about to find myself nailed to a tree in the woods. "You scared the hell out of me."

He came closer, backing me against the wall. "It's not safe to be out here, Charley. Haven't you heard? There's a killer on the loose." He leaned into me, his brilliant blue eyes causing my breath to hitch.

"I'm aware of that. I was just..."

"You were what? Going for a midnight stroll in the dark?" His eyes flashed red and then shifted back to blue as his scent intensified, triggering something deep inside me. Then he braced his hand on the wall and brought his face within inches of mine.

His timing was awful. "Samuel, I don't think this is a good time to—"

My body shivered as he grazed me, bending down to scoop Sebastian off the ground. "There you are." Then he straightened back up. "You were saying?"

I needed to get out of there before he unleashed that scent on me again. I could already feel my skin starting to heat up. "I need to go back inside and help close the bar."

He held my gaze as he stroked his cat. "You're going to make me work for it, aren't you?" With a featherlight touch, he brushed the backs of his fingers over my cheek, lowering his gaze to my mouth before bringing his eyes back up to mine. "You're flushing."

Feeling like I was about to burn up inside, I slid out from under him and headed for the door. "You and your cat have a nice night."

"Coy doesn't suit you, Charley," he said as I walked away.

The word made me cringe.

I stopped, realizing this wasn't what I wanted. What I wanted was him. "Samuel—" But by the time I turned around, it was too late. He was already gone.

SEVEN

By six a.m., the line was already halfway down the alley, and we weren't even scheduled to start for another half hour. The co-op was doing more business than ever. With the tension in town between humans and vampires settling down, donations were up. We had more vampires than we needed to keep the fine citizens of Crimson supplied with blood. I just hoped that the rumors of competition Patrick mentioned were just that—baseless rumors.

"How'd your date go last night?" I asked Patrick when he sat behind the desk to set up.

He glanced up from his briefcase. "You see a smile on my face?"

It was more of a cocky grin. "At least someone is getting lucky these days."

"Baby, it ain't luck. But you gotta put yourself out there if you want to get laid, which is something you should seriously consider."

My mind went back to the alley last night. "Do I seem coy to you?"

"Coy? Girl, there ain't nothing coy about you. A little tight, maybe."

"What do you mean by tight?"

He twirled his finger at me. "You need to loosen up that tape you got wound around your legs and go find that vampire who's been sniffing around here."

I think I'd blown that opportunity. Samuel was probably getting tired of "working for it" as he described it. He'd probably already moved on to one of the many women in town just dying to be ravished by a gorgeous vampire, and suddenly the thought made me extremely uneasy.

There was a soft knock on the door, and Mabel Gentry cracked it open and peered inside. "Is it time yet?"

"Thirty more minutes," Patrick said, getting back to organizing the vials.

I gave him a chastising look and opened the door all the way. "Come inside, Mabel."

For the first time in ages, she had a genuine smile on her face. "It's good not to have to worry about whether or not we'll get our medicine this week."

"Let's hope it stays that way," I said.

Her smile flattened. "Why? Do you think the blood will dry up again?"

"I didn't mean to worry you. The co-op will be just fine." The truth was, there was always the fear of something blowing the co-op to smithereens. Lack of donors, getting raided, a dangerous pathogen slipping into the supply. There were any number of risks, but not today.

"Don't you worry," Patrick said to her. "We got you."

She took her two vials and walked out the door as the next member walked inside. One by one we handed out precious vials of relief to every person in line, knowing that at any time, the next catastrophe could occur and send everyone back into a world of hurt. But for now, we were all content. That was half the battle when dealing with pain and illness. Come hell or high water, I intended to keep it that way for as long as possible.

* * *

It was Lucy's night off, which worked out fine since that shiner on her face probably looked worse than the day before. It would still be there when she came in tomorrow night, but Sundays brought in a light crowd. Fewer people to heckle her about it. I'd also decided to let Tucker tend bar again. I couldn't hide her in the kitchen forever, and the pack had confirmed that the SUV belonging to those thugs had indeed driven out of town last night.

"Charley!" Beau called from the other end of the bar. He was having a conversation with a customer.

I walked over to them. "What's up?"

"CJ was just telling me about a couple of women who went missing down in Little Crimson."

"Vampires?" My immediate thought was that we had two more victims, but so far, the killer had only attacked humans.

CJ took a swallow of his beer. "Yep. Roommates. Neighbors of mine, and good ones too." He shook his head slowly. "They went out Thursday night to grab a drink and haven't been seen since."

"Are you sure they're missing?" I said.

"That's what I hear."

The bar suddenly went quiet. I looked up to see what had gotten everyone's attention and saw Mag standing just inside the door. I guess a lot of people around here knew who he was, and based on their reactions, his reputation preceded him.

Dog looked through the order window and spotted Mag walking toward the bar. Without taking his eyes off the wolf, he beckoned me into the kitchen with a crook of his finger.

"I'll be back in a minute," I said to Beau.

The second I walked through the door, Dog practically jumped down my throat. "What the hell is he doing here?"

"My guess is he wants a drink."

He glowered at me for a few seconds before heading toward the kitchen door. "Well, I'm getting him out."

"Wait!" If he went out there all hotheaded, a fight would break out, and I'd seen enough of those in my bar over the past few weeks to last a lifetime. "I'll serve him a drink and hopefully he'll be on his way."

Dog chuckled and snarled at the same time. "Not likely."

"Then I'll ask him politely to leave. If he still doesn't get the message, he's all yours."

He took his anger down a notch. "Fine!"

"Don't bark at me. We're on the same team here."

"Sorry, but that asshole sitting out there"—he pointed to the window—"is pressing his luck."

"I get it. You've got history. Just let the man have a drink and we'll take it from there."

He nodded once and walked over to the refrigerator, grabbing a head of lettuce from the product bin so hard he nearly crushed it in his hand. "He's got twenty minutes."

"Thirty," I said, hurrying out of the kitchen before he could argue about it.

When I got back up front, Mag was chatting up Tucker. Stools at the bar were prime real estate on Saturday nights, so he must have persuaded the previous occupant to move.

"Mag," I greeted him when I walked behind the bar.

His eyes wandered down to my chest and back up again. "Charley."

It was a good thing Lucy was off tonight. She would have been all over him.

Tucker gave him a shy smile. "Magnus was telling me he just came back to Crimson after being gone for several years."

"Call me Mag, darlin'." He winked at her and downed his

shot of whiskey. "What time do you get off? I'll stop back by and have a drink with you."

"She's closing tonight," I said. He'd just finished his one drink, but something told me he wouldn't appreciate being told to leave five minutes after walking through the door. I'd give him the full thirty, as long as he didn't start trouble.

I nodded to his empty glass. "You want another shot of Jack?" I'd cut him off after that.

He grinned. "The lady already knows what I like."

"I just have a good memory."

I went to grab his glass, but Tucker beat me to it. "I got it." Her schoolgirl smile suddenly disappeared when she realized she'd practically snatched it out of my hand. "Unless you want to get it for him."

"You go right ahead." I patted her on the shoulder and continued down the bar.

Beau leaned into me when I walked over to where he was standing. "I thought you weren't going to let that guy in here anymore."

"No. I said I'd give him a chance to prove that he isn't as bad as Dog makes him out to be. He's got about twenty more minutes to do so. Then he's leaving." Even if he did behave, Dog came first around here. If he was uncomfortable with Mag, the wolf had to go.

Tucker had clearly fallen for his charm. She had her elbows planted on the bar and a wide smile on her face, hanging on every word Mag was saying to her. If I didn't run some interference, the girl was a smooth line away from having her panties around her ankles after closing.

"I need to have a word with Tucker in private," I said to Beau. "Can you handle the bar by yourself for five minutes?"

He shrugged. "Sure."

I walked up to Tucker and grabbed her arm. "Excuse us for

a minute," I said to Mag. "We need to check the stock in the back room."

"Stock?" She gave me a strange look as I ushered her out from behind the bar.

By the time we got to the back room, she seemed genuinely confused. "Is there a problem?"

"Not if I can help it." I let out a long sigh. "Here's the thing, Tucker. When it comes to women, that man out there is trouble, and you looked like you were steering straight toward it."

"Who? Mag?" Her confused look suddenly lifted. "Oh! I'm sorry, Charley. I can be a little dense sometimes. But I get the message loud and clear. He's all yours."

"What? No!" My head shook in frustration. "That is *definitely* not what I'm trying to say. Look, Tucker. You're a grown woman, so you can do what you want. But I know things about Mag, and trust me, I don't think he's your type." Come to think of it, maybe he was. I didn't know her well enough to have a clue about what she liked. For all I knew, she preferred men who walked all over her. "Do what you want," I said, heading for the door. "Just don't say I didn't warn you."

When I went back up front, I caught Mag watching me as I crossed the room. He didn't bother to hide it either.

He jiggled his empty glass at me when I walked past him. "How about another shot?"

"I think you've reached your limit." I glanced at Dog staring at him through the order window. "You might want to get going."

"But I'm not done looking at you yet."

Was he serious?

I gave him my full attention. "Are you actually trying to hit on me?"

"That depends."

"Oh yeah? On what?"

He set his glass down and nudged it toward me with his

index finger. "On if you're the kind of woman who likes a quick fuck." He leaned over the bar. "But something tells me you're not." It was a statement, but there was a question in his eyes. The customers sitting on either side of him wasted no time getting up and out of striking range.

I stared at him, a little lost for words. By the time I found my voice again and prepared to give him a piece of my mind, I heard the front door open.

Samuel walked in and strolled over to the bar, planting himself on one of the vacated stools. "Charley."

I held his gaze for a moment as the memory of his fingers brushing against my cheek came rushing back, but I shook it off when I caught Mag watching me.

I grabbed a bottle of the best scotch in the house and poured Samuel a drink. After setting the glass down in front of him, I turned back to Mag. "It's time for you to go."

When the wolf wouldn't budge, Samuel took a sip of his drink and looked at him sideways. "I believe the lady asked you to leave."

"I don't need any help," I said to him, continuing to stare at Mag. Dog came out from the kitchen next. "I don't need yours either." Damn it. It was my bar, and I didn't recall asking for anyone's help.

Dog kept his distance but stayed put.

Mag locked eyes with me for a moment before finally standing up. He threw some money on the bar and smiled at me, then gave Dog a scowl as he turned and walked toward the door. "It's nice to see you again, Charley," he said without looking back. "Let's do it again sometime."

Dog came over and looked me in the eye. "That's the Mag you haven't met yet. The one I know."

"Okay, you were right. He's an asshole." I glanced at Tucker. "What did I tell you?"

Samuel finished his drink and stood up. "Can we have a word in private?"

After telling Beau to hold down the fort for a few minutes, Samuel and I went to the back room. "Is something wrong?"

He seemed annoyed. "What's this I hear about a body on your doorstep?"

"How did you—?" I shook my head. "Never mind." Half the town must have heard about it by now. "His name was Keith Barnes. He was one of my customers. I found him when I got home yesterday afternoon."

His face hardened. "Why didn't you mention it last night?"

"I wasn't aware I had to."

He continued to stare at me intently. "Tell me what happened. Leave no detail out. Not even the smallest one."

Jeez, he was more thorough than Murphy.

"I came home yesterday afternoon and found him dead on my porch with his throat ripped open." I shrugged. "There's nothing more to tell."

His eyes narrowed like he wasn't convinced I was telling him everything. "Was anything left with or found on the body? Any strange marks or symbols?"

"You mean other than his throat being ripped open? I'd say those were strange marks."

"I'm serious, Charley."

"Believe me, so am I." I'd be scrubbing blood off my porch for days.

He kept staring at me, but now it was like he was looking straight through me.

"Samuel? What's going on?"

A brief smile appeared on his face as his eyes refocused on mine. "I'm just concerned about you."

I wasn't in the mood for another safety lecture, so I ended the conversation and turned to leave. "Candy does enough worrying about me for everyone else, so save your breath."

He stepped in front of me before I could walk out. "Does that mean you won't be inviting me to move in?"

"Tempting but I'm not looking for a roommate."

He came closer, backing me against the wall. The intensity in his eyes was almost too painful to look at. "Oh, Charley. Neither am I."

I froze. Trapped by his gaze. It was like he was reaching into me and stroking me from the inside. Before I could put a coherent thought together in my mind, he pressed his lips to mine and kissed me gently but thoroughly, leaving me aching for more.

He pulled away too quickly. "I won't let anything happen to you, Charley." His expression turned thoughtful for a moment. Almost confused. "I don't think I could bear it."

I wanted to pull him against me. Take in his scent and kiss him until neither one of us could breathe. But then suddenly he was backing away from me, the conflict in his eyes easy enough for any fool to read.

"I have to go."

It was like a punch to the gut. "Go where, Samuel?"

Without another word, he gave me a last look and slipped out the back door, leaving me pressed against the wall with a hollowness in my chest. I had no idea what had just happened, but it left me breathless, and I wanted more.

EIGHT

There was a rather loud knock on my door. I rolled over and looked at the time. It was three a.m. "What the hell?"

I stumbled out of bed and pulled on a pair of jeans, trying to figure out if I'd been dreaming or if someone was actually stupid enough to knock on my door at this hour.

The knock came again, only this time it was louder.

Fearing something bad had happened, I hurried down the hallway into the living room. "I'm coming," I muttered, peeking through the front window to see who it was. I'd just found a dead body on my porch two days earlier, so I wasn't about to blindly yank the door open. And where was the pack?

Desiree Dubois was at my front door. I looked closer and saw Katherine Belltower and the Winston sisters next to her. The Squad was standing on my porch.

I heard a key insert into the lock. The door opened a second later, and Candy walked inside with the four witches right behind her.

Had she lost her mind?

She startled when she saw me standing by the window.

"Good Lord, Charley, you scared me! I didn't know if you heard us knocking, so I used my key."

I gawked at her. "For all that is holy, *what* is going on?"

A sly grin slid up her face as she looked at the time. "It's the witching hour, honey. It's time for a lesson."

My jaw dropped. "I've died and gone to hell. That's what this is."

Desiree brushed past Candy and continued into the living room. "Hell doesn't exist, dear. It's a fairytale." She glanced around, pulling the collar of her shirt together as if a chill had rolled through the room. "The house has changed. It feels... empty."

Candy shot her a warning look. "You don't live here, so why don't you keep your comments to yourself."

Mia Winston clapped her hands briskly. "Chop, chop! Let's get started. The hour is passing."

Magic was at its most powerful during the witching hour. At least that's what my mother used to say. And now I had five witches standing in my living room at three a.m.

I heard footsteps on the porch and saw Loki, the pack's second-in-command, standing outside the open door. "Is everything okay?" he asked, looking at the ladies.

Fine question to ask me now.

"Yeah, everything's fine." I wasn't sure what they had in store for me, though. "I'll yell if I need you."

"You can go back to patrolling," Candy said, shooing him away. "If you hear banging coming from the house, just ignore it."

Banging? What kind of lesson was this?

I was dead tired. "Are you sure we can't do this at a normal hour?" None of them dignified my question with an answer. "Then let's get this over with."

Candy went toward the kitchen. "Lose the attitude, honey. The killer has his eye on you, and I intend to make sure you don't become his next victim." She stopped to look back at me. "Unless you've changed your mind about staying at my place?"

I put on a saccharine smile. "Ready when you are."

Rex swooped down from the refrigerator, and Desiree let out a yipe as his talons grazed her cherry-red hair and plucked a few strands before flying through the open door.

She gasped. "Get that crow!"

"No one's touching him," I said, closing the door. Rex lived here; she didn't. "He got startled, that's all."

Fay looked horrified. "But he has Desiree's hair! She's vulnerable!"

I hardly expected Rex to be up in that tree casting spells with a few strands of the witch's hair.

"You're being paranoid," Candy said. "Let's just get on with it while we still have time."

I squinted at her. "What exactly is *it*?"

Katherine reached into her bag and pulled out a jar. It was painted black, and I could hear something moving around inside. "Something to fortify you from the inside out."

A shiver ran through me as I pulled my eyes away from the jar to look at Candy. My dear beloved friend who would never do anything to hurt me, I kept telling myself. "What is she talking about?" I wanted to climb into Candy's lap and hide.

She gave me a commiserative smile. "You trust me, don't you, honey?"

I trusted her with my life, but I had my limits. "What's in the jar?"

Katherine started to unscrew the lid but stopped short of opening it. "You'll have to swallow it quickly so it doesn't escape." A dark laugh slipped from her mouth. "If that happens, we're all in trouble."

"Candy?" My legs took an involuntary step back.

She took a deep breath and exhaled slowly. "We need to activate the magic inside you."

"I'm not sure I'm okay with this," I said, glancing at the jar again.

"Don't be foolish," Mia said. "You're an Underwood, and an Underwood witch must be seasoned properly."

Candy's smile grew more commiserative. "Every witch has a little flicker in their belly just waiting to explode into a bonfire. But like I've said before, you've got some napalm in you. With all this killing going on around here, now's as good a time as any to bring it to the surface."

"But I told you, I've been practicing. I have it under control." It was a lie I was willing to tell because whatever was in that jar was moving. Candy knew me well, though. Annoyingly well. By the look on her face, she was calling my bullshit. "Fine. What do I have to do?"

Desiree grinned mischievously and clapped her stubby little hands. "Delia would be proud." Then her eyes darkened as she turned to Katherine. "Quickly before she changes her mind."

Candy suddenly lost her smile. "Let's take our time." I could feel her nervous energy wrapping around me.

"We don't have time," Katherine replied. "Half the hour is already gone. Outside. Now!"

"Where are we going?" I asked Candy as she ushered me toward the door.

"The ritual will be more powerful under the moonlight," she said.

They practically pushed me out the door and down the steps. I kept expecting the pack to intervene when they saw me being manhandled by a bunch of witches, but I was on my own. There wasn't a wolf in sight. I kept reminding myself that Candy wouldn't do anything to hurt me, but it wasn't her I was worried about.

We stopped in the center of the yard. The moon must have gotten the memo because it was brighter than usual. Almost too bright. But then it was the witching hour.

Katherine came closer to me and held the jar at arm's length. "Like I said, swallow it quickly."

I glanced at it and let out a nervous laugh. "You're not going to tell me what's in there, are you?"

She gazed at me for a moment. "It's better this way. Trust me, Charley. It won't hurt you if you surrender to it."

And if I didn't?

My eyes shifted to Candy as Katherine started to unscrew the lid again. "You've done this, right?" She was a witch. Surely, she'd partaken in the ritual herself.

"Not exactly, but I'm not from these parts. But your mama did," she quickly added when she saw the look of panic in my eyes.

The world came to a screeching halt when Katherine shoved the jar closer and lifted the lid. I caught a glimpse of something black and fuzzy scurrying over the edge before retreating back inside. Katherine grabbed me by the nape of my neck and pulled me forward, pressing the jar forcefully to my lips. She dropped it and stumbled, a look of fascination rolling over her face as my eyes flew wide.

The spider crawled past my lips toward the back of my mouth, making me gag as it continued down my throat. I couldn't breathe. Desperately, I tried to open my mouth to hack it back up, but my lips were sealed shut.

"Don't fight it!" Katherine came closer and looked me in the eye. "Swallow it!"

Candy knelt next to me and took my hand when I fell to the ground. "It's all right, honey. I've got you."

The next thing I remembered was the sound of growls coming from every direction. The faces of witches and wolves staring down at me were the last things I saw before everything went black.

* * *

I had no idea what was happening to me, but it felt like a dirty war was taking place in my gut. The spider crawled along my stomach, biting at my insides. But the worst part was seeing it vividly in my mind as it wreaked havoc inside me.

Somewhere in the distance, I heard the faint voices of the witches mixed with the thunderous growls of the wolves. But Candy's voice filled my head like a mantra.

Hold on, Charley. It's almost over.

It was torture. Death would have been kinder.

I fought to open my eyes, praying it would stop. And then I saw her as clear as day. My mother was stirring something in a large pot under the moonlight. In a cauldron.

Charlotte, it's time for dinner.

The pain faded as the movement in my stomach ceased. I climbed to my feet and walked toward her, a familiar humming filling my ears. I peered over her shoulder as she stirred, catching her reflection in the black liquid filling the cauldron. Her face was the same, but her eyes were pits filled with white mist.

I stumbled back when the liquid in the cauldron started to boil. Something was coming to the surface.

She gripped my arm and pulled me back toward her.

Don't you dare show fear. You're a witch, Charlotte. An Underwood.

My mother suddenly started to shrink as a leg poked through the liquid. The spider's eyes broke the surface next, shiny and black like spheres of onyx. The rest of it emerged and climbed over the edge of the cauldron, scurrying down the side toward the grass as it continued to grow.

My feet froze as it engulfed her, leaving me paralyzed and mute to watch helplessly as it fed, reducing my mother within seconds to nothing but a pile of clothing on the ground.

Whatever it was finally released me. I grabbed a branch and tried to smash the spider, hitting it repeatedly. As I prepared to deliver a final deadly blow, a sharp pain hit me in the stomach. I dropped the branch and doubled over. Something was raging through me. The spider's venom. I couldn't breathe.

I was dying.

* * *

My eyes popped open. The moon had been replaced by the morning sun. Katherine lay on the ground next to me with blood trailing down her face. I scurried away from her and looked up at the witches, shocked and confused.

They helped Katherine to her feet and dusted her off, dabbing her face with their sleeves. She seemed okay, but what about all that blood?

I stared at the blue light coming from my hands. "What did I do?"

"You won," Katherine said, glancing down at the dead spider on the ground. It was flattened. It was also missing some legs. "You went to battle and came out on the other side. It's done."

Candy reached down to help me up. "The fire in your belly has always been there, but it's lit now." She grabbed my hand. "Don't go pointing that finger around willy-nilly. You could take someone's head off if you're not careful."

Mortified, I looked back at Katherine. "I'm sorry."

She straightened her hair and reached for the dead spider. "Don't ever apologize for being what you are."

"But—"

"Never!"

I nodded slowly, not fully understanding what had just happened. "It was so strange. My mother was there and—"

Desiree stopped me. "Never talk about the ritual. It's for you only."

"Ooo*okay*."

I looked around the yard, wondering where all the wolves had gone. I'd seen them, so I knew they'd witnessed what had happened. "Where did the pack go?" I was surprised Dog wasn't standing there when I'd opened my eyes.

"Witches only," Candy said. "We sent them on their way, but Dog wasn't as easy to get rid of. He's inside the house."

I went in to find him. He was passed out on the couch when I walked into the living room. "Dog?"

His eyes flew open. He jumped to his feet as the wolf morphed in and out. When he realized it was me standing in front of him, he ran his hands over his startled face and took a few steadying breaths. "Fucking witches!"

They must have knocked him out good.

Candy walked in behind me. "Sorry about that, Dog, but that's what you get for not leaving when politely asked. What happened out there wasn't for your eyes."

"Careful." He glowered at her. "A witch's magic can backfire when used on a wolf."

She disarmed him with a pat on the back. "I guess I'll just have to make it up to you. In the meantime, I don't think either one of us will be worrying about our girl over here much longer. She's on her way to becoming a certified witch. With a little more training that is."

A little more? I wasn't swallowing any more spiders, if that's what they had planned. I did feel like I was about to jump out of my skin from all the energy coursing through me, though.

I went back to the door to see what the Squad was up to in the yard, but they were gone when I looked outside. Rex flew down from the tree and landed on the porch railing with a few strands of cherry-red hair still gripped between his talons. Then I looked up at the sky. It had turned dark, and raindrops were just a moment away.

NINE

I was still buzzing with energy by the time I got to the Stag that evening. Every time I touched the metal edge of the sink behind the bar, a mild shock ran through me. Dog kept his eye on me through the order window like he half expected me to start levitating or something.

As much as I tried to pick Candy's brain about what had happened to me in my yard that morning, what it all meant, she refused to talk about it. Said it was my experience to figure out, and if I wasn't careful, it would slip away with the words coming out of my mouth. I'd lose all memory of it completely, and eating that spider—which I was convinced wasn't a hallucination—would have been for nothing.

Beau had been breezing up and down the bar all evening like a well-oiled bartending machine. He was unusually pleasant. Not that he wasn't generally an easygoing guy, but tonight something definitely had him feeling good.

"What's up with you tonight?" I asked him.

He grinned and flipped a glass into the air, catching it on its way back down. "Why? Can't I just be in a good mood?"

Murphy hadn't shown up over the weekend to question him

again about Kim Widby, so that was something for him to be thankful for. But I knew him better than that. "Who's the lucky girl?" He was definitely sleeping with someone new.

His grin grew wider. "Just someone I met last night."

"You were working last night."

"Yeah, and then I went to a party. The best ones don't start until after midnight. You remember those days, don't you?"

I narrowed my eyes at him. "What are you trying to say? That I'm past my prime, too old to pull an all-nighter?" Becoming a business owner at a tender age had curbed any desire to stay out all night drinking. These days, my idea of fun involved a television and a cozy bed.

"I'm going over to see her after closing tonight for a little... you know."

"A second date? Must be serious."

His brow twisted. "Date? Who said anything about a date?"

I tossed a bar rag at him. "You're disgusting."

A patrol car pulled up in front of the bar and Murphy got out, killing Beau's good mood.

"I think I'll take my break now," he said, throwing the rag in the sink.

"Don't worry about it. I'll handle him." I walked around the bar to head Murphy off as he came through the front door.

Murphy glanced at Beau before looking back at me. "I need a word with you."

"It's Sunday night, Tom. Can't it wait until morning? I'm shorthanded at the bar." That wasn't true. It was a slow night, and Tucker was coming in soon.

Ignoring me, he walked to the back of the room. I followed him because the sooner I listened to what he had to say, the sooner I could get rid of him.

He lowered his voice. "I just wanted to stop by to let you know you're not a suspect anymore."

"In Keith's murder?" A short laugh burst from my mouth.

"You didn't seriously think I killed him?" I figured that kangaroo interrogation in his office the other day was just a formality. Another way for him to bust my chops.

He leveled his eyes on mine. "I told you, Charley. No special treatment. You're damn right you were a suspect."

I decided not to tell him he was crazy because that would have prolonged the conversation. "Then why did you clear me?" Because he knew I wasn't a murderer, that's why.

He leaned closer. "The medical examiner over in Adlersville confirmed that there's a ninety percent likelihood that the bite came from a vampire, and as far as I know, you aren't a bloodsucker."

I glanced around the room. "Watch your mouth in my bar."

"Okay. You aren't a *vampire*. Is that better?" He settled down. "The wounds are almost identical to the ones found on Patrice Henderson and Kim Widby, so all three were likely killed by the same perpetrator."

"Then I guess Beau is off the hook too. Last time I checked, he didn't have a set of fangs either."

He got his usual agitated look. "Ninety percent isn't conclusive."

"Except when it comes to me." I shook my head at him. "Jesus, Tom. You know damn well neither of us did this."

"Look, I don't think Beau Henry is our killer, but technically he's still a suspect."

I huffed in disbelief. "Because he slept with Kim Widby a month ago? Come on, Tom. Beau has slept with half this town."

He was getting more frustrated with me. I could see it in the way his face was starting to heat up. "Damn it, Charley, we've got a serial killer on the loose. Anyone who looked at the girl is a suspect." He ran his hand over his face and let out a sigh. "And you're on the killer's list. Why else would he leave a body on your porch? He's playing with you."

I was starting to have another theory. If it was a vampire,

maybe the co-op had something to do with why the killer left me a message. It was too much of a coincidence to ignore. Maybe those rumors about competition were more than just talk.

"What makes the medical examiner an expert on vampire bites anyway? I still say it could have been anything with fangs."

Murphy shook his head. "You really are a piece of work, Charley."

"And you haven't answered my question."

"He's an expert because he *is* a vampire. Are you satisfied now?"

I'd admit, it was compelling. "The medical examiner is a vampire? How progressive of the folks over in Adlersville."

He nailed me with a superior look. "It's pretty obvious. The killer is most likely a vampire. And he must be working with a human or someone else because a vampire didn't leave that body on your porch in broad daylight, which means we have an even bigger problem."

"And yet another reason why you're barking up the wrong tree with Beau."

Murphy snickered. "Or Beau is the human helping him."

"That's ridiculous." The conversation was heading south fast. Murphy was grasping at straws, although he was right about someone other than a vampire dumping Keith's body on my porch in the middle of the day. It also made me question even more if it actually was a vampire.

"The killer could be a woman," I said to throw another variable into the mix that would take some of the heat off Beau. "Your own partner suggested that, and until you know conclusively otherwise, you can't rule it out."

He scoffed. "A woman didn't do this."

"You don't think a female vampire can be just as dangerous as a male?" I immediately regretted saying it. Any comment about dangerous vampires was counterproductive to keeping the harmony in Crimson. But vampires had the same problems as humans. There were good ones and bad ones. Law-abiding citizens and criminals.

"It doesn't matter, Charley. You're in danger. If he was bold enough to leave that body on your porch, he's changed his M.O. He's playing games with his potential victims now."

"You don't need to worry about me. The pack is watching my house at night." As well as keeping an eye on Tucker.

His eyes took a walk around the room. "If there's one thing I've learned in law enforcement, it's that the worst ones are usually hiding in plain sight. The killer could be any one of your customers."

I glanced at the bar. "Maybe it's Mike sitting over there. He looks like a real killer to me." The only thing Mike Miller was capable of killing was a beer. And he wasn't a vampire either.

"You think this is funny?"

"No, Tom. I don't think any of this is funny. Not one damn bit. Now, why don't you go do your job and find the killer before he or she strikes again." The look he gave me could freeze hot coals, so I walked it back. "Sorry. I'm just a little on edge these days."

He nodded firmly. "Good. It might keep you alive."

I could have told him that I wasn't as helpless as he thought. That I was becoming more like my mother every day. But that would have only made it worse. Made him come down harder on me. He hated what my mother was. Tried to control her by disparaging her work with rituals and spells. And for a moment he succeeded, until the magic in her blood grew stronger than her desire to please a tyrant who'd somehow gotten his hooks into her. I'll never forget the day she finally woke up. Took Candy's advice and told him it was over. It was like a fog had lifted from her eyes. To this day, I still couldn't fathom what she saw in Tom Murphy.

It was time to get rid of him because I was feeling uncomfortable with the way he was staring at me. Like he was about to start in on me again. "I need to get back to work, so if there's nothing else."

"Nothing else?" He took a step closer and gave me an incredulous look. "We're not done with this conversation by a long shot."

A wave of nausea hit me when he came closer. He was practically in my face. I could barely hear the sound in the room as it faded to a whisper, replaced by Murphy's nagging rant as his mouth kept moving. He just wouldn't shut up.

"Get away from me, Tom."

He stepped forward when I backed up, gritting his teeth. "You're just like your mother, Charley. Irresponsible and foolish."

His words faded as my entire body started to vibrate. A moment later, they came roaring back to life in my ears.

"You can't stay at the house alone, Charley. You'll get yourself killed."

I squeezed my eyes shut and shook my head, trying to get the repeat of his words out of my mind.

You'll get yourself killed.
You'll get yourself killed.
You'll get yourself killed!

I couldn't listen anymore. It was like the walls were suddenly closing in on me and my head was about to explode. But there was a different voice in my head now.

That's right, Charley. Explode!

He was still in my face when my eyes reopened. "Get out of my bar!" I ordered, surprising myself.

Murphy let out a mocking laugh. Then he started to move backward. The front door swung open, and he was sucked outside. Before I could make sense of what had just happened, I was looking at him through the window.

With a stunned look, he stared back at me. His blank

expression morphed into anger a moment later as he went for the door.

I hurried toward the kitchen when he walked back inside and pointed his finger at me. He looked like steam was about to come out of his ears.

"Get back here!" he yelled across the room.

"Don't tell me what to do," I said without turning around. The way I was feeling, I was liable to point a finger right back at him, and Candy had warned me about that.

I pushed the kitchen door open and made a beeline for the other side of the room. Tom tried to follow me inside, but Dog stepped in his path.

"Get out of my way, Holt!"

Dog let out a growl when Murphy reached for his holster. "You gonna shoot me?" There wasn't an ounce of fear in his voice.

Murphy backed up. "You just threatened me."

"He's protecting me from you," I said, keeping my distance. Tom Murphy had done some unpredictable things before, but he'd never come after me like that. I'd really pushed his buttons this time.

He shot Dog a snide grin. "It's a police officer's word against a shifter's. Who do you think they'll believe?"

Dog nodded to Beau and Tucker standing in the hallway just beyond the door that Murphy was still holding open. "Them."

I glanced down at my shaking hands as a faint blue light emitted from my skin. "Get out of here, Tom. It's over." I needed to sit down before I lit up like a glowstick. That would only add fuel to the fire.

Murphy glanced at several customers who'd gotten up to see what the fuss was about. "What the hell are you looking at?" Then he turned his hostile gaze back to me. "I don't know what just happened out there, but don't you ever touch me again."

"I didn't lay a hand on you, Tom. All I saw was you running out the front door." He was moving backward but...

He gave Dog a departing glare before finally turning to leave. "This conversation isn't over, Charley!" he yelled on his way out.

I sagged with relief when he was gone and sank into a chair.

Dog motioned for Beau and Tucker to get back to the bar. Then he gave me a questioning look. "What just happened out there?"

"I assaulted a police officer, that's what happened."

He chuckled. "From what I saw, you asked him to leave and he left."

"You saw it?"

He nodded to the order window. "Every glorious second."

"Christ, Dog! Murphy isn't going to just let this go. He'll be all over me until I confess to him that I'm a witch."

He shrugged. "So, tell him. It's not a crime. This is Crimson, for God's sake." He went over to the sink and poured me a glass of water. "You need to stop letting that man get to you. He's got no right climbing up your ass every chance he gets."

I took the glass from his hand. "Well, he climbed pretty far up there tonight."

"It's time to let it go, Charley. For your peace of mind. But I don't give a damn about Murphy's peace," he muttered.

Dog was right. I did need to let it go. Forgive Tom Murphy for making my mother and me both miserable for years. But damn it! Those were my formative teenage years. Like hell I'd forgive him, but I'd work on the letting go part. I just hoped Murphy wasn't about to stage an intervention to exorcise the demon out of me. The witch.

I took a sip of water. "I'll work on it."

"What was he doing here anyway?"

I attempted to stand up but sat back down when I got a little lightheaded. "He dropped by to let me know I'm no longer a suspect in Keith Barnes's murder."

He raised his brows. "And that made you angry?"

"He just wouldn't shut up. One minute we were having a half-civil conversation, and the next he was laying into me about staying out at the house alone." I shuddered. "It was like he was inside my head. Berating me to the point where I just snapped."

He laughed. "Remind me not to lecture you."

"He also said the medical examiner is ninety percent sure it was a vampire who attacked Keith and those women, but we already knew that."

Dog seemed relieved. I couldn't blame him. Shifters had escaped the brunt of the bigotry around here, but all it would take was a bad wolf to make them public enemy number one.

I looked up when I heard a familiar voice out front. The kitchen door swung open a moment later, and Candy walked in. "What in Hades happened? Beau said you had a run-in with Tom Murphy." She walked over and reached for my hands. "Good Lord. You're shaking like a vibrator."

I sagged deeper into the chair. "You know that warning you gave me about not pointing my finger at someone?"

She dropped my hands. "You didn't?"

"I didn't have to. All I had to do was think it and say a few words. The next thing I knew, Tom was flying out the front door." She and Dog looked at each other, and I could tell they were both fighting back a laugh. "This isn't funny."

Candy winked at Dog. "Maybe just a little. He had it coming to him. But clearly we still have some work to do on you."

"No kidding." I tried to stand up again, but I was still lightheaded.

Dog grabbed me before I went down and ran his hand over my arm. "Jesus, Charley, you're burning up."

"It's all that energy running amok inside of her," Candy

said, lifting my chin to examine my eyes. "Murphy must have really gotten under your skin this time. Good thing you didn't point that finger at him."

Dog grunted in agreement. "That's what I said. You need to go home, Charley."

Candy dropped my chin. "Dog's right. It's Sunday night, and the bar is almost empty anyway."

I didn't argue with them. My head was still hurting, and the thought of getting dizzy behind the bar with that wall of liquor bottles behind it was enough to convince me. "I think you're right. I'm calling it a night."

I finally managed to steady myself and followed Candy out of the kitchen, telling Beau and Tucker to hold down the fort on my way to the door. After walking outside, I headed straight for my truck.

Candy looked at me like I was certifiable. "Where do you think you're going?"

"Home." I reached for the door and got a massive shock when I touched the metal handle. "Ow!"

"You're not going anywhere but to the Cauldron with me." Before I could argue with her, she threw her hand up to shush me. "Just for the night. Besides, I've got something I want to give you."

TEN

When we walked into the Cauldron, my eyes went directly to a giant ball of light suspended in the middle of the room. It was a blue sphere moving clockwise with a ring of white light circling it in the opposite direction. I could hear a faint sound coming from it that I initially thought was ringing in my ears.

"What exactly am I looking at?" It was fascinating, but I had no idea what it was.

Candy glanced up at it. "That thing? I'm just saging the place. I needed to clear all the bad juju in the shop, especially after the mayor was in here the other day." She shuddered. "The things I do to pay the rent."

"Don't you need actual *sage* to sage a room?"

"I like to cleanse without all that obnoxious smoke. It makes my throat scratch. This is a whole lot more efficient anyway, and it gets rid of all that other stuff along with it."

"Other... stuff?"

Without elaborating, she went straight for the stairs. "Come on. Let's go have a look at something."

I followed her up to the second floor and down the hallway to a room on the left. I'd never been in that room before and never asked what was in there. But Candy seemed to have a lot of hidey-holes around the shop, including that oversized closet in the back room on the first floor with all those mystery vessels on the shelves.

When I walked inside, I immediately stopped to take it all in. It looked like a small library, with bookcases against three of the walls. "I didn't know you liked books so much." I'd been getting her the wrong gifts all this time.

She shrugged. "I try to get in a little reading in every night. Keeps me sane."

Tucked into the corner by the window, there was a wicker chair shaped like an egg suspended from the ceiling. In the other corner was a giant lump of fluorescent-green vinyl. "Is that a beanbag chair?" I'd seen them in old movies from the seventies, but I'd never come across one in person.

"Yes ma'am." She went over to one of the shelves and ran her finger over the spines of the books. "Now, where is it? I saw it here just the other day."

I sank into the beanbag chair. "It's kinda comfortable."

"I like the way it molds around me while I'm reading," she said while she kept looking for something. Her finger finally stopped on one of the books. "Here it is."

I struggled to get out of the chair and met her at the shelf. "What is it?"

It was a book about birds, something I didn't know she was interested in. She opened it, revealing a hidden compartment in the center. Tucked inside was a small box. "It's something your mama wanted you to have."

She slapped my hand away when I reached for it. "Patience, grasshopper." Then she got a sly grin on her face. "This isn't a toy."

Now I really wanted to get my hands on it. "What's in the box, Candy?"

"Like I said. It's something Delia left you." She took a deep breath and finally opened the small box. It contained a ring. "Now that you've gone through the ritual, I can give it to you." Before handing it to me, she gave me a warning. "But don't go wearing it yet. You've got to learn a thing or two first, or that ring will end up wearing you. It'll get you into trouble."

I eagerly grabbed it from her and slipped it on my finger. "What kind of trouble?"

"Now, see?" She put her hands on her hips and shook her head. "You don't listen."

"Sorry." I slipped it off to examine it. It was a large sapphire stone set in ornate silver, and it looked a lot like the pendant Candy wore around her neck. "Are they a matching set?"

"Might as well be." She reached for her amulet and rubbed the stone between her fingers. "And you've seen what this can do. It's powerful stuff, Charley. Not fit for untrained hands. Your mama didn't want you to have that ring until you were in full control of your magic, which you are not."

"Then why are you giving it to me now?"

"Because it's yours." She grumbled for a moment like she was having second thoughts about it. "I'm asking you to put it somewhere safe, and when you're ready, you can wear it proudly. You're not ready, Charley, but you will be soon, if I have anything to say about it."

I gazed at the beautiful stone. The ring felt heavy in my hand, but it was really just the sadness of the memory of my mother. It should have been her giving it to me.

Candy let out a deep sigh. "I'm bone tired, and after that ritual this morning, I know you are too. Why don't you go to bed."

I stuck the ring back in the box and went to the spare room. But instead of going straight to sleep after climbing into bed, I pulled the ring back out and slipped it halfway on my finger. I couldn't help it. I just wanted to gaze at the blue stone. Before I knew it, my eyelids grew heavy, and I was cradled in the magic of that ring while I drifted off.

* * *

When I heard a knock on the bedroom door, I sat straight up. The small box fell off the bed and hit the floor, and my eyes went to the ring that had somehow slipped all the way on my finger. It was probably the reason I'd had such wild dreams all night.

I grabbed the box and stuffed the ring inside, quickly setting it on the nightstand. With all the commotion, Odin tumbled over the side of the bed, but instead of landing on his feet like a normal cat, he hit the floor with a thud.

Candy cracked the door open and stuck her head inside, spotting Odin walking toward her. "I've been looking all over for that cat. I was about to whip out the crystal ball to track him down."

"I think I kicked him off the bed by accident. I hope I didn't give him a concussion."

"He's got enough padding to withstand a drop from the top of the building." She smirked at him as he slipped past her legs into the hallway. "I saved you some eggs and bacon in the kitchen if you're hungry. The shop is open, so I need to get back downstairs."

The shop is open?

"What time is it?" I glanced at my phone on the nightstand. "Crap!" I'd overslept. Well, technically I didn't have to be anywhere at ten thirty in the morning, but I had a boatload of work to do at the Stag, and I'd just slept through a couple hours of time I could have spent doing it. "Why didn't you wake me up earlier?"

She winked at me. "I figured you needed the sleep." Then

she glanced at the box on the nightstand. "How late did you stay up looking at that ring?"

How did she always do that?

I climbed out of bed and pulled on my jeans. "Not very long. I fell asleep wearing it, though," I muttered. "Sorry."

And how did she always manage to get me to confess about every little thing?

"You can just leave it in the nightstand drawer," she slipped in as she was walking away. "It'll be waiting for you when you get back here tonight."

Nice try.

"I'm not coming back, Candy. This was a one-nighter, remember?" I put my shoes on and grabbed the box before she could hold it hostage. "I need to get home to take a shower and change my clothes."

She turned, disapproval written all over her face. "I didn't think it was possible, but you're even more stubborn than Delia was."

"Yep. I've been told." I brushed past her into the hallway. "It's only morning," I said when she followed me. "Don't waste your time worrying about me until it's necessary. With the sun up, there won't be any vampires waiting for me at the house." Tonight was another story, but I'd worry about that later.

I started to go downstairs, but as my foot hit the first step, Odin darted between my legs. He let out a hiss that turned into a spine-chilling growl when I accidentally kicked him. I fell forward, managing to grab a hold of the railing before tumbling down the stairs.

"Damn cat." Candy shot him a look that sent him running down the hallway. "Are you okay, Charley?"

"Other than my heart beating out of my chest, I'm fine."

She glared at Odin when he stopped in front of her bedroom door. "I need to put that cat on a diet."

"He looks more like a possum to me." As I caught my breath

and started to pull myself up, I heard a crack. The railing gave way. Before I knew what was happening, I was tumbling over the side of the staircase.

"Charley!" Candy tried to grab me, but it was too late.

I squeezed my eyes shut, waiting for an impact that never came. I reopened them when I heard Candy running down the steps. The hardwood planks were inches from my face, close enough to see every knot and scratch in the wood. But I was just floating there, suspended above the floor.

The bell sounded as someone walked into the Cauldron. "What the hell, Charley!"

My eyes darted toward the door, and my feat of defying gravity failed. I crashed down on the floor, rolling over and reaching for my nose to see if it was still on my face.

Candy crouched down next to me to examine it. "Nothing's broken, but you and Lucy might have matching shiners by tonight." Then she helped me up and glared at Rick Carter. "No thanks to you, officer. What do you want?"

He gave her a suspicious look before turning his attention back to me. "I always knew you were a chip off the old block. You're a witch just like your mother was."

Candy strolled up to him and met his hostile glare. "I don't know what you're talking about. All I saw was Charley taking a little spill." She had no problem flying her witch flag proudly, but I guess she thought it was up to me to decide if and when I wanted to do the same.

"I ain't blind. I saw it with my own two eyes." He squinted at me. "Does Tom know?"

I spotted the box on the floor and the ring a few feet away. After grabbing them both, I gave him my two cents. "Here's a newsflash for you, Rick. It's none of your business what I am. And it certainly isn't any of Tom's. If I decide to trade my truck in for a broomstick, it's none of anyone's damn business." I brushed past him to leave. "I'll call you later, Candy."

As I was walking out the door, an ambulance drove past the shop with its siren blaring. It was traveling west toward Adlersville where the nearest hospital was located.

Candy walked out behind me. "I wonder what that was all about?"

"That's why I'm here," Carter said, following us out. "I saw Charley's truck parked in front of the Stag, but when no one answered the door, I figured she was down here at the Cauldron."

It was never a good sign when the cops were looking for you. "Well, here I am. What is it?"

"That ambulance that just flew by is taking a woman over to the hospital, and it doesn't look good for her."

"Who is it?" Candy asked.

He straightened his back and cleared his throat. "That's police business. I can't say." Then he looked back at me. "When's the last time you saw Beau Henry?"

ELEVEN

I drove out to the house with my phone to my ear the entire way. I must have dialed Beau's number half a dozen times, but he wouldn't pick the damn thing up. For once, Carter had kept his mouth shut. All he would tell us was that another woman had been attacked and found in the woods, and she was hanging on by a thread in that ambulance. Then he asked all kinds of questions about Beau: when I'd seen him last, if I'd noticed any cuts or bruises on him. It was obvious Beau was still at the top of the suspect list whether he was a vampire or not. Candy was right. The cops were just trying to find a scapegoat. Someone to pin it on before the mayor came down on them hard.

My heart was racing as I climbed out of the truck and walked up to the porch. I got a flashback of Keith Barnes's body heaped near the front door. I'd probably see him lying there every time I climbed those steps, and the bloodstains were still embedded in the wood to remind me.

Rex flew down from the tree and landed on the railing next to me. He cocked his head, looking at the box in my hand. "You would have liked her," I said when he wouldn't stop staring at it.

Crows were attracted to shiny objects, and by the way he was fixated on the box, you'd have thought he could see that ring right through it.

Rex had shown up after my mother died. The irony was, she'd always said she was destined to have a crow as a familiar. But she never had a familiar. Said she didn't need one. Candy said she didn't have one either, but sometimes I wondered about her and Odin. That cat was downright peculiar.

I went inside and straight to the small room off my mother's bedroom where she kept her important things, like her books and other magical items. It was the safest place in the house for that ring, so I slid the box behind a bookend.

My phone rang before I made it back out to the living room. It was Dog.

"Is everything okay?" I asked.

"Not really. I came in a few minutes ago and found Beau hiding in the back room."

"Hiding?" I would have thought it was strange, but not after that conversation with Carter. I was sure they'd already been to his apartment looking for him. "I've been calling him for the past hour, but he won't pick up his phone."

Dog inhaled sharply. "He said the cops are looking for him."

"Yeah, I know. That's why I've been trying to get a hold of him."

"He's spooked, Charley. I think you need to get over here."

This was getting bad. Real bad. "I'm on my way."

After a quick change of clothes, I got in my truck and headed back to town. When I reached the square, I didn't see any cars parked in front of the Stag. Beau and Dog had probably pulled around back, which was where I was going. The last thing I needed was for Murphy or Carter to see my truck out front and start knocking on the door.

I pulled up next to Beau's car and went in through the alley. They were waiting for me in the back room. Dog was leaning against the wall, and Beau was sitting in a chair with his elbows resting on his knees. I could tell he hadn't slept, and his precious hair looked like a bird had nested in it.

"You look like hell, Beau. What's going on?"

He turned away from me. "I didn't do it."

"Do what?" Dog asked.

"I didn't hurt her!"

The conversation was starting off cryptic, but we didn't have time to beat around the bush. "Hurt who?"

"Tammy. The girl I went to see last night. The one I met at the party."

His booty call.

I was starting to put the pieces together, but not entirely. "You need to fill in the blanks, Beau."

"Will someone tell me what the hell is going on?" Dog was clearly getting frustrated.

"That's what I'm trying to find out," I said, watching Beau's expression carefully when I asked the next question. "Tammy was attacked, wasn't she?"

"Yeah, but she was fine when I left her." His brows pulled tight. "But how did you find out?"

"Because Carter came down to the Cauldron looking for me this morning when he saw my truck parked in front of the bar. He was asking questions about you. Then an ambulance drove past the shop and he told us another woman had been attacked." I sighed. "It didn't take a genius to put two and two together."

"What did you tell him?"

"The truth. That I'd seen you last night. But the bigger question is how do you know she got attacked?" I couldn't believe the thoughts that were suddenly running around in my head. I'd known Beau for a long time, and he didn't have violence in him.

"Don't look at me like that, Charley. I've never touched a

woman in my life. Well, not like that," he added under his breath. "My buddy, Zeke, is a janitor over at the jail. He heard Carter talking to the chief after they found her early this morning." His eyes filled with distress. "She was nailed to a tree just like the others!"

"Did Carter mention you by name?"

"No, but the cops have a pretty good description of me and my car from one of her neighbors. That's all they need to try to pin it on me. Especially after Murphy questioned me about Kim Widby."

I felt sicker by the second. "Just tell us everything that happened last night."

He got up and started to pace, running his hands over the top of his head as he wore out the floor. "Like I said, I went to see her after we closed up. We had a couple of drinks, watched about five minutes of a movie, and then... you know. But when I left her, she was tucked in bed with a smile on her face."

I heard the door open up front, followed by Lucy's voice. She was talking to someone.

"Great," I muttered.

Beau froze. "Is that Murphy?"

"Sounds like it. Lucy must have let him in."

He got a panicked look on his face. "I'll go out through the alley while you keep him distracted up front."

I thought he was making a bad joke until he started walking toward the door. "You're crazy, Beau. If you run, it'll only make it worse. You'll look guilty as hell."

"What are you saying, Charley?" He was looking at me like I was speaking Russian.

Dog stepped between him and the back door. "She's saying you need to get a hold of yourself and tell the cops the truth." Seeing the frantic look on Beau's face, he groaned and stepped aside. "Look. I'm no fan of Crimson PD, but if you go out that back door, your face will end up on a wanted sign."

I tried a different approach. "Come on, Beau. People around here know you. And they still have to prove you did it. What's the worst that can happen?"

"The worst is they railroad me and send me down to the state prison in Reidsville!" He lowered his voice and leaned closer to me. "See this face? I'll be someone's bitch before I make it through my first day down there. I can't survive that."

Dog turned his back to Beau, stifling a laugh.

But Beau was dead serious. I could see his feet warming up to make a run for it.

"You're not going to Reidsville. The worst that could happen is they lock you up for a day or two over at the jail. But without any hard evidence, I doubt they'll even have grounds for that." I chose my next words carefully. "Unless Tammy wakes up and identifies you, but that's not going to happen, right?"

He looked at me sideways. "You mean the part about her waking up or identifying me?"

I rubbed my forehead where it was starting to ache. "Look. We're going out there right now to talk to Murphy."

Before he could argue about it, Dog nudged him toward the door. He whined all the way down the hallway but shut up when he saw Murphy and Carter standing in the middle of the bar.

Murphy shot me a wicked look. First I'd handed him his ass last night, and now it appeared I was hiding Beau in my back room. Not to mention that Carter had probably opened his mouth about what he saw at the Cauldron that morning. Take your pick. There were any number of reasons for his snake eyes staring back at me.

Carter approached Beau with a set of handcuffs. "Put your hands behind your back. You're under arrest for aggravated assault and attempted murder."

"What?" Beau shot me a look. "I shouldn't have listened to you. Are you happy now?"

"Tammy Davis," Carter said. "Name ring a bell?"

Lucy was watching the whole thing with her mouth hanging open. "You got to be kidding me," she said to no one in particular. "Beau ain't no woman beater. Believe me, I know what they look like."

"Not now, Lucy," Dog growled.

Murphy's phone rang. He turned his back to us and answered the call. After a few seconds, he hung up.

"On what grounds are you arresting him?" I asked when he turned back around.

"On the grounds that we've got a dead woman lying in the basement of the hospital over in Adlersville."

Beau flinched. "Tammy's dead?"

"That's right," Murphy said. "She died fifteen minutes ago. The charges just got upgraded to murder, and we've got a witness who can put you at her house last night."

He shook his head. "I didn't do it. I slept with her, but—"

"Be quiet," Dog said. "Don't say another word until you have a lawyer."

At the mention of a lawyer, the terror on Beau's face went up a notch.

Carter cuffed him and led him toward the door. "Come on. You're going to jail."

I glared at Murphy. "Beau didn't do this, and you know it."

"That's what you said about Mutt."

His words stung. My gentle giant of a dishwasher had turned out to be a killer, but he'd been possessed at the time. I guess Murphy would never let me forget how wrong I'd been about Mutt. How I defended him all the way up to the moment when he attacked me in the alley out back.

"That was different, and you know it. What about Mag

Ryan?" The name spilled out of my mouth without much thought. "Have you questioned him?"

Dog shot me a look. "Charley."

"Don't *Charley* me. The man has a bad reputation for being careless with women. You told me that yourself." The first attack happened a while ago, but there was no telling how long Mag had been back in Crimson before he walked into the Stag.

I understood why Dog reacted the way he did. Mag was a former member of the pack, and when a pack member got himself in trouble with the law, it reflected on all of them. It was just another example of the bigotry in this town. If one was a criminal, they were all perceived as being criminals. But Mag was no longer a member of the pack, and Beau was in serious trouble. In my mind, Mag was a person of interest. The least Crimson PD needed to do was question him.

Murphy responded with a warning look. The one he usually got when I pushed him too far. When I dared to assert myself. After everything that had happened over the past twenty-four hours, I figured he'd reached his boiling point.

"You've got to help me, Charley," Beau said while Carter manhandled him out the door.

"I'll figure something out. Just stay quiet for now."

Murphy came closer and stuck his finger in my face, which was probably not a good idea considering what had happened last night. "I'll be back to have a talk with you later."

"Whatever you say, Tom." I put on my best defiant face and refused to cower. "You might want to get your finger out of my face."

His smug look vanished as he lowered his hand. "You're just like her, aren't you?"

"God, I hope so. You better leave now, unless you want to find out."

After glaring back at me for a moment, he followed Carter

out, shooting me a final stern look as he climbed into the patrol car.

Dog came up next to me as they pulled away. "I think I saw a little fear in Murphy's eyes just now. Delia would have gotten a kick out of that."

I decided not to mention my brush with levitation back at the Cauldron because that would be a lengthy conversation, and I had more important things to do. "I need to go see Bob Flanders."

He gave me a funny look. "Flanders? You're kidding me?'

"Do you have a better idea?'

Bob Flanders was a retired ambulance chaser, but he was the only lawyer in town. It couldn't hurt to talk to him about Beau.

Dog groaned. "That man couldn't argue his way out of a paper bag. Does he even have a license to practice anymore?"

"I don't know, but he's still got an office down the street." A sign with FLANDERS ESQ. was still displayed on the door. But that could have been because no one else had rented the space, so no one had bothered to take it down yet.

"I haven't seen any traffic coming in or out of that building for years," Dog said.

"Good. Then he's probably available." I laughed halfheartedly, knowing it was a long shot. "If he's over there, I'm going to talk to him. Maybe he'll have pity on Beau and give me some free legal advice."

Dog chuckled. "A lawyer giving free advice? Good luck with that."

It was past noon, so I decided to head over there to see if Flanders was in his office. "I'm going over there now. Do me a favor and call Tucker and see if she can cover Beau's shift tonight."

Someone needed to help Lucy at the bar, and I wasn't going to be available. As much as I cringed at the thought, I needed to find Ian Masterson to see what he knew about the attacks. I believed him when he said it wasn't him, but since the killer was almost certainly a vampire, someone down in Reaperstown had to know something. Who better to question than the self-proclaimed mayor of Reaperstown himself. I was going down there tonight to find that vampire because the stakes had just gone up. Come hell or high water, I was getting some answers.

TWELVE

I wasn't sure whether I should knock on the door or let myself in. The sign said they were open, and since the door was unlocked, I decided on the latter.

Bob Flanders used to come into the Stag when my mother still ran the place, but he'd become somewhat of a recluse over the years. I wasn't even sure if I'd recognize him if I passed him on the street. There were even some rumors that he was dead.

The room just beyond the front door was empty. There was a single chair and a loveseat against the wall, and the stack of magazines on the small coffee table were out of date by years. It must have been the waiting room.

"Hello," I called out. Something fell in one of the rooms down the hallway. "Mr. Flanders?" I heard someone moving around back there, but when no one answered me, I walked back toward the front door. For all I knew, there were squatters in the building, and I wasn't interested in coming face-to-face with them.

"Give me a minute," I heard someone say.

I turned around and walked halfway down the hallway. "Is that you, Mr. Flanders?"

"Hold your horses! I'll be out in a minute."

It was Flanders all right.

I went back into the waiting room to take a seat. As soon as my butt hit the chair, a man came around the corner that I barely recognized. He was older than I thought he'd be, with deep lines on his face and white hair that seemed to have a mind of its own. Poly-fil fiber came to mind. The suit he was wearing looked like he'd slept in it, and there was a red stain on his tie. I couldn't tell if it was dried ketchup or blood.

I stood up when he didn't say a word. "Bob Flanders?"

"Well, who else would I be?"

I took that as a yes.

With my hand extended, I walked over to him. "I'm—"

"I know who you are. I'm old, not blind." He grumbled something under his breath and looked me up and down. "I've known you since you were born. You've grown up, but you still look just like your mother."

"I remember you from the Stag years ago," I said, catching a whiff of alcohol. Coming here was a bad idea. "I wanted to get your legal advice about something." I glanced at the dusty sign-in book on the ledge of a small sliding-glass window in the wall. "But it looks like you're not practicing anymore. I'm sorry to have bothered you."

"Hold on." His voice cracked. "My receptionist is on vacation this week." He stared at me for a moment like he was debating whether to send me on my way. "I've got an opening this afternoon, so why don't you come into my office."

And I was so close to a clean getaway.

I followed him down the hall, hoping there was a shred of a chance he could help Beau. Or maybe refer me to a lawyer who could. How to pay for it was another thing. But it didn't cost anything for a brief consult to see what he had to say.

His office wasn't much to look at. It definitely hadn't had a good cleaning in a while, and it smelled of old cigar smoke.

Flanders quickly grabbed a pint bottle off the desk and stuffed it into one of the side drawers. "Have a seat."

I preferred to stand because I didn't plan to be there very long, but I had my manners. After sitting down, I cut to the chase. "A friend of mine was arrested this morning for something he didn't do."

He chuckled. "Of course."

"He's innocent." Hearing the conviction in my voice, he straightened up. "I was hoping you might be able to give me some advice on how to help him. Maybe give me a name of a colleague." *That didn't cost an arm and a leg*, I wanted to say.

"Colleague? My advice isn't good enough for you?"

"Well, yeah. I just thought you were retired."

"Retired? You think I'd come down to this office and stare at the walls if I could be off fishing up in the mountains? Quit wasting my time and tell me why you're here." He turned his head to cough and clear his throat. "What did your friend *supposedly* do?"

"They arrested him for killing someone."

He leaned over the desk and looked at me slyly. "Pre-meditated or manslaughter?"

"I didn't ask." No sense beating around the bush, so I laid it all on the table. "He's a suspect in the attacks on the women around here."

"You mean Patrice Henderson and the Widby girl." He sat back in his chair and stared past me for a moment before bringing his eyes back to mine. "Who is this friend of yours?"

"One of my bartenders. Beau Henry."

That got his attention. "Beau Henry? Dan Henry's kid? That boy's always been a little rambunctious, but a killer...? His father is questionable, but his mother didn't raise a murderer. Alice Henry was a good woman." He shook his head. "I've never seen that boy raise a hand to anyone who didn't damn well deserve it."

"Like I said, he didn't do it."

He eyed me suspiciously. "They had to have something in order to arrest him."

I always knew Beau's promiscuous behavior would get him into trouble one of these days, but I never thought it would decide his fate. "They connected him to the victims. He slept with two of the three women recently."

"There was a third attack?"

"A girl named Tammy Davis was found this morning in the woods. She was nailed to a tree like the others. Looks like it was the same person who attacked Patrice and Kim." Not to mention Keith Barnes, but I decided not to complicate the discussion. "She died at the hospital this afternoon."

He looked at me sideways. "Not even those idiots down at the station would be stupid enough to arrest him with just that. What aren't you telling me?"

"Beau was with Tammy last night. He swears she was alive and well when he left her, and I believe him." Now for the damning part. "A neighbor saw him leaving her place and gave a description of him and his car. That's what they arrested him on."

"That's it? A neighbor saw him *leaving* her place?"

I shrugged. "As far as I know." I looked Flanders square in the eye. "I know Beau as well as anyone, and I'm telling you, he isn't capable of doing this."

Flanders stood up. "Well, let's go get him out."

"You can do that?"

"I can try. My specialty is personal injury, but I know enough about criminal law to know that without any DNA evidence or a witness putting him at the scene of the crime, the police are walking a thin line even trying to hold him. He's a solid suspect, though, so he should probably get himself a criminal lawyer. Not someone like me."

"I was hoping you could refer me to one."

He thought about it for a minute and nodded. "I'll see if I can scrounge up a name or two. In the meantime, let's go see if we can get the boy out of jail."

On our way out the door, I asked the question that had been on my mind since walking into that ghost town of an office. "Do you even have an active license to practice law?"

He locked the door behind him. "Have I given you any legal advice?"

I wasn't exactly sure, but it didn't seem like he'd actually represented himself as an attorney. And it was his ass on the line if he crossed that line, not mine.

A faint smile crossed his face. "Don't worry. I've got a few more months on it before I officially retire. Let me put it to good use."

* * *

Jen looked up from the magazine she was reading when we walked into the station. She took one look at me and Bob Flanders and got a nervous look on her face. "Tom and Rick gave me specific orders not to let anyone in to see Beau."

"He's got a right to speak to his attorney," I said.

She glanced back and forth between us. "You'll have to wait until one of them gets back."

Flanders pulled out a business card and handed it to her. "You see that?"

She studied it for a second. "Uh-huh."

"It says Bob Flanders, Attorney-at-Law. I'm here to see my client, so I'd suggest you lead the way."

I guess he'd changed his mind about taking the case. At least long enough to get Beau out of jail. I wasn't sure how this worked after that.

Her face started to flush. "Can I call one of them first?"

He smiled at her. "You can call the mayor if it makes you feel better."

Jen was about to pick up the phone when Carter came through the front door. He frowned when he saw who was standing next to me. "What are you doing here, Flanders?"

"He's Beau Henry's attorney," I said.

Carter shot him a snide look. "Attorney? When's the last time you represented anyone who wasn't in a wheelchair or faking a neck injury?"

Flanders nodded to him. "Nice to see you too, Rick. I see you're still an asshole."

Carter reached for his holster. "Are you threatening a police officer?"

"For crying out loud, just take me to my client."

I finally broke it up when the two of them got into a glaring contest. "Maybe we should leave, Bob. When the judge finds out Beau was denied his right to counsel, he'll be free to go." Come to think of it, maybe we should have left and let Carter's unlawful behavior do the work for us.

"You're right, Charley." Flanders glanced at Jen. "You're a witness to Officer Carter denying my client his rights."

She stood up abruptly. "Me?" Then she gave Carter a confused look.

After glaring at us for a moment, he pointed his finger at Flanders. "Just you. Charley needs to wait out here."

"Come on, Rick," I said. "What do you think I'm going to do back there? Bust him out?"

He glanced at the door nervously like he was afraid Murphy would walk in. It showed who wore the pants at Crimson PD. "All right. You've got five minutes."

Flanders got dangerously close to Carter, reminding everyone in the room that he still had some shark left in him. "You don't dictate how much time I spend with my client. I'm done with Beau when I'm done."

Before things got hairy between them again, I offered a compromise. "Give us fifteen."

Carter held his tongue and nodded before continuing into his office.

When we got to the cell, Beau was standing at the bars, gripping them so tightly his knuckles had gone pale. "I knew I heard your voice, Charley." Then he looked at Bob Flanders. "Can you get me out of here?"

Flanders chuckled. "Slow down, boy. You haven't hired me yet."

"But I heard you just tell Carter you were my lawyer."

"Semantics. First you have to ask me to represent you. Then I have to decide if I want to take the case."

Beau nodded his head briskly. "Well, yeah. Will you be my lawyer?"

Flanders gave him a long look. "Let me ask you a question first. Did you attack..." He squinted at Beau. "What's the woman's name again?"

"Tammy Davis," I said, trying to move it along before that fifteen minutes expired.

Flanders waited. "Well?"

Beau let go of the bars and took a step back. "Wait a minute." He glanced back and forth between us, but his eyes finally settled on mine. "You don't think I did it?"

"Of course not," I said. "But I think Mr. Flanders needs to hear you say it."

"No, I didn't do it! She was alive and breathing when I left her house last night."

Flanders squinted at him. "So you were with her?"

Beau shrugged. "Yeah, I was at her house. We had a date."

Date my ass. He went over there for a quick in and out.

Flanders gazed at him steadily for a moment. "Did you have sex with her?"

"Yeah. I slept with her."

"Did you use a condom?"

Beau was starting to squirm. "Uh... does it matter?"

Flanders shook his head. "I'll take that as a no."

"I intended to, but I ran out." He walked back up to the bars and lowered his voice. "She's a busy girl, if you know what I mean. I figured she'd have a supply."

"Jesus, Beau. What were you thinking?" I swear he wouldn't walk away from sex even if the building was burning down.

His face twisted up as he rubbed the back of his head. "I wasn't thinking. I had other things on my mind."

Flanders watched him closely. "Charley said the police have a witness who saw you leave her house last night. Where did you go after that?"

"Home. It was late."

"And no one else saw you?"

He thought about it for a moment and shook his head. "Not that I know of."

Beau lived in a garage apartment at the edge of town. The house was a vacation rental property for a couple down in Atlanta. In exchange for cheap rent, he mowed the lawn in the summer and kept an eye on the place when it was vacant, like now.

Flanders took a deep breath. "I believe you. Let me see what I can do about getting you released."

Beau got a worried look on his face. "Make it fast. I ain't built for jail."

Even if Bob Flanders managed to get him out, he was still a suspect. That meant he needed a criminal lawyer, and they didn't work on contingency.

"I need to call your father," I said to him.

Beau's jaw dropped. "What?"

"You heard me. You're going to need a lawyer."

He glanced at Bob. "I have one."

"Charley's right, Beau. I might be able to get you out of this cell for now, but I'm not qualified to keep you out. You're going to need a real criminal lawyer."

There was a look of fear in Beau's eyes. "No way. You're not calling him. I'd rather rot in this cell."

"That's ridiculous," I said. "He's got the money to help you." There'd been a rift between them for as long as I could remember. His mother had died years ago, and the only memories I had of his father were of a stern figure who showed up at Beau's football games occasionally. The man never cracked a smile. It was like he was only there to monitor his son's performance. As soon as Beau graduated from high school and got a job, he was out of that big house.

Beau gripped the bars again and looked me in the eye. "I will never forgive you if you call him."

I was surprised by the look on his face. It wasn't the easygoing Beau I knew staring back at me, and something told me I really would lose him if I made that call. "All right. It's your neck on the line."

As we headed back up front, my confidence in springing Beau started to wane. "Do you really think you can get him out?" I asked Flanders.

"I don't know. They've got an eyewitness who can put him at her house last night and they'll probably find semen samples. Let's go have a talk with Carter and see what else they have."

"Well, I hope you can. The longer he stays in here, the more chance he'll have of saying something that'll get him into deeper trouble."

Jen buzzed Carter when she saw us coming down the hallway. He came out of his office as we reached the front desk.

"Unless you've got evidence to put Beau Henry at the crime scene," Flanders said to him, "you need to release him."

"We have evidence," Murphy said.

I turned around and saw him coming through the station door. "What are you talking about?"

He gave me a smug look and then shifted his eyes to Flanders. "Are you practicing criminal law now, Bob?"

Flanders held Murphy's gaze, and I could tell there was bad history between them. "Just get to the evidence."

Murphy shifted his eyes to me. "Your bartender isn't going anywhere."

"Why's that?" I said.

Murphy got a smile on his face. "Because DNA doesn't lie, and we have a witness."

Flanders countered. "It'll take at least a week to get DNA results. And that's if you're lucky." He shrugged. "He already admitted to being at her house last night, but it doesn't put him at the crime scene, does it?"

The two men had another standoff before Murphy dropped the bomb. "You're right. But I just took a statement from one of the nurses at the hospital. It seems Tammy Davis had something to say on her deathbed."

I glanced at Flanders, trying to determine if he was having the same sinking feeling that I was, but his face was a blank slate.

"The nurse asked her who did this," Murphy continued. "You know what she said? One name—Beau Henry."

THIRTEEN

I was stunned. On her deathbed, Tammy Davis had identified Beau as her attacker. Was it possible? I shook off the thought that was creeping into my head.

"What do we do now?" I asked Flanders as we walked down the sidewalk and stopped at the corner near the Stag.

"I'll get you some names. If you want the best, you'll have to drive down to Atlanta. It'll cost you, but we're talking about Beau's life here."

"Is there any way to convince you to take the case?"

He let out a quiet laugh. "Like I said back there, trying to get Beau out of that jail was one thing, but he needs a criminal attorney or he could end up in prison. He'd be better off with a public defender than me."

My head was starting to spin. Beau didn't have the money for a fancy criminal lawyer, and neither did I. "Thanks for trying to help, Bob. If you could text me those names and phone numbers, I'd appreciate it."

As I was walking away, he gave me some parting advice. "Beau's in a lot of trouble, Charley. Make those calls."

Tucker was prepping the bar when I walked inside. "I appreciate you coming in tonight," I said.

"It's no problem. I can use the money." She had a strange look on her face as she hurried up and down the bar, sideswiping Lucy.

"Will you watch where you're going." The bin of clean glasses Lucy was carrying nearly ended up on the floor.

Tucker hadn't worked for me for very long, but I'd gotten familiar with her moods and expressions, and the one on her face right now told me something was up.

"Everything okay?" I asked.

She flinched. "What?"

"I said, is everything okay?" It clearly wasn't. She needed to calm down before we opened so she wasn't messing up her drink orders all night. It was also time for a staff meeting to discuss the elephant in the kitchen—my conspicuously absent third bartender.

"Dog!" I yelled. "Can you come out here please."

He walked out of the kitchen with a dishrag in his hand. "How'd it go with Flanders?"

"Not as well as I would have liked." I started with the easy problem first. "What's wrong with you, Tucker? And don't tell me everything's fine. You're buzzing around like you've had half a dozen energy drinks."

She was all wide-eyed and nervous. "It's probably nothing."

I didn't like the sound of that. "Which means it's probably something, so spit it out."

"I think..." She hesitated. "I think someone's following me."

"What makes you think that?" Dog asked.

She shrugged. "I'm not sure. I thought I saw a shadow behind me while I was walking home last night. But every time I looked back, nothing was there. I just kept getting a creepy feeling like I had eyes on me."

"I thought the pack was looking out for her," I said to Dog.

"They were, but since those guys from Atlanta took off and haven't shown up again, I had them prioritize watching your place instead." He turned to Tucker. "You think they came back?"

"I doubt it. If it was them, they would have just snatched me off the street and taken me straight back to Atlanta. But I don't think I was imagining it."

I twirled my finger at her. "You can't see anything in that crystal ball head of yours?"

Her face twisted up. "It doesn't work like that."

Something else crossed my mind. "When's the last time you saw Mag?" I asked Dog.

His eyes locked on mine. "What are you saying?"

"I'm not saying anything, but he was real interested in Tucker when he stopped in here Saturday night. He offered to buy her a drink when she got off." A thought suddenly occurred to me. "He didn't show up here after I left last night, did he?"

"He had the good sense not to," Dog said.

"Have you figured out where he's been staying? Maybe you and Loki should have a talk with him." No one seemed to know where Mag had been sleeping since he got here or when he planned to leave. Then again, maybe he was back for good. Even more reason to find out what he was up to, and if he'd followed Tucker home last night.

I could see Dog's wheels turning. "I'll find him. I'll also make sure one of the pack escorts Tucker home from now on."

Now for the other business. "I'm going to need both of you to pick up some extra shifts for a while. Beau is out indefinitely." If I didn't find a way to clear him quickly, I'd be looking for a fourth bartender.

Lucy gawked. "Beau is still in jail?"

"Jail?" Tucker's eyes grew even wider. "What did he do?"

"He didn't do anything. They're just looking for someone to take the fall for the attacks that have been happening around here."

"Attacks? You mean murders," Lucy corrected.

She wasn't helping matters. Especially since Tucker didn't know Beau as well as the rest of us did, and by the look on her face, she was probably wondering if she'd been working with a killer since she came to Crimson.

"Another woman was attacked last night," I said to Tucker. "Beau is a suspect."

Lucy huffed. "Which is a bunch of crap."

"That's right. It is crap. But he's stuck in jail for now, so everyone needs to pitch in around here until he's out."

"I take it Flanders wasn't interested in helping?" Dog asked.

"He tried, but he couldn't get him out." I wasn't about to mention the part about Tammy Davis naming Beau as her attacker. There had to be an explanation.

Tucker raised her hand like a schoolgirl. "I'll do whatever I can to help out." She shrugged. "It's the least I can do for everything you've done for me."

"I appreciate that, Tucker. I'll be spending more time behind the bar myself." I gave Lucy a questioning look. "Can I count on you too?"

She got up and walked back behind the bar to get to work. "I'm not even going to justify that with an answer."

Lucy was a lot to handle at times, but she was loyal. After all the shit she pulled around here, it was one of the reasons she still had a job.

I motioned for Dog to follow me into the kitchen so I could fill him in on that nurse's damning statement. The final nail in Beau's coffin.

"What else do they have on him?" Dog asked as soon as we walked through the kitchen door.

"The nurse at the hospital gave a statement. She said Tammy Davis identified Beau as her attacker before she died."

He took a deep breath and grabbed a knife. "When I find out who's been doing this..." He hacked a potato in half. "...I'll kill him with my own two hands."

I hesitated to say it, but I needed to. If for nothing more than to hear a voice of reason tell me I was thinking foolish. "You don't think..."

"That Beau's guilty?" He jammed the tip of the knife into the cutting board and let out a bitter laugh. "That boy couldn't kill a mouse with an AK-47."

Dog was angry. We both were. I wasn't about to let Beau take the fall for Tammy Davis. But I could feel the tension building around town. Crimson PD needed to arrest someone, to take the heat off themselves and the mayor during an election year. But you didn't have to convince me it was the work of a vampire. I'd already decided I was going down to Reaperstown to have a talk with Ian Masterson, but I wasn't a complete fool. Someone was going down there with me. The question was who?

* * *

Patrick walked into the Stag around eight o'clock and took a seat at the bar.

"To what do I owe the honor?" I hadn't seen or heard from him in a day or two, which was unusual.

"Can't I stop by just to see my girl?" He nodded to the liquor bottles against the wall. "Give me a shot of bourbon, and not that cheap shit on the bottom shelf." He glanced up and down the bar. "I thought you were taking a break from slinging drinks so you could focus on being the boss. Where's your boy?"

"You mean Beau?"

"Is there another boy back there I haven't met?"

I grabbed a bottle of the good stuff and poured him a drink. "He's in jail."

"What did he do? Run a stop sign?"

I called him down to the other end of the bar, near the order window where it wasn't so crowded. "They arrested him for murder."

Patrick cocked his head. "That ain't even remotely funny."

"Damn right it isn't, but it's true. They're trying to pin Tammy Davis's murder on him."

"The girl they found in the woods?"

Lucy came over and stuck her nose where it didn't belong. "That's right. He went over to her place last night and left a deposit, if you know what I mean. They probably have his DNA and everything."

"Go do your job." I nodded to a customer waving from the other end of the bar.

Patrick waited until she walked away. "What the hell was that dimwit talking about?"

"Does the whole town know about the latest attack already?" I was surprised Patrick hadn't heard about Beau being arrested, but it would spread like wildfire by morning.

"Girl, don't you watch the news?" He downed his drink and set the glass in front of me.

I poured him another. "Not if I can help it."

"It's been on every station, but none of them have mentioned a suspect being arrested." He gave me an irritated look. "And why the hell haven't you called me by now? That's some juicy gossip."

"Really, Patrick? That's all you have to say? Beau's being railroaded, and you're more concerned about being left out of the loop?"

"I have my priorities. Now, what's this about DNA?"

"Beau went to see Tammy Davis at her house last night. A

neighbor saw him on his way out. Sometime after that she was attacked."

He took a sip of his drink and shook his head. "I always knew that boy's pecker would bite him in the ass one of these days."

So did I. Beau was a walking hormone, and now I had to fix this mess.

I leaned over the bar and lowered my voice to a whisper. "I'm going down to the Beast tomorrow night."

"The Beast?" He practically bellowed it out.

"Do you mind not broadcasting it to the whole place."

I walked around the bar and beckoned him to follow me. "I'll be in the back room with Patrick," I said to Lucy.

As soon as we got there, he turned around and looked at me like I had a screw loose. "Are you out of your ever-lovin' mind? Because you must be high to even consider going down to that place."

Dog walked in behind us. "Damn right she is."

"Don't you have a burger to flip?" The two of them were starting to annoy me. "You were eavesdropping?"

"I didn't have to. You were having your delusional conversation right next to the order window."

"Ian Masterson has to know something," I said. "I'm going down there to make that vampire talk."

Patrick sat on the edge of the desk and snickered. "How? You gonna nag him into talking?"

"I just might."

Dog gave me a firm look. "No, you aren't. If anyone is going down to that place, it'll be the pack."

I laughed. "If you haven't noticed by now, wolves aren't exactly welcome in Reaperstown. You won't make it past the front door of the Beast. Hell, you probably won't even get within a hundred feet of the place without them smelling you."

"Dog's right," Patrick said. "You walk in there all by your

lonesome, and you'll be on the menu. Maybe you should have that vampire boyfriend of yours escort you down there."

At the mention of Samuel, a shot of warmth hit me in my nether regions. But any hopes of finishing what we'd started the other night was fading fast with his absence. "I haven't seen him since Saturday night, so you can forget about that. Besides, Ian Masterson and I called a truce." He hadn't shown his face around here since the night I blew up that restaurant across the street.

"For fuck's sake, I'll go with you." Patrick groaned and hopped off the desk. "But you owe me. That list of IOUs is getting pretty damn long these days."

With Patrick's mouth, we'd both end up on the menu. He'd probably enjoy it. "That's an awful idea."

His eyes leveled on mine. "Girl, you need someone who can speak vampire, and if you haven't noticed, I am one. Besides, I know the terrain. I've been down to that freak show before."

"Why doesn't that surprise me?"

Dog crossed his arms and shook his head at me. "You won't change your mind, will you?"

"If you have a better idea, I'm all ears."

After holding my gaze for a moment, he threw up a white flag. "I'll have the pack tag along anyway. Just for backup," he quickly added when I opened my mouth to protest. "You won't even know they're there. Unless trouble breaks out."

Unfortunately, if trouble did break out, we'd be inside. The pack wouldn't even know what was going on. But it was comforting to know that at least we wouldn't be ambushed on our way through Reaperstown—all two blocks of it.

"Then it's settled," I said. "We're going down there tomorrow night."

A knot formed in my stomach as I walked back out to the bar. Tomorrow night would either get me answers about who was killing women in Crimson, or it would turn into a real shit show. Patrick was more of a lover than a fighter, so the latter was a real possibility. I would have sold my right arm for that precious sunlight bullet loaded in Samuel's gun, the only one left in existence according to him. And if Ian Masterson tried something stupid tomorrow night, I would use it on him in a heartbeat.

FOURTEEN

"Does this thing go any faster?" I'd wanted to drive my truck, but Patrick and Dog had pointed out that it was too conspicuous. Not to mention loud. I really needed to get that muffler fixed. Instead, we drove Patrick's MINI Cooper, which wasn't conspicuous at all, with its candy-apple-red paint job.

He pulled his eyes away from the road. "You want to get to Reaperstown or pulled over?"

"I'm just nervous. If I don't get out of this car soon, I'll throw up."

"You better get them nerves under control."

"Watch the road, Patrick!"

"I'm serious. You walk into the Beast and start puking, you can kiss your ass goodbye."

I took a few calming breaths as we drove down a stretch of dark road. Like the last time we went down to Reaperstown, the moon was obstructed by an overcast sky. Darkness seemed to be the norm around here, and the clouds were in on it.

"One thing." Patrick glanced at my outfit as we came to the stop sign at the edge of town. "If a vampire hits on you, and believe me, one will, act like you're into it. Then tell him you're O positive."

"What's wrong with O positive?"

"It's the most common blood type, and it ain't as tasty as O negative." He chuckled. "By the time the vamp realizes he can't find anything better, we'll be long gone."

I didn't sign up for any of this. "You owe me, Beau," I muttered.

"Where do we park?" I asked as we came to the next stop sign in front of the Beast. Just looking at the building made me question my sanity. The last time I came down here, the club wasn't even marked. The menacing vampire hanging around the entrance gave it away. But now there was a sign across the front that said THE BEAST. The letters were painted with red lacquer, appearing wet and slippery like blood, and the aura around the place warned of what was beyond that door. It made me want to tell Patrick to keep driving.

Patrick took a left and drove around to the back of the club. The parking lot was full, but he managed to squeeze his pint-size car into a gap between two large SUVs.

"I don't think this is a parking space."

He gave me a dull look. "It is now."

My nerves started to fire up again as we got out. The music coming from the club was loud enough to penetrate through the back wall of the building, so I could only imagine what it was like inside.

Patrick bent down to look at his reflection in the side mirror and smoothed his hair. "I'm lookin' good tonight. Too bad I'm on babysitting duties."

"Who? Me? I believe you invited yourself." I was thankful that he had, though. I doubted I would have had the nerve to walk inside alone.

He glanced at my outfit again. "Hike your skirt up a little. This ain't no church."

I'd planned on wearing a pair of jeans and an old leather jacket, but Patrick had other ideas. He instructed me to go heavy on the makeup and talked me into wearing a skirt that was already obscenely short. "If I hike it any higher, I'll get arrested."

"Not in this place."

I pulled it up about an inch—that was the limit to my boldness—and followed him around the corner. The music got louder as we reached the front of the building, but thankfully it wasn't as ear-piercing as I expected it to be.

There was a small entryway as soon as we walked inside and a second door that led into the club. A vestibule or whatever you called it. Against the wall was a cigarette machine, but when I got a closer look, I realized it was a different kind of dispenser. You had a choice between condoms or vials.

"What's with the condoms?" The vials made sense, just in case you wanted to take a little blood home with you. But vampires didn't need to worry about diseases.

"They're for the humans," Patrick said. "Some of the vampires in this place carry some nasty shit."

Which was the very reason we screened donors at the co-op on a regular basis. Humans were delicate in comparison.

On the opposite wall was a bulletin board. It was covered with flyers, most of them with a fringe of tear-off phone numbers at the bottom.

"Hmm." Patrick grabbed one from a flyer advertising a questionable service.

"Don't tell me you're into S&M?" I said.

He raised a brow. "Have you tried it?"

"No!"

"Then don't judge."

In the middle of the board was a picture of a young woman. Written above it in bold letters was the word MISSING. Below the picture, it said she was last seen in Little Crimson.

"So vampires are going missing too," I said.

Patrick glanced at it. "Third one in the past few weeks."

"I heard about the other two from a customer, but I didn't think it was connected to the human attacks. Why isn't anyone concerned about this?" The only person who'd even mentioned it was CJ.

He looked at me like I was dense. "Nobody gives a damn if a vampire goes missing. They consider it a public service."

"You mean these women are disappearing and the police aren't doing anything about it?"

"Like I said, no one cares about a missing vampire."

"But what if they're connected to the other attacks?"

"That's a bit of a stretch. They haven't found any female vampires tied to trees, have they?"

As I turned to look at the picture again, a large man came through the second door and snatched the flyer off the board. He grinned, revealing a set of fangs with gold caps, as he crumpled it in his hand. His short platinum-blond hair stood straight up on his head, and he had a row of metal rings piercing his eyebrows.

His grin disappeared. "You must be lost. TGI Fridays is two towns over."

Patrick looked him up and down, letting his own fangs descend. "We're in the right place. My girl here is looking for a little adventure."

The vampire's grin returned as his eyes walked all over me. "Right this way." He stepped aside and motioned us toward the second door.

My heart started to beat faster as I walked through it, the steady sound of music filling my ears. At least it wasn't so loud I couldn't hear myself think. To our right was a crowd. They were staring at a stage in the middle of the room. A round platform big enough to hold two women who were gyrating against a pole in the center. Both were topless and wore skimpy G-strings that left nothing to the imagination. Around their necks were black studded chokers with straps dangling from them. Like dog collars with leashes.

"It's a strip club?" I said.

"It never used to be, but I guess it is now."

Then I remembered Lucy saying that her brother had started coming down here because of the strippers.

Patrick took a good look around the club. "The place looks like it got a facelift by Dracula."

The entire wall behind the stage was upholstered with red satin fabric, tufted in a diamond pattern like a chair or a sofa. The rest of the walls and most of the furniture were painted black. The club was dark even by vampire standards.

"You mean it didn't always look like the inside of a coffin?"

"No ma'am."

A man near the stage grabbed one of the straps. The woman at the other end of it flashed a set of fangs when he tugged her closer. She caught the eye of another man watching them from across the room, and her fangs immediately retracted, her eyes growing dull and lifeless.

I followed her gaze to the dark figure standing at the entrance of a hallway. His eyes left the stage and panned around the club, stopping when they landed on me. "That vampire is staring at me," I said.

Patrick glanced across the room. "What did you expect? Look around, Charley. You're a novelty in here."

I doubted I was the only human in the place, but I seemed to be the only blonde. And the only woman in the room who didn't look like I shopped at a Vampires-R-Us boutique. The leather skirt and jacket I was wearing were conservative compared to what the other women in the club had on.

There was a bar to my left. "I'm not getting through this night without a drink in my hand. You want something?"

He shook his head. "I prefer to stay sober in this place. You might want to do the same. Unless you want to find yourself shanghaied," he added under his breath.

I changed my mind about the drink and surveyed the room. "I don't see Masterson anywhere. What now?"

"This was your idea, girl. You tell me." He caught a pair of eyes watching him from the other side of the room. "I think I'm gonna secure myself a little company for later on. I'll be right back, so stay put."

"Patrick!" I hissed as he left me standing there and made his way across the room. I felt like prey. A fresh slab of meat in the middle of a lion's den as a bunch of eyes turned to me. "Screw this." I headed for the bar to get that drink before I lost my nerve completely.

A tall vampire with shockingly pale skin came up to me. He was bald and had a tattoo of a serpent's jaws wrapped around his head. It looked like the snake was swallowing him. And his eyes were unsettling. I couldn't tell if they were naturally dark or if he was wearing thick eyeliner.

"That's an interesting tattoo," I said.

He didn't even crack a smile as he stood there waiting for me to order a drink.

"I'll have one of those." I nodded to a cooler behind him filled with beer. No one was slipping me anything in a sealed container.

He opened the bottle and set it down on the bar in front of me. "Seven fifty."

Expensive. I handed him a ten. "Keep the change."

Finally, he cracked a smile and leaned over the bar, getting a good look at my cleavage before bringing his eyes back up to mine. "Anything else I can get for you?" The tips of his fangs peeked out from under his lips as they parted slightly.

"I'm looking for Ian Masterson. Has he been in here tonight?" The vampire straightened back up and disappeared down the bar without another word. "I'll take that as a no," I muttered.

I took a swallow of my beer and turned around, coming face-to-face with two vampires. I practically slammed into them. "Sorry. I didn't see you there." *Climbing up my ass*, I wanted to say.

One of them wrapped his hand around my rear end and pulled me against him. "Pretty."

I shoved him. "Get your hands off me, asshole!" It was probably not the smartest thing to say to a vampire in Reaperstown.

He grinned, running his tongue over the tips of his fangs. "That's not how it works in here, sugar." Then his hand found my ass again. "We give the orders."

His buddy helped himself to the bottle of beer I was holding, taking a swig as his fangs clicked into place. "Why don't we go find a corner in the other room and get on with it?"

No one at the bar—including the bartender—seemed to give a rat's ass that I was about to be manhandled into the other room. I was beginning to understand why everyone was so opposed to me coming down here. And where the hell was my best friend?

"The lady isn't available."

Finally.

The vampire groping me turned around to look at Patrick, while his friend leaned against the bar and continued to enjoy *my* beer. "What was that?"

Patrick's fangs came out. "I said, the lady isn't available. She's with me."

The vampire held Patrick's gaze for a moment and then reached back to grab me by my jacket. Yanking me in front of him, he wrapped his arm around my neck as he pulled me against his chest. "I'll just have a taste. Then she's all yours."

I gasped when the vampire's fangs punctured my skin and a sharp pain radiated across my shoulders. As I slumped against his ice-cold chest, it faded to a warm sensation spreading through my limbs, lulling me into pleasure. But as quickly as the relief washed through me, the pain came roaring back.

The room began to disappear around me, turning pitch-black. All I could feel was fire racing through my veins. The vampire wrapped his fingers around my neck, pulling me closer to sink his fangs deeper.

I clawed at his hand, digging my nails into his skin as I desperately tried to breathe. And then everything went quiet as a light flickered in the distance. It lit up around me, and all I could hear was the beating of my own heart as I was suddenly freed from the vampire's grip. I stood there for a moment, my mind a blank. Then the room started to come back into focus, and everyone was staring at something behind me.

I glanced down at a broken bottle in my hand, the edges jagged and covered with blood. Slowly turning, my breath hitched when I saw the vampire moving down the wall, leaving a trail of blood as he slid to the floor. His neck was nearly severed.

Dropping the bottle, I looked back at Patrick, bewildered. "Did I—?"

"Girl, that was some fucked-up shit," he said, still gawking at the vampire.

"Is he dead?" Then I heard a thud as his head toppled.

Patrick grabbed my wrist. "We need to get out of here."

"What just happened?" I said as he practically dragged me toward the exit.

"You just killed yourself a vampire." He looked back at the angry mob coming after us and shoved me through the door. "Run!"

We took off, rounding the corner to the parking lot. But before Patrick could fumble with his remote to unlock the doors, someone grabbed me from behind. As I spun around, a vampire grinned at me. When I looked back at Patrick, another vampire was wrapping something around his neck. He pulled it tight, and Patrick's skin started to smoke like it was about to catch fire.

As adrenaline raced through my veins, a light traveled down my arm and shot from my fingertips. I was about to try to use it on the vampires when a familiar voice spoke into my ear.

"The wire wrapped around your friend's neck is very sharp and made of pure silver. If you continue to fight me, Charley, he'll die."

It was Ian Masterson.

FIFTEEN

"Get your hands off me!" I said to Ian as he manhandled me toward a door. "I can walk."

He shoved me into a room. "My, aren't we full of piss and vinegar." A smug look appeared on his face. "It almost got you killed tonight."

"Tell that to the decapitated vampire back at the Beast."

He glanced at my neck. "I see he got a nip in first."

I reached up, horrified when I felt the puncture wounds, the memory of those fangs sinking into my skin still vivid.

"Lucky for you he was feeling playful."

"Playful, my ass," I scoffed. "He would have done far worse if I hadn't stopped him."

"You mean killed him."

I wouldn't have believed it if Patrick hadn't said it himself during our swift retreat out of there. I'd killed a vampire twice my size.

His eyes trailed down to my neck again. "That bite is almost healed. Are you sure *you're* not a vampire?"

It was time to change the subject. "Where are we?" His lapdog, Marcus, was standing next to him, and several others were positioned around the room like sentinels. "And where's Patrick?"

"You're in my office. This is my house. And Patrick is indisposed at the moment."

By the looks of the room, it was an old house. I could smell years' worth of mildew. "This is your house?"

"Why? Do you like it?"

Enough with the pleasantries. "Are you planning to kill me?" And stake me to the stop sign at the edge of Reaperstown as a warning for anyone else who dared to enter uninvited.

His eyes grew impatient. "That depends on how much you annoy me over the next few minutes."

"I'll try to keep it to a minimum. Just tell me what I'm doing here so we can get this over with."

After taking a seat in an oversized chair, he stared at me for a moment. "You came here looking for me, Charley." He sighed and sank deeper into it. "Now you've found me."

The vampire with the snake tattoo must have called him. "You know, your bartender really needs a lesson in hospitality."

"My bartender?"

"It's your club, isn't it?"

He glanced at Marcus with an amused look before shifting his eyes back to mine. "What gave you that idea?"

I shrugged. "I don't know. The overall deplorable nature of the place?"

"You're doing an exceptional job of annoying me, Charley."

"Then we're even." I decided to tone it down a notch when his face went cold. "You're telling me you don't own the Beast?" I could have sworn he said he did during one of our previous encounters. Or maybe I just assumed it, seeing as how he liked to call himself the mayor of Reaperstown.

"I run the place. Let's just leave it at that. At least I used to," he grumbled under his breath.

"What was that?"

His lips rose slightly into a forced smile. "What do you want, Charley?"

"I came to find out what you know about the attacks in Crimson. Three women have been killed, and it's obviously a vampire."

"Three?"

So, he didn't know everything. "A third woman was attacked and found out in the woods yesterday morning, just like the others. She died at the hospital later." I tried to gauge his reaction, but he was giving me nothing. Not even a flash of his eyes or a twitch of his lips. He just sat there staring at me. "You don't have anything to say about that?"

He cocked his head. "We already had this discussion. It wasn't me."

"I'm not accusing you."

"Well, thank God for that."

"You don't have to be so smug." I wanted to wipe the grin off his face, but I also wanted to get out of the room alive. Starting another war with the vampire would be counterproductive for me and the co-op.

"Why have you taken up the investigation?" he asked. "Starting a true crime podcast?"

Arrogant bastard. "Someone's got to find the killer."

"Isn't that the job of the Crimson PD?"

I almost laughed. The cops were useless. "They arrested my bartender. He's the prime suspect."

"You mean your foolish half-wit of a partner?"

During our first encounter with Ian Masterson, Patrick was busy being possessed so Beau had stepped in regarding co-op business. "Patrick's back, so Beau is just helping out now. And he's smarter than you think."

He glanced down at the floor when a muffled string of expletives came up from the room below. It was Patrick's voice.

"Depending on how this evening goes, you might want to keep your options open regarding a partner."

I stepped closer and glared at him. "If you hurt him, I'll—"

Masterson was out of his chair and had me pinned to the wall before I could blink. "You'll what?"

He was so close I could see my reflection in his dark eyes. "Just don't hurt him. Please."

Ian finally backed off, but not before making it very clear that the ceasefire between us was at his mercy. If I didn't get my adrenaline under control, I'd probably do something reckless and get my best friend killed. Just because Patrick had fangs didn't mean he was a match for a horde of vampires like Ian Masterson.

"Look," I said when he gave me some breathing room. "I just came here looking for information. The cops don't seem to give a damn that Beau's innocent."

His brows hiked. "You're sure he is innocent? Serial killers are often quite amiable."

"You know as well as I do that the killer is a vampire. The cops are just looking for a scapegoat to keep the mayor off their ass, and you're doing nothing about it."

He shot me a wicked look, reminding me of his true nature. "Why should I care about a handful of human women getting killed?"

"Because some of them were seen at the Beast before they were attacked. If more women fall victim, it's only a matter of time before the police show up here to investigate."

He tried to shrug it off, but I could tell I'd hit a nerve. Not that the Crimson PD had jurisdiction down here. No one did. Technically, Reaperstown didn't exist. It was a lawless wasteland. But the cops could draw attention to Ian's illegal activities. Cause him serious inconvenience.

"I would think you'd be more interested in finding the killer," I said. "Seeing as how female vampires are disappearing too. I think whoever is attacking humans is also responsible for the vampire disappearances."

He laughed quietly. "But they haven't found any vampire victims, have they? It's not the same M.O."

"We both know that doesn't mean anything." Vampire bodies had a funny way of cleaning themselves up. They just seemed to vanish. Some disintegrated immediately, but others shriveled for hours before combusting and turning to ash. They rarely left much of a trace. If you thought about it, killing a vampire was the perfect crime. No body, no evidence. And good luck identifying a pile of ashes. "Those vampire bodies could have been long gone before anyone found them. Don't you care at all?"

The tips of his fangs peeked out from under his lips. "You're wasting your time trying to humanize me." With a balled fist, he knocked on his chest. "There's nothing in here but a cold black heart. Just the way I like it."

"You don't need to be human to have an ounce of compassion. Two of your own kind going missing in less than a week should concern you." I hooked my thumb over my shoulder. "And I saw a flyer tonight on the bulletin board at the Beast about another woman who just disappeared in Little Crimson."

There was a slight flash in his eyes this time. A third missing vampire must have been news to him, so I decided to keep the momentum going. "Where's the rest of your crew?" I asked, looking around the room at Marcus and a handful of others. There'd been a female vampire with him the night he came to the Stag trying to extort me, but she was absent tonight. "I don't see your female friend. Is she missing too?"

"You're really starting to bend my nerves, Charley."

"She's irritating me too," Marcus said. "Would you like me to take care of her friend down in the basement?"

My adrenaline spiked at the mention of him. It was time to remind Masterson who he was dealing with. "If you kill Patrick, you'll have no leverage to use against me." I focused on my shaking hands, but instead of summoning my power, something hit me in the gut. It was like the light had traveled inward, ravaging my stomach like a wild animal trying to free itself from a cage.

Ian waved his hand at me as I lurched. "What's all this about?"

Marcus took a step back. "She looks like she's about to hurl."

"Now, *that* will make me kill you," Ian growled.

I had no idea what was happening to me, but something was climbing up my throat. Gagging, I stumbled back, my breath cut off from the obstruction. As soon as my back hit the wall, I felt something move into my mouth and work its way along my tongue. Desperate to breathe, I reached inside and grabbed the furry object, gagging again as I gazed at the black spider leg.

Ian squinted at it, keeping his distance. "What the hell is that?"

Suddenly Candy's words came roaring back in my head.

The fire in your belly has always been there, but it's lit now. Don't go pointing that finger around willy-nilly. You could take someone's head off if you're not careful.

When I didn't respond fast enough for Ian's liking, he came toward me. The spider leg slipped from my hand, disintegrating before hitting the floor. I threw my right hand up when he came dangerously close. "Stop!"

His feet were suddenly glued to the floor. He tried to lift his leg, but he couldn't. "*What* did you just do to me?"

I'd angered him, that was for sure. "I told you to stop."

He snapped his fingers. "Take her to the basement."

Marcus came toward me. Without thinking, I threw my hand up, the one Candy had warned me about. A crackle of energy traveled down my arm and into my hand, continuing through the tip of my finger. He flew backward and hit the window, shattering the glass as he crashed through it.

In the distance, a sound was growing louder. It was the steady sound of grunts and growls coming from outside.

Ian managed to regain control of his legs and glanced at the window before training his eyes back on mine. His fangs had descended. "The truce is over."

A second window shattered, and wolves flooded into the room. Loki took one of the vampires down while the larger wolf standing in front of him locked eyes with me. It was Dog. But then two vampires came out of nowhere and slammed into him, sending him careering into the wall.

I ran into the hallway and started yanking on doors. Most of them were locked. "Patrick!" I yelled. When I tried the doorknob to the one at the end, it opened. There was a staircase that descended into darkness, and I could hear his voice down there.

"Patrick?" I whispered, slowly taking the steps.

"Don't come down here, Charley." His voice was weak.

The adrenaline racing through my veins had me shaking. I stopped for a moment to steady myself, the taste of the spider still in my mouth.

In my mouth!

When I reached the bottom step, someone grabbed me. A hand wrapped around my neck and pinned me to the wall. I was looking into the eyes of a vampire, spikes of pink hair shimmering in the light coming through the door at the top of the stairs.

"Let go of me," I squeaked out as she gripped my neck tighter.

A grin spread across her face. "I don't think so."

I guess she wasn't missing after all.

"Play nice, Irina," Ian said from the top of the stairs. "Charley's mine."

"She ain't no one's," Patrick coughed out from somewhere in the dark room. "Come and get me, motherfucker!"

Ian might have managed to get away from the wolves, but I

could hear them still going at it with his crew in the room above us. If I stalled long enough, Dog could still find us before things turned deadly.

The vampire released me and backed away. "You're in for some fun. Ian likes to play rough." Her grin vanished. "Good luck with that."

The lights suddenly came on, and I spotted Patrick near the far wall. His neck was deeply cut by the silver wire still wrapped around it, the ends gripped tightly by a vampire standing behind him. I'd never seen him look so weak. So vulnerable.

"If she so much as lifts a finger," Ian said as he came down the stairs, shutting the door behind him, "sever his head."

"I won't," I said. "Just don't hurt him."

He grabbed my arm when he caught me glancing up at the ceiling. "We should go before your wolves come looking for you." Then he practically dragged me across the room toward a door at the other end of the basement. It was pitch-black on the other side when he opened it. "Ladies first."

I didn't dare yell out for fear he'd make good on his threat to kill my best friend. "What about Patrick?" I said before walking through the door.

"Don't worry. He's coming with us." Ian nodded to the vampire detaining Patrick. "Bring him."

The door to the basement splintered off its hinges as Dog crashed through it and bounded down the stairs. Irina pulled a dagger from her boot and stepped in the wolf's path, slashing the blade at him. The vampires and wolves from the first floor came down right behind him, and the basement became a mosh pit of fur and fangs.

"Block the tunnel!" Ian barked to the vampire holding Patrick before shoving me through the door and slamming it shut behind him.

I stumbled blindly. "I can't see where I'm going."

He grabbed my arm roughly and started to drag me along with him. "Let's go!"

After what seemed like a mile, he suddenly stopped and placed my hands on a ladder. "Up!"

I did as he ordered, stopping when my head hit something hard at the top. A hatch. The night air hit my face as I pushed it open. As soon as I climbed out of the hole, I considered running, but I had no idea where Patrick was.

Ian climbed out and shut the hatch behind him, grabbing my arm again to lead me into the woods. We finally stopped when my legs gave out and I dropped to the ground. "I can't go any farther."

He glared down at me. "Get up!"

"Where's Patrick?" By now I'd realized he wasn't in that tunnel. That meant he was back in the basement. But so was Dog, and I prayed the pack had gotten the upper hand and that vampire hadn't killed Patrick.

He sneered. "I ask the questions, not you."

I climbed to my feet and stumbled back when he tried to grab me again. "Get away from me." Then I raised my hand. "I *swear* I'll send you straight back to hell if you take another step."

"And Patrick will die."

"That's funny. I don't see him anywhere. What are you going to do? Send a message to your henchvampire telepathically?"

The grin on his face flattened as his fangs descended. "You think you can take me on? Well then, let's play."

Recalling what I'd done to Marcus back at the house, I pointed my finger at Ian. "Don't say I didn't warn you."

When he started to stalk toward me, I summoned all my will to stop him in his tracks. My adrenaline suddenly spiked, stirring another wave of nausea in my stomach. Then a light appeared on the underside of my hand. In my palm. But as Ian came closer, it fizzled. The energy running down my arm sputtered, then all but dissipated. My finger sparked, but nothing happened.

I was a dead woman.

The snarl on his face turned into a grin. "Problem?" He grabbed me, and the energy began to crackle along my arm again.

Ian yowled and stumbled back. "You little—"

"I'd watch my mouth, if I were you," I said, having no idea what had just happened, other than Ian getting zapped when he put his hand on me.

The result was the same when he came at me again. By the look on his face, the second jolt was worse. I think I saw smoke coming from his hand.

He clenched his teeth. "I should kill you for that."

"You came at me first." He was smart enough not to try it again, and it seemed we were at an impasse. "This is ridiculous, Ian. We were doing just fine until you broke our truce." I stared at him for a moment to gauge his level of anger. "I don't want to be your enemy. We can co-exist, but you've got to stop attacking me every time we run into each other. Now, back off."

His eyes narrowed. "You first."

It was a huge leap of faith on my part, but it was either that or we'd end up glaring at each other indefinitely. As tired as I was, he'd win that battle.

I finally dropped my arm, half expecting him to jump me. But he just stared at me like he was contemplating what to do next.

"If I'm not allowed in Reaperstown, you need to stay out of Crimson," I finally said. Seemed fair.

He was two feet away from me before I could blink but smart enough not to lay a hand on me again. "No one tells me where I can or can't go." The look in his eyes was as dangerous as I'd ever seen it. "I own this territory."

"Then clean it up. Help me find out who's killing people around here."

"I don't give a damn about humans getting their throats ripped out in pursuit of thrills they can't handle."

It was true that Patrice Henderson and Kim Widby had both been spending time at the Beast, but what about Keith Barnes and Tammy Davis? It was more than that. The vampire was lying through his teeth.

I met his cold gaze. "You're hiding something."

He took his hostility down a notch as he stepped back. "Perhaps. But I didn't get to where I am by doing favors for nothing in return."

"Then tell me what you want."

"Oh, I will. All in good time because you owe me now."

"Owe you? For what?"

"For not picking up where we left off tonight and killing you in the future." He was in my face a second later. "And believe me, Charley, I can."

With that, he was gone. In a streak, he dashed past me and disappeared into the night. I think our truce was back in full force, but my gut told me I'd have to pay for it. Ian Masterson had just handed me a big fat IOU.

SIXTEEN

"Y'all need to get the hell out of this room," Patrick ordered.

He was going to be just fine.

The wolves had come through the tunnel and found me in the woods, which I was thankful for because I had no idea where I was after Ian Masterson ditched me. They'd also managed to rescue Patrick. He was in Candy's spare bedroom now, nursing his wounds, and he was being a lousy patient.

Candy ignored him and leaned closer to check the progress of his healing. "It's looking pretty good. You'll be right as rain in no time."

He started to climb out of bed. "I'll give you an update in the morning, from the privacy of my *own* bedroom."

"Suit yourself." She stepped aside to let him learn the hard way.

When he tried to stand, he wobbled and sat back down on the edge of the mattress. "Maybe I'll stay for a few more minutes."

The seared skin of his throat wasn't nearly as gruesome as it looked when we got to the Cauldron, but he'd be healing for a few more hours. That vampire had pulled the wire so tight, it cut halfway through his neck.

A question had been on my mind since those vampires showed up in the parking lot and incapacitated Patrick. "I thought vampires and silver was a myth?"

"It depends on the vampire," Candy said, swatting Patrick on the arm. "Isn't that right?"

"Don't push me, woman." He leaned back against the pillows and groaned. "The less pure the vampire, the more effective it is. And if you haven't noticed, I ain't exactly a saint."

I tried not to smile, or God forbid laugh, because the situation wasn't funny. But Patrick did have a salacious appetite.

"It also needs to penetrate the skin," Dog said. "It's why they used thin silver wire, so they could cut him."

All this time I thought I knew vampires as well as anyone around here, but I was getting an education tonight. Ian Masterson wasn't exactly pure himself, so maybe it would be a good idea to keep some of that silver wire handy just in case he pulled a stunt like that again.

Candy shooed us toward the door. "Let's quit hovering and go downstairs so he can get some rest."

"Yeah, why don't you do that," Patrick said. "I'll be good in a few minutes."

I looked back at him as we walked out the door. He acted all tough, but that ordeal had taken it out of him. Masterson was officially on my shit list, but I intended to play nice with him as long as he stayed on his side of the tracks.

As soon as we got downstairs, Candy turned around and gave me a look that did not pale in comparison to the warning gazes my mother used to give me. "What the hell were you doing down in Reaperstown tonight?"

"Trying to find Ian Masterson. And guess what? I found him."

Dog leaned back against the counter with his arms crossed

to watch the show. Candy was about to chew me out enough for both of them.

"Charlotte Underwood." She shook her head. "I never thought I'd see the day when you did something that stupid."

"I was trying to help Beau. He's being railroaded, and nobody but me seems to give a damn."

I detected a slight flaring of her nostrils. "Oh, I give a damn, but I give a damn about you a little more." She glanced at Dog and then brought her eyes back to mine. "And you put the pack at risk saving your ass."

"Well, I wouldn't say the pack was at risk," Dog muttered with a chuckle.

"Look," I said. "We're all in one piece. No one got killed. End of story."

She calmed down as a wicked smile slid up her face. "What did you do to Masterson? Did you light him up like a torch? I would have paid good money to see that."

I would have liked to have seen it too. "I didn't do anything to him."

She frowned. "Well, why not?"

"Because I failed miserably." I fizzled out like a dud, that's what happened. "Everything was working just fine when we got down there. I even killed a vampire at the Beast."

She froze, her gaze boring into mine for a moment that seemed to go on forever. "I believe you've lost your mind, walking into that cesspool!"

What was done was done. It was time to move on and figure out what was wrong with me. "I don't know what happened to me tonight. Ian came after me, but when I tried to use my magic on him, it just... fizzled. One minute I was throwing a vampire through a window with this"—I pointed my finger at her—"and then nothing."

She grabbed my hand and directed it away from her. "Like I told you before, you might not want to point that at anyone."

"Why? I don't know what I'm doing. What the hell good is having magic if you can't figure out how to use it?"

Candy gave me a commiserative smile. "Honey, most witches don't know what they're doing at first."

"Then what was that ritual all about?" I didn't swallow that spider for nothing.

"That was just the beginning. To make sure you had it in you. And believe me, you do. But you don't get a pass on working at it like the rest of us had to just because you're an Underwood."

"Are you telling me you were like this once?" I couldn't imagine Candy ever being an amateur at anything.

"Well, I wasn't born knowing how to use my gifts. It took a while to get the hang of it." She got a sly grin on her face. "I was so unpredictable at your age I nearly killed a man while I was giving him the ride of his life."

"Candy!" Nothing that came out of her mouth should have shocked me. "You're joking?"

"Honey, there are two things I don't joke about—paying taxes and the power of the vajayjay."

Dog rubbed the bridge of his nose. "Can we please get back to what happened with Masterson?"

I recalled the strange feeling of the energy crackling along my skin and then suddenly fading. "Ian tried to grab me, so I threw my hand up to stop him. There was a light coming from my palm, but then it just went out. It was like the energy faded along with it. But the strange part was, when he grabbed me, he got a powerful shock. Not once, but twice. It was enough to get him to back off."

She looked at me curiously. "Did anything strange happen leading up to that?"

"You could say that." The memory of that hairy thing in my mouth came back vividly in my mind. "Shortly after Ian took me to his house, I started to feel strange. Kinda sick. Then I started to gag when I felt something crawling up the back of my throat." Just the thought of it made me want to brush my teeth. "It was one of the spider's legs."

"Spider's legs?" Dog was looking at me like maybe I hadn't come out of tonight unscathed. "What the hell are you talking about, Charley?"

Candy stared at me curiously. "That's interesting. Just one leg?"

"Why? Does it matter?"

"It might. I need to have a word with the Squad."

"You do that." I suddenly felt weak. Overly tired, which was understandable considering the night I'd had. "I need to go home and get some sleep."

She looked at me like I had two heads. "You're not going anywhere. You're staying right here."

"We already had this conversation," I reminded her. "I'm not getting run out of my own house, and that's the end of it. Besides, Patrick is up in the spare bedroom. Just worry about him tonight." He'd probably be gone before she woke up.

"It's your life," she said, glancing at Dog.

He nodded to her. "The pack has her back, so you don't need to worry about her."

"Well, then get out of here so I can go to bed. But I expect a call first thing in the morning, you hear me?"

"Crack of dawn," I said on my way out.

Dog and I walked back to the Stag where my truck was parked. "Thanks for tonight," I said as I pulled out my keys. "I'd probably still be in Ian Masterson's basement if the pack hadn't shown up."

"You can thank me by not going down to the Beast again."

Not that I ever wanted to, but I couldn't make that promise. I just smiled and got in my truck. "See you tomorrow."

On the drive home, my eyes kept darting to the woods on the side of the road. I kept expecting to see something come running out in front of my truck. "Stop it, Charley," I told myself. My imagination was running wild these days, but for good reason.

The lights were off in the living room when I pulled up to the house. I usually left them on before leaving for the Stag, but I must have forgotten today. There was something reassuring about it, especially when you came home late at night. I just kept reminding myself that if a vampire was waiting for me inside, all I needed to do was order him out. But if Ian Masterson was in there, I'd have to be very specific. Once you gave a vampire an explicit invitation to enter your house, like I did the first time he showed up here, the order to get out had to be just as explicit. Forgetting that could be deadly. It was a loophole probably devised by vampires themselves.

When I got out of the truck and started walking across the yard, Rex came swooping down and sailed past me, landing on the railing at the top of the porch. "Well, hello to you too." He cawed persistently, which made me slightly nervous.

I scanned the yard, looking for signs of trouble, but nothing stood out. No movement or shadows. The moon above was particularly bright, and a strange feeling had stirred up in my stomach. It felt like butterflies laced with dread. When I continued up the steps, I was relieved that there wasn't another body dumped on my porch.

As I was about to unlock the door, I heard something fall, making me flinch. "Is someone there?"

I should have gone straight into the house, but I saw something move near a small table at the far end. An animal or something. When I went to look, something scurried over my feet. I stumbled back and fumbled for my phone, turning on the flashlight to see under the table. It was a possum. A dime a dozen around here.

After picking up the lantern it had knocked over, I walked back to the door. Rex was going ballistic on the railing behind me. "What the hell is wrong with you?" I said as I went to unlock it. But then suddenly I felt a presence. Something dark. My hand began to shake as I tried to stick the key in the lock, and I could hear Rex's wings flutter as he lifted into the air. The sound of footsteps made me turn, and I nearly collided with someone standing behind me. The keys slipped through my fingers and hit the porch. When I looked down at them, I saw a hammer dangling from the figure's hand with something shiny and wet reflecting off the steel. Blood.

"Who are you?" I said, backing up as the figure towered over me. His face was concealed by a hood, and suddenly my entire body was shaking from fear mixed with adrenaline. He never said a word, nor did he try to stop me as I slowly moved around him. It was like he wanted me to run.

Seizing the opportunity, I took off down the steps toward the truck, but I'd dropped my keys on the porch. And by the time I got my hands on the gun behind the seat, he'd be on top of me. A glance over my shoulder confirmed it. He was right behind me. Something told me a bullet would be useless anyway because I had a feeling I'd just come face-to-face with the vampire stalking Crimson.

I darted around the garage and pressed my back to the wall, holding my shaking hands out as I tried to summon my power. The other option was the woods behind the house, but my instincts told me I was as good as dead if I ran in there.

Where the hell was the pack?

My hands started to vibrate as I heard footsteps coming closer, but there wasn't so much as a spark of light coming from them. Time was up. I had to fight. I searched the ground for a weapon. Anything to fight him off with. There was a pile of concrete cinder blocks on the ground, but at forty pounds each, they wouldn't do me any good.

The footsteps stopped at the corner of the garage, just a few feet away from where I was standing. And then I saw something move. A hand wearing a black glove appeared around the edge.

I slid down the wall toward the other end and braced myself, suddenly feeling a surge of energy. It came on so fast I felt lightheaded. I shook it off and stepped away from the garage trying to steady my trembling legs as I raised my hand and took aim. A shadow appeared around the corner, but then my breath caught when someone grabbed me from behind.

A beam of blue light shot from my hand as I fell backward. It lit up the night sky, illuminating a black cloud of crows above me as my head came down and cracked against something.

My eyes fluttered open as a man hovered over me and his face came into view. "Samuel?"

Then it was lights out.

SEVENTEEN

My eyes opened when I heard banging. I was lying on my couch, and Rex was perching on the edge of a chair on the other side of the living room. He cocked his head like he was trying to examine me. Then he took off toward the kitchen, probably to destroy a cereal box on top of the refrigerator.

"Samuel?" I whispered as the events of the night came flooding back: my trip to the Beast, Ian Masterson, what had happened behind the garage.

Loki came down the hallway a moment later and bent over to get a look at me. He whistled, shaking his head as he straightened back up. "Glad to see you're not dead. Dog would have skinned me alive. *After* he beat my ass." The hair on one side of his head was caked with blood.

I pushed myself up with a groan. "What happened to you?"

"Got a rough handshake from whoever paid you a visit tonight. Nothing you need to worry about."

Then I noticed what he was wearing. "Is that my bathrobe?"

"It was hanging on the bathroom door, and it fit. Well, sort of." He ran his hand down the fluffy blue fabric. "It was either this or my birthday suit."

I was used to seeing the wolves in their birthday suits, but things tended to get weird after a few minutes.

"Dog will *still* kill you when he finds out you dropped the ball tonight," Samuel said to him as he walked into the living room.

"I was taking a piss. The bastard came up behind me and hit me before I could shift." There was another staring match between them. "By the way, thanks for the blood," he finally said to Samuel with a sneer. "I'm feeling another hurl coming on, so I better get to the bathroom."

Samuel smiled. "Next time I'll let you die."

Loki stepped up to him. "There won't be a next time, bloodsucker."

What was it with vampires and wolves? Once they got to know each other they were fine, but it was always a pissing contest until they got a steady whiff of each other's ass.

"Stop," I said. "My head hurts enough without having to listen to you two going at it."

Samuel held Loki's steady gaze a moment longer. "Why don't you run along and go patrol something so Charley and I can speak in private."

Loki broke eye contact with him and looked at me. "You okay with that?"

"It's fine. Thanks, Loki. If you get hungry tonight, help yourself to whatever's in the kitchen. There's a spare key in the bird feeder out front." No one ever thought to look for a key in a bird feeder. "You can just leave my robe on the porch," I said as he was walking toward the door.

He stripped it off and tossed it over the chair on his way out, giving me a look at his perfect ass. "Holler if you need me."

Samuel watched Rex sail from the kitchen and across the living room, disappearing out the door with Loki. "That's a very interesting crow you have there. I believe he and his friends were prepared to eat me if I tried anything funny with you behind the garage tonight."

One of the last things I remembered before the lights went out was seeing that group of crows circling the sky above me. "He's protective. You should have seen what they did to the last vampire who attacked me on my front lawn." A thought occurred to me. "By the way, how'd you get in here?" I'd never invited Samuel into my house before.

"It was the crow."

I stared at him for a second. "What do you mean?"

"He lives here, so he invited me in."

I wasn't sure how to respond to that, but I gave it a go. "You speak crow?"

"Something like that." Seeing my perplexed look, a smile crossed his face. "You had a moment of lucidity and managed to ask me inside."

I let out the pent-up breath I was suddenly holding. He had me going for a minute there.

When he came toward me, I recoiled slightly. But it was involuntary. His face was the last thing I saw before blacking out, so I guess my subconscious was reacting. "What are you doing here, Samuel?" I hadn't seen him since he left me breathless against the wall in the back room of the Stag.

His eyes darkened as he took a step closer. "You don't think I did this to you?"

I couldn't fathom it. "Of course not. Did you see who it was?"

He hesitated. "He was gone within seconds. I would have chased him down if you weren't in dire need of my help."

Part of me wished he'd gone after my assailant, but I probably wouldn't have been breathing right now if he did.

He put his hand on my shoulder to keep me from standing

up, sending a shot of warmth through me. "Give it a few minutes. The concussion hasn't healed completely."

"Concussion?" I felt the back of my head again.

"You hit a cinder block when you fell."

"You mean when I was thrown to the ground." I distinctly remembered being grabbed from behind. Samuel was becoming my Florence Nightingale. "I always seem to be waking up to you."

A grin spread across his face.

"Don't get any ideas." Not that I didn't want to, but Loki was outside and my head was still throbbing.

His brows arched. "No?"

We locked eyes. If I didn't change the subject fast, I'd do something reckless. But reckless was coming, just not tonight. "What was all that noise in my kitchen a few minutes ago?"

His intense gaze softened. "I was looking for an ice pack."

"In the cabinets?"

"I was also looking for tea. I thought I'd make you a cup, but you don't seem to have any."

He would have found some if he'd looked inside the tin on the counter marked TEA, but I was really more of a coffee girl.

When I glanced down, I spotted drops of blood on my shirt. "Did I land on the back of my head or my face?" I was afraid to look in the mirror.

"It's mine. It dripped from my wrist when I was feeding it to you."

My smile vanished. "Samuel? You gave me your blood?" I was obviously a major proponent of vampire blood as medicine, but the decision to consume it was a very personal one.

"I would have asked your permission, but you were unconscious at the time. If I hadn't given it to you, you'd be in a hospital right now. Or worse."

Of course he did the right thing. I wasn't thinking clearly. I looked at the bloodstained towel he'd wisely thought to put between me and the pillow and felt the back of my tender head. "It was that bad, huh?"

He shuddered. "Grisly. You're quite the bleeder. And that's saying a lot, coming from a vampire."

There was a moment of awkward silence between us before he finally spoke again. "I'm afraid I haven't been completely honest with you, Charley."

"I figured. I just hope you're not about to tell me you're a fugitive. Or, God forbid, a Scientologist." I laughed halfheartedly, nervous about knowing his big secret. I didn't want to hear anything that would change the way I felt about him. But I had to remind myself that he did say he was just passing through town. Once he finished his business in Crimson—whatever that was—he'd be gone, so maybe it was for the best if I got him out of my head. I was afraid it was too late for that, though.

He walked over to the window and looked out. When he turned back around, he'd pulled a pendant out from under his shirt. "This is what I am." It was some kind of symbol. A triangle with a claw in the center. The talons of a hawk or some other bird of prey gripping a shiny black stone. The metal looked like silver.

"I guess you're not sensitive to silver," I said.

"It's titanium. The seal of a hunter."

"Oh yeah? It's not hunting season in Georgia yet." I tried to make light of it, but the word "hunter" stirred all kinds of uneasy thoughts.

"I'm a bounty hunter. I've been hired to find a vampire who I believe is hiding in Crimson or very close by. I also believe he's the vampire who's been attacking women around here."

Of all the things I expected him to say, it certainly wasn't that. "What makes you think it's the same vampire?"

"Because of this." He reached for something in his pocket and handed it to me.

I gasped. "It's just like the others." It was a very old black-

and-white photograph of a young woman slumped against a tree. Her hands had been nailed to the trunk above her head, and her throat had been torn open. Even in black and white, the blood was horrific. "Who is this?"

"One of his first victims."

I handed the fragile picture back to him. "When did it happen?"

"A lifetime ago." He put it back in the protective case and shoved it in his pocket. "There's no doubt it's the same vampire. I've been tracking him for years, and I intend to end it here."

"Can I ask who this vampire is?" I shrugged. "Maybe it's someone I know?" Not that I thought one of my customers was a serial killer, but I couldn't rule it out after everything that had happened in town over the past couple of months. And then there were the lowlifes in Reaperstown. Not to mention Ian Masterson, although I doubted it was him. He could be ruthless, but he wasn't that depraved. I was prepared to scrutinize every vampire in Crimson if necessary, though. For Beau's sake.

"It's no one you know," Samuel said. "The vampire I'm hunting isn't a local. I only tracked him here recently."

"And you think this is the vampire who attacked me tonight?"

He held my gaze for a moment. "Yes."

Okay, I was sufficiently scared now.

"His day of reckoning is coming." He stared off in thought for a moment. "It's coming very soon."

It seemed very personal to Samuel. Like it was more than just a job. "Who hired you to find him?" Crimson was a small town. Nothing more than a blip on the map that all of a sudden had an ancient killer on its hands. Nobody around here would have the connections or the money to hire a hunter, and my guess was Samuel didn't come cheap.

"A man who doesn't give up," he said. "The girl in the picture's father. What that vampire didn't know is that my employer isn't human, so he's had an eternity to hunt down his daughter's killer." Samuel's expression hardened as he stared out the window again. "The killer took the wrong girl. He'll pay for that with more than just his immortality. My employer will make him suffer, and so will I."

Samuel had never given off cruel vibes. He was a cat lover, for God's sake. But the look in his eyes *was* cruel, and the tone of his voice gave me the chills. "You're scaring me."

He finally snapped out of whatever bloodlust had gotten under his skin and looked back at me. "Don't ever be afraid of me, Charley. I'll never hurt you." He turned around to give me his full attention. "Never."

"What aren't you telling me, Samuel? This is personal to you. Why?"

His blue eyes turned dark again, a flicker of ruby catching the light as a cold grin appeared on his face. "You're right. It is personal. That vampire took something from me as well. Something I can never get back." His grin vanished. "Victor Steele took my humanity. He's the vampire who turned me and left me for dead."

EIGHTEEN

Samuel was gone before the sun came up. He wasn't happy about my decision to stay at the house after what happened, so he hung out in the living room for the rest of the night. I knew Loki wouldn't make the same mistake twice, but even if he did, that vampire wasn't getting inside my house without an invitation.

While I took a quick shower, I thought about the conversation I'd had with Samuel. I was still shocked to learn that the killer in town was also the vampire who took his life. His maker. Although many vampires, most even, considered it a rebirth and enjoyed their immortality, Samuel apparently did not. This Victor Steele had drained him and left him to die. But Samuel had survived the attack. He resurrected and was left to fend for himself in a new world, with no one to teach him how to be a vampire. Now he was on a mission to fulfill his job but also to get his revenge. I didn't even know a vampire could kill his own maker. I thought it was impossible. But Samuel had explained that it was possible under certain circumstances, like when your maker abandoned or tried to kill you. Victor Steele was fair game now.

After getting dressed, I went into the kitchen. Loki was having breakfast and thankfully wearing my robe again.

"Hope you don't mind me making something to eat," he said, looking like a kid caught with his hand in the cookie jar.

"Why would I mind? I told you to help yourself. And bless you for making coffee." I could tell he was more embarrassed about dropping the ball last night than me finding him eating a plateful of eggs in my kitchen. "It's not your fault, Loki. It wasn't your average vampire that attacked both of us last night."

He chuckled nervously. "Tell that to Dog."

Loki was a tough wolf. It was the reason Dog had chosen him as his second-in-command. It took a lot to get the better of him, and he seemed to be taking it as a personal failure. "Who said anything about telling Dog?" I said. "It's over, and we all came out in one piece."

He glanced up from his plate. "I appreciate that, Charley, but that's not how it works with the pack. Don't worry, he won't kill me."

It sounded like a joke, but I knew better. Wolves had their own brand of punishment, and it wasn't always kind. But as Dog had put it to me before, it was necessary to keep the pack focused and disciplined. To preserve the hierarchy. In a strange way, their bond would be stronger for it.

I dropped the subject and poured myself a cup of coffee. Dog would find out anyway because I needed to go down to the police station this morning and report the incident. I'd been attacked by Crimson's serial killer, and since Beau was sitting in that cell, it definitely wasn't him. I just had to convince Murphy that it was the same attacker and not some new vampire blowing through town. And if Murphy didn't believe me and refused to release my bartender, I'd have Loki and Samuel as witnesses and sic Flanders on him again. Well, I'd try. Bob Flanders was probably done with the matter, but he still hadn't sent me that list of criminal lawyers.

"Don't worry about the dishes," I said to Loki. "If you want to take a shower to wash that blood out of your hair, you're welcome to. I need to get going, so lock the door behind you."

"I appreciate that, Charley, but I need to get out of here too. Lux or Max will be here tonight."

In other words, Dog would relieve him of his babysitting duties. "If it means anything to you," I said on my way to the bedroom to find some shoes, "I still trust you with my life."

* * *

When I got to the police station around nine a.m., there was only one patrol car parked out front. If I was lucky, it wouldn't be Murphy's, because I stood a better chance of convincing Carter to let Beau out of that jail cell.

Jen was at the desk when I walked inside. She had a biscuit in one hand and a cup of coffee in the other.

"Morning, Jen. Is Carter in his office?"

She took a bite of her biscuit and took her time chewing and swallowing it before answering me. "No, but Tom's here if you want to talk to him."

"Delighted." I headed for his office.

"Where do you think you're going?"

I pointed to his office door. "To talk with Murphy."

She motioned to the row of chairs against the wall. "Have a seat. I'll see if he's available."

It took a lot of restraint, but I held my tongue.

She mumbled something into the phone and hung up. "He'll be right out."

I must have sat there for fifteen minutes before Murphy finally came out of his office. He was wiping his hands on a napkin and swallowing a mouthful of food. "Hope I didn't interrupt your breakfast," I said. God forbid one of the citizens who paid his salary should need immediate police assistance.

"What do you want, Charley?" He seemed irritated.

"I need to report a crime, if it's not too much trouble."

He let out a frustrated breath and motioned me into his office.

I remained standing as he sat down behind his desk. "I was nearly killed last night when I got home. It was the same vampire who's been attacking women around here." He stared at me but didn't say a word. "Did you hear what I just said?"

"Sit down, Charley."

"I'd prefer to stand."

He leaned back in his chair and laced his fingers together over his stomach. "All right. Stand."

"You need to release Beau."

After looking me up and down, he nodded his head a few times. "You look all right to me, so I doubt it was the same vampire." He leaned forward with a contemptuous look. "*If* you were attacked at all."

I figured he'd pull something. "I have witnesses. Loki was attacked too."

"Loki?" He huffed. "You expect me to take the word of a wolf?"

"He's a citizen of this town, same as you or me, so you're damn right I do." I wanted to come across the desk at him. "Samuel Cain witnessed it too. If it wasn't for him, I'd be dead right now."

His brow tightened. "You mean that new vampire in town? What was he doing at your place last night?"

"All you need to know is that he was a witness." I glanced at his desk for a pad of paper or an incident report form. "Why aren't you taking my statement?"

Murphy just shook his head at me. "You'd say just about anything to save that boy, wouldn't you?"

I'd had enough of his backwoods policing, so I walked out of his office. Jen yapped at me as I headed down the hallway toward the cells. I was going to at least talk to Beau and make sure he was okay.

"Charley!" Murphy barked. "Get your ass back here, or I'll toss you in the other cell!"

By the sound of his voice, he meant it. He'd do it out of spite, so I went back up front. "You can't hold Beau any longer, and you know it. I'm serious, Tom. I was attacked last night." I calmed down and tried another tactic. "Either take my statement and release him, or I'll have Bob Flanders down here within the hour."

Hopefully.

Jen mumbled something under her breath and took a sip of her coffee.

"Flanders can't help you, Charley."

I didn't like the look on his face. "What do you mean?"

"Bob Flanders is in the hospital. He's in ICU, and it's not looking too good."

At first I wasn't sure I'd heard him correctly. "What?"

"His cleaning lady found him in his office this morning."

Bob Flanders had a cleaning lady? You wouldn't have known it by looking at the place.

Murphy gave me a moment to let it sink in. I was ashamed that I'd never checked on him. All I'd thought about was that he hadn't sent me that list of lawyers. I shook it off. "What happened? Did he have a heart attack or something?" Bob was up there, and a heart attack or stroke were the usual suspects.

He shook his head. "His neck was ripped open. Same M.O. as Keith Barnes."

"And the women," I added. "Looks like the killer is branching out."

Jen stood up abruptly, nearly spilling her coffee. "Charley's right. None of us are safe." Her eyes filled with panic. "I need to go home and lock myself in!"

"Take it easy," Murphy said to her. "The sun is up. If this is a vampire—"

"If?" I shook my head at him. "You know damn well it's a vampire." I looked him in the eye. "You let Beau out of here, or I'll put my bar up as collateral to hire a fancy lawyer to sue the hell out of the Crimson PD." I was hoping he didn't call my bluff, but I was desperate.

When Murphy just stood there glaring back at me, I turned around and headed for Beau's cell.

"He was released this morning," Murphy said before I made it down the hallway. "Right after we heard about Flanders."

I stopped in my tracks as his words registered. Then I continued down to the cells to see for myself. They were both empty. When I went back up front, I got in Murphy's face. "You're a real bastard, you know that?" He took so much pleasure in tormenting me. It was more than just pseudo-parental delusion. I was a stand-in for my mother with him, for all the bitterness he still harbored toward her.

Murphy didn't even flinch. "It still doesn't explain why Tammy Davis accused him on her deathbed." He turned to go back into his office. "But in any event, he has an ironclad alibi for one of the crimes now."

Instead of doing something that would get me arrested, I let it go and left the station. Tom Murphy wasn't worth my time, but finding Beau was. I climbed in my truck and drove to the Stag. Beau's car was gone from around back, so I headed out to his place.

When I got there a few minutes later, I was relieved to see his car in the driveway. I parked next to it and took the stairs up to his apartment above the garage and knocked on the door. "Beau?" I tried the doorknob when he didn't answer, but it was locked. "It's Charley. Open up."

I knocked a few more times and listened for sounds inside, but it was dead quiet. It got my heart racing. Something was wrong. After checking for a spare key under a planter and coming up empty, I noticed the kitchen window at the other end of the landing was cracked open a few inches. It was a small window, but I got it all the way open and managed to squeeze through it and land on the kitchen sink. It was just a kitchenette off the living room of the tiny apartment, a far cry from the big house he grew up in. But it was all his and a world away from his father.

"Beau?" The hair on the back of my neck was standing on end, so I grabbed a knife from the drawer and crept toward his bedroom. There was nothing out of place in the living room, except for his usual dirty clothes scattered everywhere. No signs of a struggle. But seeing his car parked outside conjured all kinds of horrific thoughts.

When I came to the short hallway that led to the bedroom, I noticed the bathroom door was closed with the light on inside. With the knife gripped tightly in my hand, I reached for the doorknob and slowly turned it. I shoved it open, waving the knife in front of me.

Beau was on the floor. "Get away!" He backpedaled until he hit the tub, and he had an even bigger knife in his hand.

"Beau! It's me!"

His hand was shaking so badly, the knife slipped through his fingers and hit the tile floor. "Charley?"

"Yeah, it's me." I steadied my own shaking hands. "What are you doing in the bathroom?"

"I... I thought you were him."

"Him?" I grabbed the knife from the floor and set it on the bathroom counter along with mine before reaching down to help him up. He was wearing a hoodie. As he climbed to his feet, I noticed dark red stains on it. "What is that?"

He ran his hands over them and got a strange look on his face. "Blood."

"I can see that. Where's it coming from?"

The strange look quickly turned to fear. "I'm in trouble, Charley. You got to help me!"

It was time for us both to calm down and take a breath. "Come on. Let's get you in the living room so we can figure this out."

I made him sit on the couch and went to the kitchenette. "I'll get you a glass of water."

"Better make it a beer."

It was still morning, but after what he'd been through over the past few days, who was I to judge? I grabbed a bottle from the refrigerator and handed it to him. "What happened, Beau?"

He drank half the beer in a gulp and looked up at me with worried eyes. "I think I'm a vampire."

"A vampire? Don't be silly, Beau. You're not a vampire."

He grabbed the sweatshirt and pulled it away from his neck. On the left side of his throat were two small puncture wounds, the source of all the blood. "Do you believe me now?"

NINETEEN

Beau and I made it to Patrick's house in record time. If anyone could take a look at that bite and ease Beau's fears, it was a card-carrying vampire. Patrick would set him straight.

It was so dark inside the house I nearly tripped over a stack of books in the living room. "Patrick?" I flipped on the lights and told Beau to take a seat. He didn't say a word as he planted himself on the couch. He'd been like that since showing me those bite marks. It was like he was scared to talk about it.

Patrick strolled out of the bedroom wearing a pair of sunglasses. "This better be an emergency."

His lack of urgency was annoying. "Believe me, it is."

"'Cuz I gotta get me some beauty sleep."

I looked at his glasses. "Are those really necessary?"

He pulled them off, revealing bloodshot eyes. "It is if helping out a friend just got you a bad case of silver poisoning."

"Oh yeah. I forgot about that. Are you feeling better?"

"Good enough to deal with this fool." After giving Beau a once-over, he shook his head. "What the hell kind of trouble did you get your ass into this time? I thought you was in jail?"

Beau suddenly came back to life and stood up, pulling his

shirt back to expose the bite mark on his neck. "Where do you think I got this?"

He didn't mention that on the way over.

Patrick leaned in to get a better look at it. "Who gave you that?"

"Wait a minute," I said. "Back up. Are you telling me you got bitten while you were in jail?"

Patrick snickered. "Was it Carter or Murphy? My bets are on Carter. I always knew that cop was a freak."

"This isn't a joke, Patrick." I stared at Beau, daring him to clam up again. "What happened?"

Beau licked his lips as his breathing got heavier. "I was sound asleep in my cell last night when something woke me up." The fearful look in his eyes returned as he whispered, "It was a vampire."

"Boy, quit your whispering," Patrick said. "He can't hear you."

"He was a big sucker," Beau continued. "At first he just stood there staring at me. I tried to scream, but my vocal cords were paralyzed. Then he gave me a message." His eyes turned to me. "He said it was for you, Charley."

"Me?" Okay, this was getting weirder by the second. "What did he say?"

He swallowed hard. "He said the clock was ticking and you have something he wants."

"Well, what is it?" According to Samuel, this vampire was his maker. What could he want from me?

"I don't know! That's all he said!"

I wanted to shake him. Beau wasn't the best at retaining details, but if that vampire did say more, it was buried somewhere in Beau's thick head.

He got a funny look on his face. The look he always got when he was hiding something.

"Beau? What are you not telling us?"

He shook his head and took a seat again. "I'm not crazy."

Patrick chuckled. "Right."

"You're not helping, Patrick." I sat down next to Beau and patted his thigh. "Come on. Tell us the rest."

His eyes focused on the floor as his brows pulled tightly together. "Something happened, but I can't explain it. I think my eyes were playing tricks on me." He went quiet for a moment like he was trying to find the right words. "One minute I was looking at this big guy with fangs, and the next, I was looking at myself. It was like I was looking in a mirror."

"Boy, you got glamoured," Patrick said.

Beau looked horrified. "Glamoured? What the hell for?"

"Because he was fucking with you. Comes in handy sometimes."

A revelation hit me. "It also explains why Tammy Davis pointed a finger at you just before she died. He glamoured her into thinking it was you who attacked her." The pieces were quickly coming together. It had been so easy for Victor Steele to frame him. First Beau put himself under suspicion with his wandering dick, and that vampire sealed his fate. "He must have been watching you the night you went to her house." What it didn't explain was why. And why give Beau an alibi by attacking me and Bob Flanders? It was like he was playing with us.

"Did anything else happen?" I asked him.

He looked at me like I was thick in the head. "Hell yeah. He bit me. Now I'm a vampire."

Patrick scoffed. "You ain't no vampire. It's almost noon. You'd be good and crispy after that drive over here."

The light in Beau's eyes returned. "That's right. So then I ain't a vampire!" Then his smile vanished as he ran his hand over his neck. "But he still bit me. Should I be worried?"

"Not unless you liked it," Patrick muttered. "Then you got a different kind of problem on your hands."

"Hell no, I didn't like it. You said it yourself, he glamoured me with his vampire gaze."

Patrick looked at him sideways. "That's what they all say."

"You're lucky to be alive," I said. "The same vampire attacked me last night, and he's nothing to mess with."

That got Patrick's attention. "What?"

"He showed up at my house and tried to bash my head in. If it wasn't for Samuel, he probably would have succeeded."

"I thought Dog had his wolves sniffing around your place twenty-four seven."

"He took out Loki. Knocked him unconscious before he could shift. We're not dealing with your average vampire here."

"Thank God for Samuel," Beau said. "I'm starting to like that vampire."

Patrick was eyeing me when I looked at him. "What was Samuel doing at your place last night? You wasn't gettin' you a little somethin' somethin', were you?"

"I was not," I said with false indignation. "He just showed up at the right time." I debated whether to tell them the real reason Samuel was at my house. The reason he came to Crimson. To hunt down the vampire we were talking about. To get revenge on his maker. But it wasn't my information to tell. Samuel hadn't actually told me to keep it to myself, though he didn't say otherwise either. Since it was personal, I decided to keep my mouth shut.

"Are we done here?" Patrick asked.

I looked at Beau. "Are you satisfied now that you're not turning into a vampire?"

"I guess." He rubbed his neck, not looking entirely convinced.

"Good. I need to get me some sleep." Patrick headed back toward his bedroom but turned and lowered his sunglasses to look at me. "You might want to find out why that vampire is fixated on you."

***

Tucker was ten minutes late showing up for work, and she seemed off. But that was the norm for her lately. The woman needed to loosen up. She set her bag down and immediately went over to the window to look out.

"You're late." I threw her a glance but didn't make a big deal out of it. The bar didn't open for another twenty minutes anyway.

"I'm sorry, Charley. I left my apartment a few minutes late."

I noticed her rubbing her hands together nervously. "Is something wrong?"

She shook her head. "I've just got that creepy feeling again."

"Like someone's following you?"

She hesitated before answering me. "I saw something."

"And?" I said when she went quiet.

She stared out the window again. "I think I had a vision this morning. I saw a woman, and she was in a real dark place." She finally pulled her eyes away from the window to look at me. "She was a vampire."

"How do you know that?"

"Because she had fangs."

I looked at Dog who was listening through the order window. "Three female vampires have gone missing. It has to be related to the human attacks. It's too much of a coincidence."

He nodded. "It's kinda looking that way."

"Now I need to convince Ian Masterson. He refuses to acknowledge a connection."

"What makes you say that?"

"Because I brought it up last night and he dismissed it. Maybe if more vampires start to disappear, he'll take it seriously and help us stop Victor Steele."

Tucker cocked her head. "Who's Victor Steele?"

I cringed as soon as the name spilled out of my mouth, but

there was no putting the cat back in the bag now. "He's the vampire doing it."

Dog was out of the kitchen and standing next to me a moment later. "And you know this how?"

"Samuel told me last night." I was digging a deeper hole by the second. "He was hired to find the guy. It's why he came to Crimson. Apparently this vampire has been killing women like this for years."

His eyes narrowed. "You mean Samuel's a hunter? Loki left that part out." He shook his head. "I knew there was more to that vampire's story, but I didn't expect this."

"How do you know what a hunter is?"

"There are hunters for everything, Charley, including wolves. And witches, by the way."

I'd heard of witch hunters, but I thought they only existed in dark fairytales.

"Don't climb up Loki's ass about it," I said. "He didn't know. Samuel waited until after he left to tell me what he was."

Tucker looked like she was getting more confused by the second. "What are you two talking about?"

"It's a long story." A story I wasn't getting into right now because we were about to open. "Keep this conversation to yourself."

She slowly shook her head. "My lips are sealed."

"Good. Now, go prep for tonight." Customers were already waiting outside for us to open. "By the way," I said as she went behind the bar, "Beau is out of jail. He'll be coming in soon." If he hadn't reconvinced himself he was a budding vampire.

"I don't like any of this, Charley," Dog said. "And I sure as hell don't like you getting in the middle of it. I also heard what happened to Bob Flanders. Looks like this vampire is striking at anything that moves."

I motioned for him to follow me back into the kitchen when people started walking into the bar. As soon as we were out of earshot, I gave him the next news. "Victor Steele has it out for me."

"Oh yeah? What gave it away? Finding Keith Barnes murdered on your front porch or the attack last night?"

"I'm serious, Dog."

He stepped closer and looked me in the eye. "So am I. You're going to get yourself killed if you stay out at that house alone."

"No, I won't." At least not immediately. "He's not trying to kill me. For some reason, he's trying to intimidate me."

He ran his hand over his face in frustration. "What the hell are you talking about, Charley?"

"He broke into the jailhouse to pay Beau a visit. And to deliver a message to me. I have no idea who this vampire is, but apparently I have something he wants. It might have something to do with the co-op, and he's targeting my friends and customers to intimidate me. Which reminds me. I need to tell Candy to be careful."

Dog chuckled. "Good luck to the bastard." Then his face went still. "Did he do something to Beau?"

"He bit him! Now Beau thinks he's turning into a vampire. Patrick talked him off the ledge, but this is Beau we're dealing with."

Tucker stuck her head through the order window. "Can I get some help out here? Beau hasn't shown up yet, and the bar is already getting busy."

"We'll continue this conversation later," I said to Dog. "And don't mention anything to Samuel about being a hunter if he comes in here tonight. I want to tell him myself that I opened my big mouth."

As soon as I went back out to the bar, Beau came through the front door. He was wearing all black and had a turtleneck sweater on. The sunglasses were the last straw. I grabbed his arm and pulled him into the hallway. "What are you doing?"

"What does it look like? Working."

"You're not a vampire, Beau. So lose the ridiculous sunglasses."

He took them off, exposing his bloodshot eyes. They were so red it was disturbing to look at. "You want me to go out there looking like this?"

I took an involuntary step back. "When did this happen?"

"This afternoon after you dropped me off." He rolled his shoulders uneasily and then pulled the sweater away from his neck. "The bite mark hasn't healed yet, so I wore this."

Could Patrick have been wrong? "Did you go outside this afternoon?"

"Yeah." He shrugged. "For a... second or two. The sun was pretty bright. Maybe that's what irritated my eyes."

"Maybe you should take the night off. You've been through a lot, and I don't think you should push it."

He looked at me like I'd just given him his walking papers. "I can work, Charley!"

"Okay. Calm down. You can stay, but keep the sunglasses on. Tell everyone you got them dilated at the eye doctor this afternoon."

It was starting to get crowded when we went back up front, and we were barely open. Tucker was running up and down the bar like a chicken with its head cut off.

"I better get back there," Beau said. "Tucker's about to have a meltdown."

I needed to call Patrick to tell him to stop by the Stag tonight. Just in case, I wanted him to confirm that whatever was happening to Beau was normal. A minor side effect of being bitten by a vampire. Before I could pull out my phone, Mag walked in.

"Great."

When he looked over at the bar, Tucker couldn't contain her smile. He grinned and headed straight for her.

Dog came out of the kitchen, hot under the collar, and cut him off. He must have smelled the wolf the second he walked in the place. "What are you doing here?"

Mag threw his hands up. "Relax. I just stopped in for a drink." He glanced at the bar again. "And to say hello to my girl."

His girl? "Tucker?"

"Evening, Charley. You don't mind if I sit down for a few minutes, do you?" He shot me a smile and continued over to the bar, nudging between some customers to get to her.

When Dog went to follow him, I grabbed his arm. "Don't. It'll cause more trouble than it's worth. Just let him have his drink so I can get rid of him."

The truth was, other than pissing Dog off with his mere presence, Mag hadn't actually caused any trouble the few times he'd shown up here. Dog came first and always would, but I believed there was a way to keep the peace at the Stag without angering either of them. The idea of Mag and Tucker was disturbing, though. But she was an adult and she'd tended bar in a strip club down in Atlanta. I doubted this was her first rodeo with a guy like him.

I lingered for a minute, watching Mag keep an eye on Tucker like a hawk while she hustled up and down the bar. When I'd seen enough, I asked her to take a break so we could have a word. I just wanted to know if it was true, or if Mag was full of shit and simply looking for an opportunity to pounce.

"Is something wrong?" she asked when I got her into the kitchen. I wanted Dog to hear this.

"Nothing's wrong. I just wanted to know if you're seeing Mag?" I probably should have stayed out of it, but my employees were like family, and everyone knew that family was supposed to butt into each other's business.

She looked back and forth between us. "Why? Is it against company policy to date a customer?"

"No, Tucker, it isn't. I just want you to be careful."

Dog growled under his breath. "He's bad news, Tucker. Trust me. You don't want to mess with that wolf." He went back to the cutting board and resumed chopping the lettuce. "But you're a grown woman. Suit yourself."

She shrugged. "We're not dating or anything, and Mag has been nothing but nice to me." A slight smile edged up her face. "We're just having fun."

I knew that look. Regardless of everyone around here thinking I was one step up from a nun, I'd had that same look on my face once or twice. They were either sleeping together or about to. "Like Dog said, you're a grown woman. But don't say we didn't warn you."

"I appreciate your concern, but everything's fine. Really."

"Then you better get back out there before Beau starts yelling for you."

I waited until she was out of earshot. "Do me a favor, Dog. Walk her home tonight yourself."

He sighed. "If it'll make you feel better."

"It will."

When I went back out, I spotted Beau standing behind the bar looking in the mirror. He was staring at himself, but he wasn't doing his usual preening. His head was cocked, and he looked ridiculous with those sunglasses on.

I pulled my phone out and dialed Patrick's number. Something was definitely up with Beau, and I needed Patrick to take another look at him. After several rings, it went to voicemail. I left a message and hung up. Then I went to the back room to check on those orders I never seemed to have time to follow up on. But first, I checked the back door to make sure it was locked. I must have checked it three times in the span of twenty minutes. If Victor Steele was coming for me, I damn sure wasn't going to make it easy for him.

TWENTY

I was slightly more at ease on the drive home. After what had happened last night, the pack would be on high alert. That vampire wasn't getting past them again. And speaking of vampires, something told me Samuel would be out there somewhere too. If not to keep an eye on me, then to catch Steele. There wasn't a safer place for me to be.

When I pulled up to the garage, I surveyed the property. Even with the wolves out there, I was still a little jumpy. But all was quiet. I didn't even see Rex up in the tree.

I got out and hurried across the yard and up the steps, nearly having a coronary when that possum scurried across the porch again. "You better be glad I don't have a gun in my hand," I said to him. "You scared me."

"Rex?" I called when I walked inside. "Are you in here?" It wouldn't be the first time I accidentally left him in the house on my way to work. I expected him to swoop past me and out the door, but he didn't.

I flipped the light switch, but nothing happened. The bulb in the lamp must have burned out. At least that's what I told myself when I shut the front door behind me. I walked halfway across the room when I heard the squeak of the rocking chair in the corner.

"Try the lamp on the table."

Immediately recognizing the voice, I froze. But then I turned around to face the shadow across the room. The last time I invited him into my house, I never got the chance to correctly revoke that invitation. But I was going to get it right this time. "Ian Masterson, you need to please get the hell out of my—"

He grabbed me before I could get the last word out, pulling me to his chest. "Wait!"

I didn't have a choice. His hand was over my mouth. I bit down hard, but it didn't even faze him. That was another thing to remember about vampires—they had an incredibly high tolerance for pain. For once, my adrenaline wasn't off the charts, but there was energy building inside me. Unfortunately, he had my arms pinned to my sides. It was like trying to shoot a gun without being able to aim.

"I'm not here to hurt you, Charley. If you zap me again, I'll kill that bird of yours."

Rex?

"Now, I'm going to take my hand off your mouth, but if you scream, that crow's neck will snap like a toothpick."

I turned around to glare at him when he released me. "Where is he?"

"Safe and sound, unless you *piss me off*."

So much for the safety of my house. "How did you get past the pack?"

He snickered. "Tainted meat."

I gasped.

"Relax. I brought friends. It was surprisingly easy to slip in past the commotion. You really do need better security." He glanced at the door. "The mongrels will be checking in on you soon, so let's not waste time."

I was getting tired of his fickle mood swings. One minute he was attacking me, and the next he was being half civil. "What do you want from me, Ian?"

He walked over to the window and lifted the edge of the curtain with his finger to peer out discreetly. "I need your help."

Did I hear him right? The vampire who'd tried to extort me and dragged me through that tunnel wanted my help? "You have got to be kidding me."

Before I could take another breath, he zipped across the room and pinned me to the wall by my neck. Then he brought his fangs dangerously close. "Do I look like I'm kidding? Let's just say I'm calling in that IOU."

My adrenaline was definitely flowing now. "Will you please let go of me?"

He gave me some breathing room and stuck his finger in my face. "Do not push me, Charley."

"I wasn't trying to, but you have a funny way of asking for help." I rubbed my neck where he'd pinned me. "Trust is a two-way street, you know. Just tell me what you want?"

"This vampire who's attacking humans has to be stopped."

"No shit." Now he was interested in stopping the bastard? "Last night you blew me off when I asked you for information. Why the sudden change of heart?"

His eyes flashed. "Because he's crossed a line."

It suddenly hit me. "Another vampire went missing." It wasn't a question, and he didn't deny it. "One of yours?" He looked like he was about to fly into a rage, but he reined it in and just stared at the wall. His anger was simmering beneath the surface, though. "If you want my help, you have to be upfront with me."

When he turned to look at me, I saw a flicker of humanity in his eyes. It vanished a second later. Maybe there was hope for him after all.

"Irina is missing."

"You mean your friend with the pink hair? The one who

assaulted me in your basement last night?" He was really reaching if he thought I gave a damn about that vampire. Good riddance to her. "What makes you think she's missing?" I shrugged. "She didn't seem like the shy type to me, so maybe she's shacking up with someone else."

Backing me up against the wall was starting to get old, but at least he didn't touch me this time. "She belongs to me, and no one takes what's mine."

Then it dawned on me. "You're her maker."

"And you're going to help me get her back."

"How am I supposed to do that?"

He grabbed my hand and practically shoved it in my face. "With this. As much as I hate to admit it, I can't take the bastard down alone. We're going to do it together."

Ian was in for a disappointment when he found out it was hit or miss with my magic. Mostly miss.

"You don't understand. It's not like I can flip a switch when I need to use it."

He backed off but kept his eyes glued to mine. "I've seen you in action, Charley. So don't play stupid with me."

Something didn't add up. Ian was no slouch in the vampire department. He ran Reaperstown, the dregs of vampire society around these parts, so why was he coming to me for help?

"You're not telling me everything, so why don't you start there. Who is this vampire to you?" He stared at me for a moment. Probably trying to figure out how to manipulate me so he didn't have to tell me the truth. But now that he needed my help, he'd have to show some manners, which would be a stretch for him.

"He took over the Beast. Bought the place last month, with cash." He let out a sarcastic laugh. "I've been trying to buy the damn place for years."

"Back up." I wondered if I'd heard him right. "You're telling me the vampire who's attacking women around here owns the Beast?"

"The former owner lives in Atlanta. Someone made him an offer he couldn't refuse. Twice what the club is worth. A vampire named Victor Steele." Victor Steele again, but Samuel didn't mention that he'd bought the Beast. "Ninety percent of the vampire blood that runs up and down the East Coast comes from his operation," Ian continued. "He *is* a beast."

My heart sank. "He's a drug dealer?" Maybe the rumors Patrick heard were right. "Why is he setting up shop in a place like Crimson? There's nothing here."

"Oh, but there is. Vampire blood is just one of his revenue streams."

When he went quiet and looked like he was about to zip it, I pushed him to keep talking. "Tell me why he's here!"

"Because Crimson is the perfect hunting ground. The humans he attacked were for his own amusement. And to quench his thirst. A vampire has to feed after all, and one like Steele likes to catch his food. But the female *vampires*..." He shook his head slowly. "They're a gold mine." His eyes went dark again. "Now the bastard has gotten greedy. He's broken our agreement and taken what is mine."

My head was starting to spin from all the information he was giving me. "Just spell it out for me."

"Victor Steele is trafficking female vampires. Selling them to the highest bidder." He got a faint grin on his face as he came closer. "Do you have any idea how much a wealthy human will pay for a bottomless supply of vampire blood? And for the ninety-nine percent who can't afford their own personal blood slave, he's waiting in the wings to sell it to them by the vial. At a much higher price than either of us, by the way."

A sickening thought entered my mind. The pieces were coming together in quick-fire revelations. The mention of vampire trafficking had done it. What were the odds of it being a coincidence?

"And you just turned a blind eye?" He averted his gaze from me. "He went on a killing spree in this town, and you did nothing about it. Not even when he abducted vampires in Little Crimson."

"We had an agreement." He brought his eyes back to mine. "I overlooked his indiscretions and his business practices, and he tolerated mine. What was I supposed to do? Leave town?"

Every word out of his mouth reminded me of what he was. Ian Masterson wasn't much better than Victor Steele. A vampire without a moral compass.

"He tried to kill me last night, and he would have succeeded if Samuel hadn't shown up." I bit my tongue about Samuel's connection to Steele. "But I guess my death would have just been the cost of doing business for you. Just another dead human."

His gaze softened. "I wouldn't say that. I would have missed our... banter. But I doubt he intended to kill you."

"Really? Why is that?"

"Because if Victor Steele wanted you dead, you wouldn't be breathing right now." His eyes narrowed. "He's playing games with you, Charley. The question is why?"

"You said Victor Steele bought the Beast last month?"

He looked at me sideways. "Yes."

The first attack happened before Tucker walked into the bar looking for a job, but she said she'd been in the area for months before showing up at the Stag. "Where is this vampire from?"

The suspicion in his eyes was growing. "Atlanta. Why?"

That all but confirmed it for me. "I don't suppose you have a picture of him?"

His brows twisted. "Why the hell would I?"

"I think I just figured out why that vampire has it out for me." I needed to get Tucker to a safe place. If I was right, Victor Steele was the infamous Mr. K. The King.

TWENTY-ONE

I pulled out my phone to call Tucker. To tell her to stay put until one of the pack got there. It kept ringing and finally went to voicemail. I left a message and started to dial Dog's number, but Ian yanked the phone out of my hand and tossed it on the couch.

A moment later, Dog burst through the front door. Rex sailed into the room and flew past the wolf, digging his talons into Ian's face, barely missing his eyes.

"Fuck!" Ian stumbled back, shoving me to the floor.

I backpedaled toward the open door as Dog latched onto the vampire's throat. As I started to get up, a surge of adrenaline nearly knocked me back down. My hands were shaking and lit up in a blue glow.

When I turned around, Dog had one of his massive paws braced against Ian's chest, pressing him to the floor as he tore at his neck. He was about to tear the vampire's head off.

"Don't kill him!" I yelled. "We need him!"

Dog stopped but kept Ian pinned to the floor. Seeing the panic in my eyes, he stepped back, releasing him.

Ian flashed his fangs as he gripped his throat. "You're dead, wolf!"

"Hardly," I huffed. "What did you expect? You attacked me. And for the second time in twenty-four hours."

He climbed to his feet, glaring at Dog as he shifted. The others came running through the door a moment later.

"Where the hell were you?" Dog growled. There was murder in his eyes.

Loki shifted. "Fighting off a bunch of vampires out there," he growled back. Then he turned his eyes to Ian. "You son of a bitch."

"That's enough," Dog said, stepping between them before it got ugly again.

Loki shot Ian a look that sent a chill down my spine. A look that said *this isn't over*. Then he headed down the hallway and returned a minute later wearing my robe again.

It was starting to stink like wet canine. "I'm getting you your own robe," I said to him. Dog, on the other hand, had no problem standing buck naked in the middle of my living room.

I looked up at the refrigerator where Rex had landed. "Snap his neck, eh?"

Ian glanced at the bird. "It worked, didn't it?"

"I should have let Dog chew your head off."

After pointing a finger at Ian warning him not to move, Dog fixed his eyes on me. "You want to tell me what's going on here? And where the hell is Samuel?"

"I don't know where Samuel is." I was wondering that myself.

Ignoring Dog's warning, Ian stepped closer and met him eye to eye. "Where are my vampires?"

Dog shrugged. "Beats the hell out of me. Probably halfway home to their coffins by now."

A muscle in Ian's face twitched as he clenched his fists tighter, but we didn't have time for this.

"More importantly, where's Tucker?" I asked Dog. "She's not answering her phone." Since she hadn't called me back, I assumed the worst. What twenty-six-year-old didn't answer their phone immediately or at least check their voicemail? The message I left was pretty clear it was urgent.

Dog finally pulled his eyes away from Ian's. "I walked her home and came straight here when Loki sent out an SOS. Why?"

"Her ex-boss from Atlanta is responsible for the attacks."

Dog tilted his head. "Don't you think that's a little far-fetched, Charley? What makes you think that?"

"Because Ian here just confessed."

"I didn't confess to anything," he said. "Tucker who?"

"Victor Steele is Mr. K," I said. "He's punishing me for hiding Tucker."

Suddenly Dog was curious. "The vampire Samuel has been hunting?"

Ian crossed his arms. "A hunter? Really? I knew there was something sketchy about that vampire."

"There's nothing sketchy about Samuel," I said. "He's performing a public service, as far as I'm concerned."

Ian scoffed. "A vampire who hunts his own kind is a bottom-feeder."

If he only knew that Victor Steele was Samuel's maker. I kept that little tidbit to myself.

"Get to the part about Steele," Dog said to Ian. "How do you know so much about him?"

Ian stared back at him defiantly but didn't respond, so I cut to the chase. "Because Victor Steele bought the Beast last month."

Dog nodded. "I guess that is suspicious, but you'll need more than that to convince me he's Tucker's former boss."

"According to Ian here, Steele is a drug dealer from Atlanta, and he's trafficking vampires. It's exactly what Tucker told us about her ex-boss."

The skepticism on his face melted away as he looked back at Ian. "If this is true, why tell us about it now?"

The look in Ian's eyes was unsettling. "Because he took one of mine."

"The vampire from the basement last night," I said. "The one with the pink hair."

Dog cocked his brows at Ian. "I take it she's a favorite of yours?"

"Tell him the rest," I demanded.

Ian practically snarled. "Victor and I had an agreement. I stayed out of his business, and he stayed out of mine."

I filled in the blanks to move the conversation along. "The vampire blood trade is getting a little crowded around here. Apparently, Victor Steele controls most of it on the East Coast."

"Ninety-nine percent to be exact," Ian said. "But he's getting greedy *and* cocky."

I laughed. "Sounds familiar. You should talk."

Extortion was Ian's middle name. He'd tried to shake me down for thirty-five percent of the co-op's receipts. It would have shut us down. The earnings from our little non-profit would be pennies to a big-time operator like Victor Steele, but major dealers didn't appreciate competition on any level. Aside from wanting to punish me for harboring Tucker, he must have found out about the co-op and decided to teach me a lesson for that as well. I'd say I was at the top of his shit list.

"As long as he stayed clear of what was mine," Ian continued, "we had no problem with each other. But he's gone too far, so he needs to go."

Dog's temper started to rise again. "You haven't explained what you're doing in Charley's house. Make it good, vampire."

"Victor Steele is nothing to play with," Ian said. "He's dangerous in ways you can't imagine. He won't just go away like a bad rash. We'll have to kill him." His eyes landed on mine. "As much as I hate to admit it, I can't do that alone. It will take magic, and Charley here just so happens to be made of it."

"I can't just point my finger and fire," I said. "I'm unpredictable."

"That may be, but your friend Candy *is* predictable."

So that was his plan? "You tried to abduct me tonight just to blackmail Candy into helping you? She'd volunteer if she knew Victor Steele was after me."

"We'll only get one shot at him, and we need a sure thing." Ian glanced at the wolves. "Throw in the pack, and we might stand a chance."

Loki snickered. "The chance to kill a vampire? Count me in."

Dog gave his second-in-command a look, and Loki lowered his head. Then he looked back at Ian. "If this is a setup, I'll take you apart limb by limb myself. Understood?"

Ian huffed. "You may have won tonight, but don't get too comfortable. The next time your wolves meet my vampires, the outcome will be very different."

"Can you two please lower the testosterone. We have bigger things to deal with." I grabbed my phone and headed for the door.

"Where do you think you're going?" Dog said.

"Tucker's apartment. We need to find out if Victor Steele took her or if she's just a heavy sleeper."

Dog followed me out, motioning to the wolves to fall in line. Loki dropped down on all fours when we got outside and led them into the woods, leaving my robe pooled on the ground where he'd been standing.

"Where are they going?" I asked Dog.

"Back to town. We'll follow you."

"We?" I glanced at Ian. "You're leaving me alone with him?"

Dog looked down at his naked body. "It's going to be a long night, Charley. I'll grab my clothes and meet you there. You'll be fine." He shifted his eyes to Ian. "Won't she?"

A satisfied grin spread across the vampire's face. "As long as you show up at the apartment."

"Fine." I wasn't about to admit it, but it eased my fears somewhat to have a vampire sitting next to me on the way over to Tucker's place. But I would have preferred it wasn't one with a history of trying to harm me. The small talk on the drive over would be interesting.

* * *

Dog was waiting for us when we got to Webers' Thrift Shop on Fourth Street. He seemed amused when he saw my face. "Interesting drive over?"

"Sure," I muttered before Ian caught up to me. "If you like listening to long-winded speeches about what he plans to do to Steele when he gets his hands on him." It was like I wasn't even in the car. "Where's the pack?"

"They're here."

I glanced around the deserted street, getting a feel for how eerie the alleyway next to the building was. If this wasn't such a small town where everyone knew their neighbors, it would have been downright creepy to come home alone late at night.

Tucker's place was on the second floor and had a private entrance on the outside of the building. If she didn't answer the door after some persistent banging, I had no idea how we were going to get in. But I'd worry about that when we got to the top of the stairs.

Dog made it up to the landing first, with me and Ian right behind him. He knocked, and the door cracked open. "So much for breaking and entering," he said, pushing it slowly open. He went inside to see if the apartment was clear before motioning us in. "She's not here."

I went in, but when Ian started to follow me, I looked back at him. "How can you enter the apartment without an invitation?"

"It's just a thrift shop," he said.

"It's Tucker's home."

Ian glanced around the deserted room. "Not anymore."

My mouth dropped open. "Don't even say that. We're going to find her."

"Optimistic, aren't you?" He continued inside.

The studio wasn't much bigger than the back room at the Stag. There was a small kitchenette on one side and an alcove with a double bed on the other. Off to the right was a tiny bathroom no bigger than a small closet. Taking a shower in the minuscule stall must have been a real feat.

"This is more of a dump than I thought," I said. "When this is over, I need to help Tucker find a better place to live."

Ian let out a short laugh. "If he hasn't killed her by now."

"Shut up," Dog growled.

I doubted the vampire planned to kill Tucker. She was too valuable to him. With her ability to see things, I was pretty sure he'd have other plans for her. Plans to exploit her that included a cage.

Dog flipped the light switch. "There's no sign of a struggle. It looks like she came home and walked back out willingly."

"It's a little too clean." I walked over to the refrigerator and pulled it open. There was half a six-pack of beer inside from a local brewery two towns over and some leftover takeout. Then I noticed something in the sink—two bottles of beer. One was half full, but the other one was empty.

Dog came up behind me and grabbed one of them out of the sink. He had a strange look on his face. "Fuck."

"What's wrong?"

He set the bottle back in the sink and took a deep breath. "There's another possibility." He nodded to the bottles. "That beer. It's Mag's favorite. He's been drinking it for as long as I can remember."

I looked down at the sink again, realizing what he was suggesting. "You think it was Mag who showed up here tonight?"

Ian sat down on the couch and laced his fingers behind his head. "What's this? A little indiscretion?"

"I said, shut up!" Dog growled again.

Ian was on his feet in an instant, face-to-face with Dog. "I'm getting tired of you barking at me, wolf."

"Enough!" I muscled my way between them, hoping I didn't end up as a casualty if Ian snapped.

Dog backed down first and pulled out his phone to make a call. "Find Mag and bring him to me," he said to whoever was on the other end and then hung up.

"Do you really think Mag would do this?"

His brows arched. "You're the one who asked me to walk her home tonight when you saw the way he was looking at her."

"Yeah, but I just didn't want him to—"

"To what? Come inside and have his way with her? She's an adult, Charley."

I knew that. But there was something naive about Tucker that made me want to protect her.

He stared at me for a few more seconds, letting the message sink in. "That may not have been his motive. I know that wolf. He finds trouble. I wouldn't put it past him to be working for Steele."

"You think he delivered her to Victor Steele?"

Ian slowly clapped his hands. "Well done. Fantastic job of protecting the woman."

I turned around and pointed my finger at him. "Will you please shut up!"

Ian suddenly flew backward and hit the wall, clawing at his throat as his mouth opened and closed like a fish out of water. He tried to speak, but nothing came out.

Dog gawked at me. Then he stepped in Ian's path as the vampire lunged toward me. He grabbed Ian by the shirt and got in his face. "If you ever try to touch her again, I'll snap your scrawny neck!"

Before I could blink, Ian had Dog in a death grip from behind, his fangs nearly puncturing Dog's neck. The wolf emerged, and Dog slipped through the vampire's hands. A moment later, it was chaos in the tiny studio.

I ran outside, stumbling onto the narrow landing as Ian slammed into a wall. As I turned around, the door shut in my face, and the two of them went at it for the next few minutes while I stood outside rooting for the wolf.

When the ruckus finally stopped, I dared to crack the door to look inside. Ian was near the bed, gripping his arm, while Dog stood on the other side of the studio wiping blood from his neck.

"Have the two of you gotten it out of your systems yet?" We didn't have time for another pissing contest. "Because I'm leaving." They both came out of the studio as I was walking down the steps. "Tucker's life is in danger, and all you two can do is fight like a couple of high school jocks." I stopped when I got to the bottom of the stairs and looked back up at them. "Well? Are you coming? We're going to the Cauldron."

TWENTY-TWO

I should have called Candy from Tucker's place to let her know we were coming, but the Cauldron was only a few blocks away and we were already in the truck by the time I thought about it. And thank God for that. With Dog's large body taking up most of the passenger seat, Ian was practically in my lap while I drove. I almost kicked the vampire out and made him ride in the bed of the truck.

Candy was a night owl, so I wasn't surprised to see a light on in the back of the shop when we parked and got out. Instead of knocking on the door, I pulled out my phone to let her know we were outside. As I was dialing her number, something darted across the room inside.

"What the hell was that?" Dog said, doing a double take.

Ian squinted at the window. "I believe it was a naked man."

Candy didn't answer her phone, and it looked like she was busy with a client. "Wait here," I said, deciding to venture inside. She'd murder me if all three of us walked in on one of her sessions. The sand ticking away inside that giant hourglass on the display case gave it away. It made me want to reconsider going in there, but this couldn't wait until morning.

As I was sticking the key in the lock, Candy came out of the back room in a hurry. She looked at me through the door and then at Dog and Ian standing near the truck. Then she pointed to the back room, and the man quickly disappeared the same way he came. She did not look happy as she came toward the door a moment later.

"Before you yell at me, let me explain," I said when she pulled it open. "This is an emergency."

After motioning me inside, she gave Dog and Ian a look that stopped them in their tracks when they tried to follow me in. "Someone better be dead or dying," she said after shutting the door on them. Then she glanced at Ian through the glass. "And what the hell are you doing with that vampire?"

"Tucker's gone." I figured I'd start with that and work my way up to telling her about Victor Steele.

She nestled her fist into the side of her waist. "What do you mean she's gone? And more importantly, why are you telling me at one o'clock in the morning?"

I looked at Dog and Ian through the window. "Can you let them in first? They're important to the story."

She glanced at the door to the back room and sighed. "Fine. I'll tell my client to go out through the alley."

I motioned for them to come inside. Dog had no problem entering, but Ian stopped on a dime before his foot crossed the threshold.

"Uh... Candy," I said before she could disappear through the door. The Cauldron doubled as Candy's house, so an invitation was required.

She came back over and got a sly grin on her face. "Oh, I forgot. Ian Masterson, this is a one-time invitation to enter my abode."

While she went to the back to finish her business, Ian's attention was immediately drawn to the stripper pole in the corner of the shop.

Naturally.

He walked across the room and ran his hand up and down the pole, grinning like he had Candy all figured out. "She's a real pro, isn't she?"

Candy walked back into the room and looked him in the eye. "That pole is titanium gold, vampire. You better believe I was a pro. Just not the kind you're used to."

He wisely held his tongue when he saw the look on her face. Ian was a lot of things, but stupid wasn't one of them. And right now he was desperate for her help.

She got back to the matter at hand. "What's this about Tucker?"

"Let me back up a bit." I tried to think of where to begin and how to minimize the chastising I was about to get for not telling her everything right away. "We know who the killer is. He's a vampire named Victor Steele."

Her head tilted slightly. "And how do you know this?"

She was on to me. I could see it in her shrewd eyes.

I cringed at the next words that came out of my mouth. "Because he attacked me Tuesday night." *Tuesday* sounded worse than *last night*, but it was one a.m., so technically it was Thursday now. "Samuel showed up and chased him off before he could do any real damage. Turns out he was hired to find the killer. That's why Samuel came to Crimson. He's a hunter."

She started to speak but closed her mouth for a moment as it all sank in. "Well, that's a lot to process. And I'm just hearing about it now?" There was disappointment written all over her face. "I knew something was up when I didn't hear from you yesterday."

"I wasn't avoiding you, Candy." Maybe just a little. "I was trying to get Beau out of jail all morning, and then I got busy at the Stag." I released a long breath. "Bob Flanders is in the hospital, by the way."

"I heard. The man's lucky to be alive."

"At least it provided an alibi for Beau," I said. "The police had no choice but to let him go. I was going to call you when I got home, but then Ian showed up at my house."

Her eyes narrowed. "Where is Samuel? I'm surprised he isn't sticking to you like glue after what you just told me."

"I don't know. He was gone when I woke up yesterday morning."

Dog and Candy both gave me curious looks.

"He stayed the night after the attack. In the living room," I clarified so they would quit looking at me like that. "I haven't seen him since." It did seem odd, though. But Samuel had a job to do. Killing Victor Steele was his top priority. And it was a given that the pack would be stepping up their watch on my house after what had happened, although they'd been doing a lousy job of it lately.

Ian snapped his fingers to get everyone's attention. "Now that we've established that you're *not* sleeping with a vampire, although I highly recommend it, can we move on? Time is ticking."

After shooting him a hateful look, I continued with the bad news. "To make matters worse, I'm convinced Victor Steele is Tucker's former boss from Atlanta."

Candy stared at me blankly for a moment. "Let me get this straight. You're trying to tell me that your new bartender used to work for the vampire who's nailing women to trees around here?"

"Isn't that what I just said?"

"Oh, it is. I'm just having a hard time believing it." She glanced at Dog.

He inhaled sharply. "Yep. That's pretty much the gist of it."

Ian didn't mince words. "We need to kill the bastard, and you're going to help us do it."

Candy gave him a dull look. "Say please."

His lips curled into a snarl as his fangs clicked into place. "Please."

"No one's helping you do anything if you don't lose those fangs," I said.

He retracted them and grinned widely. "Better?"

"Perfect. Now, focus. We need to figure out where Steele is holding those female vampires. That's where we'll find Tucker."

Candy squinted at me. "Female vampires? What are you talking about?"

"Victor Steele is the new owner of the Beast down in Reaperstown. According to Ian, he also moves most of the vampire blood on the East Coast, and he's trafficking female vampires for wealthy clients. Isn't that right, Ian?"

"Yes. Sells them to the highest bidder." He shrugged. "You know. Why buy the milk when you can own the cow."

Dog took a deep breath through his nose. "You lowlife son of a bitch!"

"Here we go again," I muttered, stepping out of the way.

Dog plowed into the vampire, shoving him past the display case and into the wall, his long braid snaking into the air from the impact. Ian bounced back, and Dog wrapped his huge hand around the vampire's face to slam his head into the wall again, sending the picture hanging next to him crashing to the floor.

The sound of his skull hitting the wall made me cringe. If it were possible to give a vampire a concussion, that would have done it.

Ian straightened back up and shook it off, wheezing out a laugh. "I should kill you for that."

I chuckled. "Good luck."

Fed up with it all, Candy stepped over the shattered glass from the picture frame and got between them. "The easiest way to get kicked out of the Cauldron is to start breaking shit." She reached for the amulet around her neck. "You both need to settle down before *I* start swinging."

A growl came from Ian's throat at the sight of the shimmering sapphire. She'd used it on him before, and it had made an indelible impression.

Candy gave Dog a pointed look. "You can take yourself right back over there next to Charley." Then she turned to Ian. "You were saying?"

"Steele and I tolerated each other." His fangs kept pulsing in and out, like the beat of his black heart. "But now he's taken one of mine, so he must die."

"He's got one of mine too," I said, "and he's going to regret it." Tucker worked at the Stag. That made her family.

Dog's phone rang. He answered it, and after listening silently to whoever was on the other end, he hung up and shoved it back in his pocket. "The pack can't locate Mag. He's dropped off the radar."

"Mag?" Candy looked back and forth between me and Dog. "Don't tell me he's mixed up with all this? Although it wouldn't surprise me."

"Dog seems to think he might be working for Victor Steele," I said. "He's seeing Tucker, and he was at the bar tonight."

"He was also at her apartment when she got home," Dog added.

I barely knew the man, but based on everything I'd heard about his past, I didn't trust him much either. But this was a serious allegation. Something that needed proof. "It looks suspicious, but we don't know for sure if Mag is involved."

Dog let out a bitter laugh. "I do."

Candy frowned at him. "You don't think Mag took her?"

"If he's working for Victor Steele, it's a distinct possibility."

"Like I said," I continued, "we need to find out where Steele is holding those vampires." My eyes landed on Ian. "Well?"

"I don't know where they are, but it's possible he's holding them under the Beast. There's an extensive basement down there. More like an underground compound." A wicked grin slid up his face. "We call it the dungeon. It's used for certain activities that require discretion."

"You mean prostitution," Candy said.

"Prostitution?" He laughed under his breath. "Money is useless down there. Let's just say it's where humans and vampires get together to discuss common interests. At least it used to be. No telling what it's used for now."

"Cut the bullshit," Dog said. "It's where humans get off on getting bitten by vampires."

Ian shrugged. "If you will. It's all consensual."

"Right," I said. "Until you find yourself drugged and end up in a cage."

"I wouldn't put it past the vampire." Ian's eyes went black. "Victor Steele will turn Reaperstown into a cesspool."

It already was a cesspool, but Ian Masterson had a warped perception of what was or wasn't decent. He was just concerned about his livelihood and getting his "property" back.

"How do we get in there?" I asked. "Maybe I can go back to the Beast and pretend I'm looking for a 'date' down in that dungeon." I regretted the suggestion the moment it came out of my mouth.

Candy's eyes shot to mine. "Over my dead body."

"Mine too," Dog said.

Ian, however, had a sly look on his face. "That's actually not a bad idea. I'll tell Victor I'm there to offer Charley in exchange for Irina."

"Did I knock a few screws loose in your head?" Dog said to him.

Ignoring Dog's malicious glare, Ian seemed to be pondering the idea. "Before we go rushing in there, we need to confirm that the women are actually down in that basement."

I huffed. "It's the obvious place. Where else would they be?"

He looked at me over his shoulder. "Atlanta is less than two hours away. He could be sending shipments down there on a daily basis."

Shipments?

"He's right," Dog said. "We need to get down there to confirm it. It'll also give us the lay of the land if we have to storm the place."

Ian squinted at me. "How good of an actress are you?"

"Why?"

"Because I need to convince Steele that I own you. That I've claimed you so you're mine to barter with."

"Claimed me? You mean your property?"

"Something like that. It means I've given you my blood, and no other vampire can touch you without my permission. Not even Victor Steele."

I snorted a laugh. "That wouldn't stop him. He didn't seem to have a problem touching one of your progeny."

"It's not the same. I gave Irina her freedom years ago. Released her. But she's remained loyal, and I still consider her mine."

Figures. Freedom with strings attached.

Technically, most vampires in Crimson were still bound to their makers in one way or another. But times had changed. They weren't dependent on them and were free to live their lives any way they chose. It was the twenty-first century, after all.

Candy groaned. "I'll do it. I'll go down to that hellhole with Ian so he can offer *me* up."

A snide chuckle escaped his lips. "Don't take this personally, but I can't walk into the Beast with a woman of your—"

She pointed a dangerous finger at him. "Careful."

"—temperament. Besides, it's Charley he wants. It seems he's gotten bored with his game of revenge and would like to get his hands on her now." He turned back to me. "I'm afraid you're it, sweetheart. I'll offer you in exchange for Irina, but on my terms."

"What terms?"

"I'll simply convince him I still have my own business to settle with you first. One more night to have a go with you before I hand you over." The salacious look on his face sent a chill down my spine. "Based on our history, it won't be too difficult for him to believe. Then we'll have a look around and leave him with a tempting taste of you in his mouth."

That was just gross.

"Can't you just go in there without me and make the deal? Tell him you have me locked up in your own basement or... dungeon. It certainly wouldn't be far-fetched."

Ian slowly shook his head. "Without an incentive, he could balk at the offer. Vampires are heavily influenced by sensory stimulus. If he sees and smells you, it'll be a done deal. I guarantee it."

"Okay, can you stop with the references to tasting and smelling me. It's giving me the creeps."

"It should," Dog said. "He's out of his depraved mind. You walk in there with him, and Steele will kill you both on the spot."

"No, he won't, you fleabag." Ian toned down the aggression. "He wants Charley alive. At least for now. Besides, there's nothing Victor loves more than money, and he needs my network and connections up here to make more of it. But I'm not stupid. Once he turns my *loyal* colleagues against me in Reaperstown, he'll come for me next. He's already started to test the waters by taking Irina. But for now, he still needs me. He'd be a fool to cross me again before the time is right. And as I've said, he can't touch Charley if he thinks I've claimed her."

"It should be pretty easy for a powerful vampire to smell another one's property," Candy said. "He'll know you're lying."

I gaped at her. "How do you know about all this?"

"Honey, there isn't much I haven't seen. Unless this Victor Steele can smell Ian all over you, he might call your bluff."

Ian slowly turned to me with a faint smile. "Candy's right. It'll be safer if you take a sip before we go in there."

"No way." I wasn't letting a drop of that vampire's blood pass my lips.

He shrugged. "Suit yourself."

Dog got in his face. "And if you're wrong about all this?"

"Then we fight like hell."

"I don't like it." Dog was a second away from throwing a major wrench into the already fragile plan.

Ian held his gaze. "By all means, speak if you have a better idea."

There wasn't one, so I settled it. "All right. I'll drink your... blood." I could barely say the word without gagging. "But just a drop." It was either that or Crimson would go down the drain. Steele would have us all kneeling at his feet, or we'd become his prey.

Candy and Dog gazed at each other for a moment, but neither argued with me. I'd already made up my mind, and they knew it.

Dog rubbed the bridge of his nose and sighed. "Once we confirm the women are in that basement, how do we get in there without being detected?"

Ian thought about it briefly. "There's a series of tunnels that run under Reaperstown. They were built to be used as distribution channels for contraband, but they're not in use anymore."

Yeah, since the police turned a blind eye to the goings-on down there. It would take a murder to send them down to the Beast. But that would require evidence, and vampires like Steele and Masterson didn't leave any.

"Right," I said. "Now they're just used to abduct people." He'd dragged me through one of them the other night. "How convenient that your house is connected to them."

"They do come in handy. And lucky for us, one of them leads straight to the compound under the Beast. The door has been sealed shut from the inside for years, but I'm sure we can manage to break through it. We'll just need a distraction so they're not waiting for us on the other side when we do."

Candy was fiddling with her amulet as she listened. I knew that look on her face. An idea was brewing. "I think we can come up with a distraction." Her eyes flicked to mine. "What did you do with that ring I gave you?"

"It's at the house. Why?"

"Because it's time you learned how to use it. You're not walking into that place without some weapons in your arsenal. We need to gather the Squad. First thing in the morning, after the sun comes up, you need to go out to the house and get it."

I shook my head. "Tomorrow will be too late."

"We won't be much good to Tucker if we're dead, honey. We need to prepare."

"She's right," Ian said. "We'll go to the Beast at sundown tomorrow."

I felt sick just thinking about Tucker being stuck with that monster for another night, but if we didn't go in with a solid plan, none of us would walk out of there. "Okay. I'll be back at sunup with the ring."

"Back?" You'd have thought I had two heads, the way she was looking at me. "Honey, you are absolutely not going back to the house tonight."

"I'm not getting run out of my own home." How many times did I have to say it. "And after what happened, the pack will be all over my property. Isn't that right, Dog?"

Candy huffed. "Where were they when you got attacked?"

"It won't happen again," Dog growled.

"It better not," she warned, looking back at me. "I still wish you'd stay here and get that ring in the morning."

Dog cocked his head. "What ring are you talking about?"

She stroked her amulet again. "Just a little something passed down from mother to daughter. A family heirloom that's going to help Charley lose her training wheels." Her eyes shifted to Ian. "I don't do favors like this for just anyone, especially for vampires who try to bite me." A smile spread across her face. "Uninvited, that is. I'll be expecting something in return one day. You got a problem with that?"

A sparkle of ruby flashed in his eyes. "I look forward to it."

TWENTY-THREE

"I'm staying tonight," Dog said. "I'll take the couch if I get tired."

"Suit yourself." I scanned the woods on the drive over to the house, praying I didn't see any glowing eyes staring back at me, other than wolves. "I'll probably keep you company. I doubt I'll get much sleep tonight."

A deer ran across the road, making me hit the brakes and skid sideways. When I came to a stop, I put the truck in park and dropped my head back against the seat. I was trying to hold it together, but the floodgates were about to open.

"You okay?" When I shook my head, Dog got out and walked around the truck and opened my door. "Get out. I'm driving."

He kept glancing at me as we continued down the road. "Is your adrenaline doing a number on you again?"

Rolling my head toward the window, I closed my eyes as a wave of nausea passed through me. "I think it's just my nerves about tomorrow night."

"You don't have to do this, Charley."

"Yes, I do. I doubt that vampire will stop until he gets what he wants. I won't let him take over this town, and he's not dragging Tucker back to Atlanta either." I was getting her out of there if I had to die trying. On the other hand, the vampire with the pink hair was on her own. Her fate was in Ian Masterson's hands, so good luck to her. "What do you think my mother would have done?"

"In this situation?" He chuckled. "The same damn thing, only Delia would have stormed the place without even confirming if Tucker was in there. Your mother was fearless but a bit of a hothead. Just like someone else I know."

I wouldn't say I was fearless, but there wasn't much that scared me. But *this* scared me.

"I really miss her sometimes," I said.

He inhaled deeply. "Yeah, so do I."

The house was dark when we pulled up to the garage. I'd forgotten to leave the living room light on when we left.

As we got out, Dog sniffed the air. "Stay here."

"Why? What's wrong?"

Without answering, he threw his hand up to stop me. I followed him anyway. When he got halfway up the steps, he looked at the porch near the front door and came to a dead halt.

"What is it?" Halfway across the yard, I got a sickening feeling in my gut. "Dog?"

"Stay back, Charley." His voice was firm.

Ignoring him, I picked up the pace. He physically stopped me halfway up the steps. "Let go of me, Dog!" I shoved him away and continued up to the porch. My heart started to race when I saw a pile of ashes near the front door with something lying in the center of it.

I gave myself a moment to try to process what I was looking at. Then I crouched down and picked up the titanium pendant, absently thinking about how small the pile of ashes was. "This is

Samuel's seal." I shook my head, not fully comprehending what was right in front of me.

Dog walked up and rested his hand on my shoulder. "Charley..."

I dropped the seal and stood up, glaring at him. "What?"

He grabbed me when I started to walk away. "What are you doing, Charley?"

I nearly stumbled down the steps as I pulled my arm out of his grip, the horror of what was happening hitting me like a freight train. I felt sick. "I need to kill him. I'm going to find Steele and take his head!" The pain was starting to come now. Welling up inside of me like a dam about to burst. It came in waves, the sickness washing through me. "I have to kill him!"

Dog caught me as I collapsed against his chest. "We'll kill him together, but not tonight. That's what he wants. You won't get any justice for Samuel if you walk right into Steele's waiting arms and get *yourself* killed."

He picked me up and carried me back up the stairs, stepping over the ashes to open the front door. Then he took me straight to my room and set me down on the edge of the bed. "You need to get some sleep, Charley. I'll gather the ashes so we can bury them properly."

Sleep? I felt like someone had taken a sledgehammer to my chest. Samuel was gone and I was supposed to sleep? We'd ended before we even had the chance to begin.

"I need to find Loki. Are you going to be okay in here?"

I looked up at him. "The pack? How did Steele get past the pack again?" I was starting to think Candy was right about me not being safe out here, even with a bunch of wolves supposedly standing guard.

"He must have shown up here after we left for Tucker's place." His fists were clenched so tight I could see the bones telegraphing through his skin. "I should have had some of the pack stay behind."

I shook my head. "He would have just left the ashes at the Stag for me to find." Saying the words left a lump in my throat.

"All the same, I'll be watching the house personally from now on."

I could see Dog's frustration. But Steele was smart. Cunning. It didn't matter. One of us would be dead after tomorrow night. Either me or that vampire.

"Victor Steele was Samuel's maker," I said as Dog was heading for the door.

He stopped and turned. "What?"

I don't know why I told him. I guess I just wanted someone other than me to know. I wanted everyone to know, so when one of us got to kill the bastard, we'd be doing it for Samuel. The lucky assassin could say Samuel's name as the blade severed Steele's throat.

"Samuel told me the other night. He was hired by the father of one of Steele's victims, but he was hunting him down just as much for his own revenge."

Dog had a skeptical look in his eyes. "Why would he kill his own maker?"

"Steele never intended to turn Samuel. He attacked him and left him for dead, but he survived."

He nodded knowingly. "He created his own enemy instead. Fate's a bitch."

My stomach turned from the memory of seeing Samuel's remains on my porch. "Whose fate?"

"We'll make him pay, Charley. I can promise you that. Now, try to get some rest." He looked back at me before walking out the bedroom door. "You want a cup of tea or something?"

Tea? Why did everyone think a cup of tea would make everything better?

"I'm fine." I lay down on the bed, wondering if I'd ever sleep through the night again. Everything was crumbling around me, and there was nothing I could do about it. Until tomorrow night when I intended to kill that vampire. Then I'd go after every one of his accomplices. His progeny. I'd do more than finish the job Samuel started. When I was through with Victor Steele, his dirty DNA would be wiped off the face of the earth.

"Come and get me, vampire," I whispered, stuffing a pillow under my head. "I'll be waiting."

* * *

I woke up abruptly, shaking. Someone had been calling my name, but the room was empty. It must have been a dream. I'd actually managed to fall asleep, but now I was wide awake.

The bedroom door was shut. Dog must have closed it so he wouldn't wake me up if he decided to bunk down on the couch. My phone said 3:03 a.m. when I pulled it out to check the time. When I swung my legs over the side of the bed, I spotted my shoes and socks on the floor. Dog must have taken them off after I fell asleep.

I got up and went down the hallway. The house was dark, and Dog wasn't in the living room. He must have been out on the property somewhere, probably still beating himself up for something that wasn't his fault. When I walked over to the front door and opened it, the porch was clean. Samuel's ashes were gone, along with the pendant. There wasn't a trace that he'd ever been there, but the image still burned painfully in my mind.

Suddenly feeling like I couldn't breathe, I stepped out onto the porch and took in the fresh air. There wasn't a wolf in sight, but they were out there somewhere. I could feel their eyes on me.

As I was about to go back inside, I caught the flap of wings from the corner of my eye. Rex was flying across the yard toward me, his single white feather glowing in the moonlight as he came in for a landing on the railing.

"You want to stay inside with me tonight? I could use the company." When I reached my hand out, he hopped away from me. "What's wrong? Are you going to leave me too?"

He cawed and continued to hop down the railing toward the end of the porch. Then he took off and sailed over the shed at the far end of the property. He kept flying over it, like a hawk circling prey. When he flew back to the porch, he repeated the same strange behavior of hopping down the railing. Then he flew in the air and started circling the shed again.

I walked down the steps, trying to recall the last time I went barefoot in the yard. For a moment, the cool feel of the grass distracted me from the grief. But then it came flooding back. As I turned to go back up to the house, I heard something. It was that same voice that had woken me up, but it was more like a memory in my mind.

I looked up at the sky where Rex was still flying over the shed and started to walk toward it.

"Charley?" Dog appeared next to the garage. "Where are you going?"

Following the voice inside my head, I ignored him and walked faster, suddenly falling into a run. By the time I got to the old shed, there were tears running down my face. I pulled the door open. Samuel was sitting on the floor, naked, with his back pressed to the wall. His skin was shockingly pale, and his eyes were dull and lifeless. With his head tilted to the side, I could see a set of fang marks on his neck.

"Samuel!" I dropped to my knees next to him and grabbed his hands. Samuel's skin had once been warmer than any vampire I'd ever touched before, but now it was ice cold. "What happened to you?"

Dog rushed into the shed behind me. He pushed me aside and bent down to help Samuel up. "Can you walk?"

Samuel nodded. "Get me into the house."

His voice was barely a whisper. Unrecognizable. But it matched the one inside my head.

Loki appeared in the doorway next. "Jesus. What happened to him?"

"Get out of the way," Dog growled.

He threw Samuel's arm over his shoulders and dragged him through the door. Loki took his other side, and they carried him across the yard and up the steps to the house.

"Take him to my bedroom," I said as they were about to set him down on the couch.

Dog gave me a strange look. "You mean the spare?"

I shook my head. "To my bedroom." I wasn't taking my eyes off Samuel until I knew he was okay.

After taking Samuel to my room and laying him on the bed, Dog examined the bite wound on his neck. "He's been nearly drained."

I grabbed the blanket from the chair and covered his naked body. "Drained? Why would someone drain him?"

A vampire's blood was of no use to another vampire, but I couldn't think of any other creature capable of doing this.

"To kill him," Loki said.

Dog nodded. "But they didn't kill him. Whoever did this took him to the brink and then stopped."

I sat down next to Samuel and gazed at him. "They wanted to torture him. Victor Steele did this."

Samuel had lost consciousness, but he was starting to stir again. His lips parted, and then his fangs descended. His eyes barely opened and settled on mine. I could see in his gaze what he didn't have the strength to ask for.

I rubbed my wrist anxiously. "He needs to feed."

I was bitten back at the Beast by that vampire I'd killed, but I'd never been fed on before. If all the hype was true, it would probably be more pleasure than pain. But I didn't care if it was excruciating.

Dog's face went cold. "No way."

"He'll die if he doesn't feed."

"You don't know what you're doing, Charley."

"He's right," Loki said. "If Samuel sinks his fangs into you and can't control himself, you're as good as dead."

"Or worse," Dog growled.

Samuel groaned and tried to reach for me, but he was too weak. His arm dropped back down to the bed.

I looked into his pleading eyes. "You said you'd never hurt me. I believe that."

"I'll leave you to talk some sense into her," Loki said to Dog. "I need to get back outside."

After he left the room, Dog started in on me again. "You're not doing it, Charley. I'll take the truck down to Reaperstown and find him a donor."

"Look at him. There's no time for that."

He took a step closer. "You can hate me all you want, but I won't let you take the risk."

I stared at the bed for a moment and then looked back up at him. "I love you, Dog, but you need to leave this room."

"I love you too, Charley. That's why I have to do this." He grabbed my arm and started to pull me away from the bed.

I yanked it out of his grip and looked him in the eye. "Get out of here, Dog. Leave!"

Dog suddenly flew backward into the hallway, the door slamming behind him. I quickly locked it and stepped back, staring at it in disbelief as Dog banged on it and yelled from the other side.

I thought the bedroom door would come off its hinges, but the pounding suddenly stopped, and Dog walked away. I guess he'd accepted that it wasn't his decision to make.

When I heard the front door open and shut, I went over to the bed and brought my wrist to Samuel's mouth. "Feed. Take whatever you need." My heart was racing, half from excitement and half from fear.

Samuel caught the scent of my skin and his eyes fluttered back open. There was a flicker of life in them again. And a moment later, he struck.

TWENTY-FOUR

I winced from the sharp pain radiating up my arm, but it faded quickly. It felt like a drug had been injected into my veins, turning my limbs into languid extensions of flesh. My eyes closed as I sank into the mattress and let the sensation wash through me.

"So this is what all the fuss is about," I whispered, drifting deeper into the pleasure as Samuel continued to feed.

Minutes passed, maybe hours, before my eyes fluttered open. Samuel's fangs released my wrist as the color in his skin returned. He rolled over and gazed down at me, his beautiful blue eyes even brighter than before and still hungry.

I traced my finger along his bottom lip, catching a drop of blood at the edge. "You came back to me."

His eyes wandered to my mouth. "How could I not? Your blood is like fire."

Before I could take another breath, his lips pressed to mine. He kissed me deeply, the taste of my own blood mellowing to something sweet in my mouth as my thighs parted to accommodate the heaviness of his hips.

His blue eyes faded to black and then lit up like rubies. "I want you, Charley."

I wanted him more. More than I'd ever wanted anyone before. But when his fangs grew longer, panic set in.

I slipped out from under him and climbed off the bed, backing up toward the wall. "You're scaring me, Samuel." Biting my wrist was one thing, and I did enjoy it thoroughly, but the thought of his fangs sinking into my neck terrified me.

They retracted instantly as he got up, the sight of his naked body causing my breath to hitch. It was difficult to pull my eyes away from his perfectly sculpted muscles, the crease of his hips drawing my eyes lower.

"I won't hurt you, Charley." He took a step closer, the tips of his fangs descending just past the edge of his lips. "But this is who I am. A vampire."

The heat in his gaze hammered at my stomach, all the way down to that spot between my thighs that wouldn't stop throbbing. "Does that mean you're going to bite me?"

His chin lowered as a smile slid up his face. "I might."

My back hit the wall when his eyes turned wolfish, nearly sliding down to the floor from the growing weakness in my legs. "Okay," I whispered.

In two long strides, he was a breath away from me. His fingers laced between mine, splaying my hands against the wall as he brushed his lips over mine, teasing me with a flick of his tongue. A moment later, he worked my jeans open and shimmied them down my hips. His eyes never left mine as he slipped his hands under my shirt and found my breasts. Then he kissed his way up my neck and cheek, stopping at my ear. "Can I take you back to the bed now?"

I nodded, wrapping my legs around him as he lifted me up and carried me across the room. After setting me down on the edge of the bed, he pulled my shirt off swiftly, removing my bra with one hand while cupping my breast with the other. "You're perfect," he whispered, raising my chin to kiss me while his thumb grazed my nipple.

My body arched into his touch, caught in the shivers racing across my skin. "Samuel," I whispered against his lips as I lost myself in the sensation.

He pushed me back against the bed, parting my legs as he gazed at the soft flesh. "I'd like to bite you now." Bringing his eyes back up to mine, he brushed his fingers along my inner thigh with a featherlight touch, stopping inches below that glorious place that was aching for him. "Here."

I swallowed hard as that same featherlike touch seemed to work me from the inside. The sensation consumed me. There was such intensity in his eyes, I could barely look at them. "Please."

A moan escaped me as he draped my thigh over his shoulder and sank his fangs into my tender flesh. My body was a pile of tinder, a flame igniting inside me, taking me over the edge as I surrendered to it. I came in waves, over and over, until he pulled back, my blood glistening on his lips. I wanted to taste it again, but I wanted to feel him inside of me more. "Now," I demanded, holding his gaze.

With a forceful thrust, he slid deep inside of me, bringing me to the edge again before easing back out. He teased me to the brink repeatedly until I found myself on top of him. I moved against him, riding him until I could no longer think. Then he gripped my hips and moved me faster against him until I felt like I'd splinter apart. I locked eyes with him as he held me in place and pushed deeper. A moment later, I disintegrated around him, disappearing into the ether.

When I finally came back down to earth, I collapsed against him and fought to catch my breath. I looked away from him, resting my cheek on his chest as I tried to hold back the tears brimming in my eyes. "What did you just do to me?"

Samuel rolled on top of me and brushed a strand of sweat-drenched hair out of my eyes, his finger lingering to trace the outline of my lips. "I just made you mine."

Looking back into his eyes, it hit me. He'd just ruined me for any other man who'd dare to touch me. And I found I was relieved. In that moment, I never wanted anyone else to ever touch me again. He had me completely.

His tongue gently moved inside my mouth as he kissed me. Then his scent intensified, and his skin felt almost hot against mine. "You're so warm."

"It's you." He rolled onto his side and leisurely ran his hand along my stomach. "Your body is acclimating to mine. It recognizes me now."

I propped myself up on my elbows. "You weren't serious when you said you made me yours?" I thought he was just being figurative, not to mention sexy as hell, but wolves often marked their mates. Did vampires do the same?

His lips rose into a smile. "Completely. But I won't hold you to it if you get sick of me. You're free to dump me whenever you'd like." He kissed me again, this time reducing me to liquid.

"We should probably go find Dog," I said when his eyes heated up again and his hand traveled lower. I could have stayed in bed with him for a week, but I was afraid Dog would come back into the house and break the door down, thinking Samuel had drained me, if we didn't emerge from the bedroom soon. It had probably taken every ounce of his restraint to leave earlier.

Samuel sat up and looked down at his naked body. "I'm not exactly dressed for company."

"Let me see what I can find." I went into my mother's bedroom and dug through her dresser. She never threw anything away, and I was hoping that included clothing from an old boyfriend. I found a T-shirt and some unflattering jeans that looked like they might make it past Samuel's hips.

I went back into my bedroom and handed the clothes to Samuel. "See if these fit."

He eyed the outfit. "You expect me to wear that?"

"It's either that or my bathrobe, but Loki might be wearing it." I probably should have dug those old clothes out for that wolf instead of letting him ruin my favorite robe.

He put them on without further commentary. The pants were snug, but they did the job.

When we went into the living room, I was relieved to find it empty. We'd been in the bedroom for a while, so I could only imagine what was going through Dog's mind. But he was always pushing me to live a little. To put myself out there.

Loki was sitting on the hood of my truck when I walked out on the porch. Dog was standing next to it. He walked across the yard and met me at the top of the steps, giving me a long look before brushing past me to go into the house.

Samuel nodded to Dog as he walked through the door. "I appreciate your help tonight. I owe you."

"You don't owe anyone," I said to him as I followed Dog inside. "You've done enough around here." Samuel had saved my ass more than once.

Dog grabbed my wrist and flipped it over, examining the faded bite marks. "So you did it."

"Obviously. Look at him."

Samuel was practically glowing, but it wasn't just my blood doing that.

Dog gazed at me for a moment, and his eyes began to soften. He wasn't an easy wolf to read, but I knew him as well as anyone. He could see it in my eyes. He knew exactly what had happened in that bedroom, and I think he was actually happy for me.

"We need to talk about what happened to Samuel," I said, changing the subject before the conversation got weird.

Dog finally stopped looking at me and turned back to Samuel. "Explain?"

"I went to settle a score with an old acquaintance," he said. "Let's just say it didn't go well."

I had a feeling I knew who that acquaintance was, so it was time to fess up. "I told Dog about Victor Steele. That he's your maker. He also knows you're a hunter."

There was slight disappointment in Samuel's eyes when he looked at me. "So much for discretion."

And so much for our budding romance if I didn't put it into perspective for him. "I'm sorry, Samuel. I thought you were dead." I glanced around the room and brought my eyes back to Dog. "What did you do with those ashes?"

Dog walked out to the porch and came back inside with one of my large Tupperware containers. The one I *used to store cereal* in. "I couldn't find a box."

I took it and opened it to show Samuel the ashes. "Who is this?"

Samuel looked inside. "Some unfortunate sap. Sacrificed to scare you, I assume."

"Well, whoever he is, he's going down the toilet."

Samuel grabbed my arm as I headed for the bathroom. "I believe this is mine." He snatched his seal from the container, shaking off the ashes before placing it around his neck.

Coming to my senses, I closed the container and handed it back to Dog. "Just get rid of this please."

While Dog took it back outside, I filled Samuel in on the rest. "Ian Masterson paid me a visit last night. He told me all about Victor Steele, including the part you left out."

He cocked his head. "What part?"

"The part about his vampire trafficking business."

Samuel nodded. "Yes. Just another reason to kill the bastard. I didn't think it was relevant to our conversation the other night."

"It's relevant all right," Dog said as he came back inside. "Victor Steele bought the Beast down in Reaperstown last month. He set up shop in the basement when he discovered half the population of Crimson is vampire, and half of those vampires are women. Inventory." Dog gave him a curious look. "By the way, why aren't you dead? Why send the decoy ashes instead of the real thing?"

"Because I'm still useful to him alive. He wanted Charley to think I was dead so she'd come for him." He looked me in the eye. "Then he intended to kill me right in front of you." His eyes closed briefly before continuing. "The bastard drained me to the brink. He thought I was too weak to escape and left me alone with one of his rookies. That rookie is rotting in hell right now. Then I used what strength I had left to make it back here."

"You know why he's after me?" I said.

"You mean because of Tucker? At first I had no idea, but after he weakened me and chained me up in that dungeon below the Beast, we had time to chat." He came closer and cupped my cheek with his hand. "You, my darling, have become his new toy."

"I don't get it," I said. "Doesn't he have more important things to do than taunt a nobody like me? Why didn't he just grab Tucker off the street after she got here and have done with it?" The pack didn't have eyes on her twenty-four seven, so he'd had plenty of opportunities to have one of his thugs snatch her. "It just seems counterproductive for a vampire like Steele to waste his energy on me."

Samuel gave me a weak smile. "You don't understand, Charley. This is a game to him. He'll go after the people you care about next."

It suddenly hit me. "He already has, and not just you." And Keith Barnes, a customer. "He framed Beau for the attacks around here. And after letting Beau sit in jail for days, he attacked someone else and gave Beau an alibi. But why do that?"

"As I said, it's all a game. Victor Steele doesn't need to cover his tracks by framing someone else for the attacks. He couldn't care less if the police find out he's the killer because they can't touch him. No human can. But I'm sure he took great pleasure in seeing you hurt over your employee and friend facing a murder charge." His face took on a deadly serious look. "There are two things you never want to do to a monster like Steele—take what is his or lie to him. In his mind, you've done both. The fact that you're a *female nobody* makes it worse. You've made it his mission to waste his energy on you. But make no mistake. In the end, he wants you dead almost as much as me."

"Right," Dog said. "Which is why we have to kill him before he takes another shot at Charley or someone else in her life."

We needed to confirm a couple of things first. "Did you see Tucker in that basement?"

Samuel tilted his head. "Is she missing?"

"I'll take that as a no."

"How about the vampires?" Dog asked. "The females he's trafficking. Are they down there?"

Samuel nodded. "Probably. He kept me chained up in a small room, but I could hear women's voices down the corridor. I can't confirm if Tucker was one of them, though."

"Did you see anything else?" I asked. "Like how many men he has down there?" I was sure Ian Masterson was familiar with the layout of the place, but we needed to know how heavily guarded it was. No sense taking on an army we couldn't possibly defeat.

"I can't say. He sensed me coming and ambushed me the moment I made it into the basement." His face went cold. "Apparently, his blood is still in my veins after all these years."

I didn't dare tell Samuel that Ian and I planned to go in there tonight, and to be honest, I was second-guessing the idea myself. After what had just happened between us in that bedroom, I wouldn't have put it past him to lock me up to save me from myself. But we needed to confirm that Tucker was down there, and I needed to see with my own two eyes who we were dealing with. It was time to meet the infamous Mr. K.

Samuel glanced out the window. "I should go. The sun will be coming up soon."

"I don't want you to go." I wanted to close the curtains and shut the world out. Keep him here with me. But Candy and I had a date with the Squad that afternoon to teach me how to use that ring. Then I was going down to Reaperstown with Ian Masterson as soon as the sun started to set.

Samuel took my hand and gently kissed the center of my palm, sending a flutter through me. "There's nothing I would like more than to stay, but I can't. He'll find me eventually, and I don't want to be here when he does." He nodded to Dog. "A word?"

"If you're about to bark orders about the pack keeping an eye on her," Dog said, "save your breath. It'll be Fort Knox around here from now on."

Thank God he didn't open his mouth about the plan tonight, but I still needed to make sure Samuel didn't show up at the Stag until *after* I left for that meeting down in Reaperstown.

"Come on," I said to Samuel. "I'll walk you out." When we got out to the porch, I kissed him like it might be the last time.

After pulling his lips away from mine, he held my gaze for a moment. "Is everything okay?"

"Why wouldn't it be?" I hated lying to him. It felt awful, but this was a matter of life and death. "I want you to do me a favor. I want to tell Candy and Beau about us before they see us together, so would you mind meeting me back here tonight instead of coming into the Stag?" I smiled at him. "I don't think I could hide it from them."

He smiled back at me. "Midnight?"

"Perfect."

He walked down the steps and looked back at me for a moment before disappearing into the morning twilight. There would be no more secrets between us when this was over. I just hoped he'd forgive me for what I had to do tonight.

Dog stared at me when I walked back inside. "I have nothing against Samuel," he said, "but loving a vampire comes with tradeoffs."

Love? The word stirred butterflies in my stomach and terrified me at the same time. "You're the one who's always telling me I need to put myself out there. I'm just taking your advice."

"I know you, Charley. I know that look on your face. Are you sure you want to walk down that road with Samuel?"

I didn't have to even think about it. Did I want to spend my days without him? Well, if the nights were anything like the one we'd just had, then I was all in.

TWENTY-FIVE

When I walked into the Cauldron a little before noon, Candy was helping a customer at the counter. The woman glanced over her shoulder when she heard the chimes on the door sound.

Chimes?

"Now, remember," Candy said to her. "Just a pinch. If you get too heavy-handed with it, you'll get more than you bargained for."

"Good morning," I said.

The woman shoved a small jar in her purse when I walked up. "Don't be so nosy, Charley Underwood."

"Me? Nosy?" I watched her walk toward the door with a steady clip, fighting with the veil of pink beads strung across it. The chimes went off again as she finally exited the shop. "I see you put the beads back up?" They came and went with her moods. "What was Adelle Spencer doing in here?" The woman was first in line over at the Baptist church every time there was a call to arms to stop the "ungodly" from taking over the town. I was pretty sure she considered both of us heathens.

Candy grabbed the money off the counter and stuffed it in a

box on the shelf behind her. It was her version of a cash register. "She's having some trouble shedding a few pounds. Said her husband isn't showing much interest anymore." A grin slid up her face. "I didn't have the heart to tell her it isn't the weight—it's Abigail across the street at the café."

"Maybe you should give me a jar of that stuff."

She looked me up and down. "You're perfect just the way you are, honey. Besides, that stuff's dangerous if you don't use it right. Use too much of it and it'll have the opposite effect. How much do you want to bet Adelle Spencer will be back in a few days complaining about how much weight she's gained?"

"Then why'd you sell it to her?"

"Because she's been badgering me about it." She started to grumble. "Coming in here every other day and practically accosting me at the market. The woman is worse than a pit bull. But I'll take her money and point out that she didn't follow my directions when she bitches about it."

I couldn't help but laugh at the thought of that godawful woman stepping on the scale and seeing red.

Noticing the smile on my face, Candy got an inquisitive look. "You look awfully cheerful for a woman who's about to do something foolish tonight. What have you been up to?"

My shoulders shuddered with mock dread. "Is that better?"

Her eyes narrowed. "Uh-huh."

I was dying to tell her about me and Samuel, but that would have sent her into an endless loop of questions we didn't have time for. We would have a nice chat about Samuel after Victor Steele was dead.

"What's with the chimes on the door?" I asked, to change the subject.

"I've had them for a while." She shrugged. "I figured with that vampire on the loose it couldn't hurt to have some warning when someone walked into the shop, especially after dark."

Made sense. And it only added to the witchy feel of the place.

I pulled the ring box from my pocket and set it on the counter. "So, where do we start?"

"In the woods." She grabbed the money box from the shelf and headed for the back room. "Let me put this up, and we'll be on our way."

"Isn't the Squad meeting us here?"

She glanced over her shoulder at me. "Not this time, honey. We're going to them."

* * *

We drove for what seemed like an hour, but I knew it had to be less than half of that. The deeper you got into the notorious woods, the more time seemed to become irrelevant. It messed with your head. Made you wonder what day it was.

Candy clutched the steering wheel of her Jeep. And it wasn't just any Jeep. She drove a vintage baby-blue Grand Wagoneer gifted to her by a gentleman friend from her old dancing days. She rarely drove it. She preferred to keep it covered and parked behind the shop, but today was an exception.

"Damn dirt road! I'll have to have her hand-washed to get all the dust off her wheels."

"I offered to drive," I reminded her. Technically, my truck was vintage too, but no one would have called it a gem like the Wagoneer. Candy kept that thing spotless.

She shook her head as we bounced along the uneven road. "You probably won't be in any condition to drive back to town when we're through with you, and I'm not driving that truck of yours."

I couldn't blame her for not wanting to drive it. The stick was a bear to shift sometimes.

I'd never actually seen the house where the Squad lived. I knew where it was, but it was too far back in the woods for anyone to see it from the road. You had to go down a private dirt drive to even get a glimpse of it, and it was best not to do that without an invitation. Local kids had been coming down here for years. With enough liquid courage, a few had tried to get close enough to the house to look through the windows. But they never got beyond the trees circling the property. At least none that I'd ever talk to.

The house came into view as we rounded the bend. It was your typical two-story Victorian that looked completely out of place in the middle of the North Georgia woods, especially with that turret at the top. One of those octagon-shaped rooms that you saw on castles. There was a figure standing up there next to the window, watching us as we drove up to the house. It looked like a man.

Candy put the Jeep in park and looked up at him. "So much for a sneak attack."

"They know we're coming, right?" You didn't want to sneak up on a bunch of witches living in the woods.

She chuckled. "Of course they know."

As soon as I got out of the car, I felt a heaviness come over me. It was like the barometric pressure had dropped and a headache was coming on. Even the light outside seemed dimmer than when we drove up. We were definitely at the right house.

"Did you bring the ring?" Candy asked.

"No, I left it on the counter at the shop." I deadpanned her. "Of course I brought it." I glanced at the creepy surroundings. "Let's just get this over with before I change my mind."

She lifted her brows. "You mean about going down to Sodom and Gomorrah tonight?"

"Nice try." I motioned for her to lead the way. "Shall we?"

There were tall weeds mingled with rose bushes and

foxgloves on either side of the front porch, and there was an herb bed on the side of the house that looked like it hadn't been tended in a while. It was all very odd and untamed, just like the Squad. A giant oak tree towered over us as we headed for the steps leading up to the front door.

Candy's eyes darted around the unkept yard. "If you see something move, just ignore it and keep walking."

"What?" My eyes immediately went to the tree line.

She hurried up the steps and knocked on the heavily carved door. Through the glass pane, I could see a figure walking toward us, but when the door opened there was no one standing on the other side.

"They're expecting us," Candy said to the empty space just inside the door.

After following her inside, I glanced over my shoulder as the door shut behind us. "Who were you talking to?"

She ignored me and led the way down a long hall. There were several small rooms on either side, each one decorated in progressively drabber decor. The house gave off a funeral parlor vibe, but I guess it was a matter of taste.

We eventually turned into a room at the end that looked like the kitchen. The first thing I saw was a wooden table with a large mortar and pestle in the center. The thing was big enough to crush a human skull. And there was a giant hutch that spanned the entire back wall, with shelves covered with glass jars. I didn't even want to know what they contained, and I swear I saw something move inside one of them.

Mia Winston was standing at the stove, stirring a large pot while she hummed a tune. We stood there for a moment waiting for her to turn around. Not wanting to startle her—which was wise—Candy cleared her throat loudly.

The wooden spoon went still in the witch's hand, but she kept her back to us.

Candy finally spoke up. "Hello."

Mia turned around and aimed the wooden spoon at us. Katherine walked into the kitchen a moment later and grabbed it from her hand. "Is that any way to greet our guests?"

"Guests?" The witch looked back at us with narrowed eyes. "Why would you invite guests when we have an appointment this afternoon?"

"The appointment is with them." Katherine shook her head. "That vision ointment you've been experimenting with is starting to fry your brain."

Desiree came in through a second doorway on the other side of the kitchen. "I thought I heard our visitors." Her eyes popped with excitement. "This is going to be fun."

"Then let's get on with it," Candy said. "We don't have much time."

A loud bang came from somewhere in the room. It sounded like it was coming from inside the walls, and I swore I heard a voice. "What was that?" I noticed a staircase that must have led to the second floor, and a door next to it that probably led to the basement. The muffled voice came again.

"Is there someone down there?" I nodded to the door.

"Nothing you need to concern yourself with," Mia said. "It's just the old plumbing acting up."

Plumbing my ass. "And who is that upstairs?" I was about to be at the mercy of the witches while they *schooled* me in magic, so I wanted to know who was in the house before I put myself in a vulnerable position.

"Up where?" Katherine asked.

Candy glanced at the ceiling. "In that funny little room upstairs."

Without so much as a word, Kathrine's eyes shifted to Desiree.

"Oh, all right!" Desiree stomped across the kitchen and up the back staircase.

When I opened my mouth to repeat the question, Candy put her hand on my arm and muttered, "Let it go, Charley."

I guess Candy wasn't the only witch in town with practices that required discretion.

Mia dipped a ladle into the pot on the stove and emptied some liquid into a cup. "Tea?" She held it out to me.

"Thanks, but I'm good." Whatever was in that cup wasn't making it past my lips. But when her face dropped into a frown and Candy glowered at me for being rude, I took it. "What is it?"

Mia brightened up. "Herbs from the garden. It's my own special brew."

When she kept staring at me, I took a sip. It had a little bite to it, but it wasn't bad. "It's kinda tasty." I took a few more sips as it started to grow on me.

Katherine smiled. "Let's begin the lesson, shall we?"

My nerves started to fire up as we followed her down the hallway to the living room. It was a large room with a high ceiling, and there was a fireplace with a painting hanging over it. A portrait of a woman. "Who's that?" I asked.

She glanced at it. "Victoria Wilderbrandt. The first witch to come to Crimson. She built this house."

I studied the painting for a moment. She looked young and vibrant. More like my mother than the witches of the house. "What happened to her?"

Katherine's smile faded. "What do you mean?"

I shrugged. "I just assumed she's no longer with us." If she was, she'd be in the record books. Witches came to Crimson shortly after it was founded in 1892.

"Charley's just curious," Candy said when the witch kept staring at me with a hostile gaze.

I couldn't tell if she was thinking, or if she was about to put me in my place for saying something offensive, whatever that could have been.

Katherine's glare softened. "Of course she's gone." She finally broke eye contact with me and walked over to the window to look out. "Tell me about the spider."

Candy must have told her about what happened at Masterson's house. About the spider leg and the misfire I had. "I had a run-in with Ian Masterson the other night."

"The vampire?"

"Yeah. My magic went haywire when I tried to use it on him. I was doing just fine fending him off until that spider leg worked its way up my throat and crawled out of my mouth." The feel of it on my tongue was still vivid. It made me shudder. "When I tried to used magic on Masterson a little while later that night, it just fizzled out."

"She was supercharged when the vampire touched her, though," Candy added.

"He got the shock of his life when he grabbed me. The strange thing is, I've used it since then." Like when I blasted Ian at Tucker's place and Dog later when he wouldn't leave my bedroom. "It seems to come and go at will."

"The spider was missing two legs after the ritual, if I recall," the witch said without turning around. "The two that were inside you. Since one escaped, that means you have only one left."

Only?

Candy let out an impatient sigh. "Get to the point, Katherine. Time's ticking."

"The point is, there's still hope for Charley. Still a chance for her to tame the spider and keep it trapped inside of her forever."

I shook my head. "Are you crazy? I don't want to keep that thing inside of me."

"Oh, but you do. The spider is the essence of your power. A gift from mother to daughter. All it takes is a single piece of the spider. Just one leg." She pulled her eyes away from the window and walked over to me. "Where's the ring?"

I pulled it out of my pocket. "What now?"

She took it and slipped it on my finger, squeezing my hand tight until it hurt. "You face the final challenge. The spider will test you. If it wins, the last leg will slither up your throat and disappear forever. Your magic will be lost. But if you win, it will become a part of you until you take your last breath." Then she held her hand out.

"What?" I said.

"Give me your phone."

I stepped back. "Why?"

"You can keep it with you," Candy said. "It might not work so well when this is over, though."

My phone wasn't cheap, so I reluctantly gave it to the witch.

Katherine smiled. "Now we can begin. But remember. That ring is only as powerful as the witch wearing it. It's a conduit for your magic."

The room suddenly started to go wonky as the cup of tea slipped from my hand and hit the floor, shattering. My eyes closed for a moment as I tried to steady myself. When they reopened, Katherine was standing inches away from me.

"There's just one question you need to ask yourself, Charley—are you a rabbit or a crow?"

TWENTY-SIX

As the word *crow* slipped from Katherine Belltower's lips, I drifted into darkness. It felt like a night terror. I knew I was awake, but my eyes seemed to be glued shut. When I finally managed to open them, I was in the middle of a forest. There were towering trees all around me. I was on my knees, inches deep in debris, the glow of the sapphire ring lighting up the leaves covering my hands.

When the light started to fade, I looked up. Through the thick canopy, I spotted a black cloud forming in the sky. It continued to grow, blocking out the sun until only a halo of light escaped its edges to illuminate the forest around me.

After climbing to my feet, I steadied myself against a tree. Whatever was in that tea still had me woozy, but I was able to walk. Either I'd stumble onto a road and hitch a ride back to town, or I'd find my way back to that house and wring Mia Winston's neck for drugging me. This game had gotten old before it had even started, and I needed to get to the Stag to shore things up for the evening before my appointment down at the Beast.

I made it about twenty feet when I heard rustling behind

me. A shiver ran down my spine as I stopped and slowly turned, but there was nothing there. The sound came again when I took another step. This time I glanced back quickly. I gasped when I saw something move under the thick layer of leaves. About ten feet back. It had stopped abruptly as soon as I turned. But there was definitely something under there. A squirrel or a... snake.

"Hey!" I yelled, trying to flush it out.

The leaves were still, so I took another step. This time I turned before I heard the sound again, and something was tunneling toward me at a fast speed.

I backpedaled, searching the ground for a weapon. As I reached for a tree branch, my ring began to glow brighter. But the light faded when my heart started to beat wildly. The leaves had parted, and a leg poked out from under them. An hourglass-shaped figure with a pair of shiny black eyes started to emerge, making clicking noises that rattled the leaves on the forest floor.

A spider, and it was huge.

I shut my eyes, trying to shake off the hallucination. At least I hoped it was a hallucination. Probably from that tea. But then the strange clicking sound traveled across the ground, vibrating into my feet and up through my torso. It was real.

The sound grew louder, and my eyes flew open as the spider fully emerged. Only one of its legs was missing this time. The one still inside me. I guess the one that climbed up my throat the other night found its way back to the mother ship.

I dropped the branch when a sharp pain stabbed me in the stomach and my throat started to burn from something crawling up. When it scurried toward me, I thrust my hand out, the one wearing the ring, but nothing happened. There wasn't even a faint tingle in my fingers.

My back hit a tree when the spider inched closer. I swallowed hard, forcing the bristly leg back down as the burning sensation in my throat intensified.

The spider is the essence of your power.

The moment it hit my stomach, a surge of adrenaline raced through my veins. A bright light traveled down my arm and into my hand, shooting out from my palm. The leaves on the forest floor lifted, whirling into a tornado around me. And then they suddenly exploded. The spider flew into the air and began to spin, bursting into a cloud of black confetti that floated upward. I waited, expecting it to shower down on top of me, but it just vanished into the sky.

My legs shook from the energy as I slumped against the tree. It took a moment to subside, but then I started to walk again, hoping my instincts would lead me out of the godforsaken woods.

Before I made it ten feet, something fell in the distance, rattling the forest floor. When the ground shook again, and then a third time, I fell into a run. Something massive was stomping through the woods, and it was coming toward me.

The forest grew denser as I dodged trees, running aimlessly as the frequency of the thunderous steps increased. Branches cracked behind me as something plowed through them, and a giant shadow seemed to block out the sun as it tried to break through the canopy. It was gaining speed.

My shoulder nicked the trunk of a tree, spinning me around just in time to see a tall pine in the distance tip sideways and crash to the ground. It shook me back into a run. Through the dimness, I saw a bright spot up ahead. I'd almost reached it when my foot caught a thick vein of tree roots in my path, sending me flying forward. I hit the ground and rolled into a small clearing, but when I tried to climb back to my feet, my peripheral vision started to blur. Darkness closed in, and I fell back to the ground.

It seemed like the blackout only lasted for a moment, but it was hard to tell. I was still alive, though, and the ground had stopped shaking. Whatever it was, it was gone, and I was alone again in the forest.

"Okay!" I yelled to anyone who was listening. "The game's over! I'm done!"

After climbing to my feet, I looked around. I was standing in the center of a circle. With my eyes focused and my ears perked, I took a stroll around it. The circle was bordered by large stones, and there were others marking the four quarters. Unless a herd of squirrels had built that fire pit in the center of it, my guess was it belonged to the Squad. A ritual space for conducting magic. My mother had carved out a little spot in the woods behind our house, but it was a fraction of the size of this one.

Something rustled just beyond the circle as I came back around to the spot where I'd blacked out. I held my breath and prepared to run again, but then I spotted a tail sticking out from behind a tree. The critter revealed itself and waddled over to the edge of the stones. It was a possum.

It started to climb over the stones but stopped, and its eyes didn't look right. Instead of black, they were amber. And they were trained on me in a way that made me uneasy. I tried to get a better look at it, but as I approached, a deep growl came from its throat. It wasn't a sound I'd ever heard a possum make.

Before I could put some distance between us, it started to grow. The animal's bones snapped as its fur darkened. There was something human in its eyes as it stood up on its hind legs and continued to morph. Before I knew it, A creature was towering over me, its massive paws armed with long claws. Its fur was tipped with sable, and its pointed ears were pinned back against its head. It looked like a cross between a bear and a wolf. Or a lycan.

I took off, listening to the sounds of grunting and huffing behind me. Before I made it over the edge of the circle, I felt a sharp stab to my shoulder. I lifted into the air and was slammed to the ground, shock and adrenaline quickly dulling the pain from where the creature's claws had dug into my skin. But the pain came roaring back when I saw it hovering over me, and a thick drop of saliva hit my face.

It must have stood ten feet tall on its hind legs. When it lowered itself toward me, I tried to throw up my hand, but the wound to my shoulder was excruciating. I rolled out of the way as it dropped down toward me, the air rushing from my lungs when it hooked its claws into my arm and dragged me back.

I closed my eyes, drifting, absently wondering who would take over the Stag if I died? What would happen to Rex? Would Samuel and Dog go after the witches?

Come back!

My eyes flew open when I heard the voice in my mind. The beast lowered its head and brought its snout within inches of my face. Its breath was hot against my skin, stinking of rot and death as it sniffed me. Then it suddenly started to back up, giving me room to escape out from under it.

Wincing, I dragged myself a few yards with one arm when it turned and walked back toward the stones. Was it leaving? As if reading my mind, it swung its head around and charged at me again. I managed to climb to my feet, but as I started to run it sank its teeth into my leg, snapping a bone as it brought me down like prey. The pain was blinding, and the burning in my throat returned.

My head came down on a stone at the edge of the circle, causing my vision to blur. But as I rolled over on my back to face the beast, the agonizing pain began to fade. Warmth built in the core of my stomach and radiated out toward my limbs.

"Thank God," I whispered as relief washed through me. But reality set in a moment later when the shadow of the beast loomed over me again.

Suddenly, vibrations began to travel across my shoulders and down my arms, lighting up my hands in a soft glow. The creature swung its head back and forth to look at the light coming from my palms, but the spider leg dug into my throat and dulled the glow as it climbed higher. I swallowed it back down, forcing it deep into my stomach, and the ring lit up in a blaze of blue. The beast stumbled back as the light snaked around my hand, forming a pool of blue mist in the center of my right palm. Then it spread through my body and filled my left palm with the same strange mist.

The creature growled, its eyes lighting up like rubies as it came toward me with its lips curled back. But I couldn't run. The pain had subsided, but the bone in my leg was shattered. It towered over me, staring at the blue light with fascination.

Then the softest voice whispered in my ear. *The eyes.*

My hands started to vibrate. They were shaking violently as the mist whirled in my palms. The creature lost its fascination and let out a bone-chilling roar that echoed through the forest. As it lowered its sharp fangs toward me, my hands came together. The mist formed a sphere, circling frantically inside the cage of my palms until light shot out between the gaps in my fingers like a sunburst.

The beast spread its jaws, and I aimed higher, opening the tips of my fingers to release the light. The mist flowed from my palms like a river and seeped into its eyes, filling the creature's head until light emitted from every orifice of its skull. It shot from its ears, nose, and mouth and continued down its throat to its stomach, setting the beast aglow.

I crawled away when the creature began to shake so violently it was difficult to track it with my eyes. Then it let out an ear-piercing howl before crumpling to the ground in a heap of skin and bones.

I lurched, fighting the urge to vomit. That spider wasn't getting out of me that easily. Not after what I'd just been through. When the urge passed, I fell back to the ground and closed my eyes, praying that it was over. That something else wasn't waiting for me.

My eyes reopened when I heard a flutter. I caught a glimpse

of black wings above me that quickly disappeared into the trees. A flood of light filtered through the canopy as the dark cloud parted and a sea of crows descended from the sky. They sank their talons into the skin and bones of the creature and carried them into the forest.

I tried to climb to my feet, expecting my leg to give out, but the bone was fine. It wasn't broken. The injuries to my shoulder and arm were gone too. Even my clothes were intact. I wasn't sure if any of it had been real. But then I glanced at the ground and spotted a long claw. Lying next to it was a black feather. It had all been real. How far would the witches have taken it if I hadn't been able to kill that thing?

My relief turned to anger as I shoved the claw in my pocket and glanced around trying to decide which way to go. I spotted a path to the right of the circle that I could have sworn hadn't been there earlier, so I followed it.

It took about ten minutes to find my way out of the woods. The house came into view as soon as I emerged from the tree line. My first instinct was to walk inside and shove that claw up Katherine Belltower's ass before pouring some of that tea down Mia Winston's throat, but I didn't go through hell just to get myself killed by angry witches.

I calmed down as I crossed the field and saw Candy waiting for me on the porch.

"How was it, honey?" She looked concerned but relieved when I walked up.

"Did you know what they planned to do to me in those woods?" I couldn't imagine it.

Her face went cold. "What the hell happened out there?"

I guess she didn't.

"Nothing." I walked past her into the house and headed straight for the living room where Katherine was sitting on a godawful sofa sipping a cup of tea. I doubted it was the same tea I'd had.

"Congratulations," she said, without looking up at me. "No one can take your power now."

"Damn right they can't. And by the way..." After grabbing my phone off the coffee table, I pulled the claw from my pocket and tossed it down in front of her. "...I'm a fucking crow."

TWENTY-SEVEN

Candy kept glancing at me the whole way back to town like she was about to burst, but I was still too steamed to talk about it rationally. To not say something I couldn't take back.

"I'll give you one day to be mad at me," she said as we pulled up to the shop.

"I'm not mad at you, Candy. I just can't talk about it right now. I've got to get my head straight for tonight."

Having that discussion would be one hell of a distraction from all the things I needed to focus on for that meeting with Victor Steele in a matter of hours. I was distracted enough thinking about Samuel and what happened between us. Not to mention what he would do when he found out I went down to the Beast.

She put the car in park and looked at me. "You're still going, aren't you?"

"Of course I am." I reached for the door handle. "You don't need to worry about me, Candy. I had a reckoning out in those woods, so I think I'm good now." My magic still needed a hell of a lot of work, but I prayed it would come more natural to me now. Tonight would be a good test if things went south, and things always went south lately. "Do me a favor. If Samuel comes looking for me tonight, tell him I had to drive over to Adlersville to pick something up." Regardless of me telling him not to stop by the Stag tonight, if he sensed I'd been in trouble that afternoon, I had a feeling he'd come out of the gate running as soon as the sun went down. I guess you could say it was both a gift and a curse of taking a vampire as a lover.

She grabbed my arm before I could get out. "Did something happen between you two?"

I finally looked her in the eye. "A lot has happened. We'll have breakfast in the morning, and I'll tell you all about it. I promise." Then we'd debrief and plan our attack on the Beast to stop that vampire once and for all. "I need to get going." It was 6:45, and I needed to be out of there before it got totally dark just in case Samuel did decide to show up. I was suddenly glad he wasn't a dusk-tolerant vampire.

"All right," she said. "I'll be down in a few minutes to see you off."

"It's not like I'm going off to college, Candy. I'll see you in the morning."

She gave me a pointed look. "You'll see me tonight. We'll all be waiting for you to come back in one piece. If you don't, we'll be coming down to Reaperstown after you."

I climbed in my truck and drove back to the bar, trying to get all my ducks in a row before walking in there. I may have gotten Candy off my back, but I still needed to navigate through Dog's last-minute roadblocks. I also needed to change clothes in order to play the part, so I grabbed my duffel bag and got out.

Lucy looked at me funny when I walked inside. "What happened to you?"

I looked in the mirror behind the bar. My hair was disheveled, and there was a leaf sticking out of it. Candy didn't bother to tell me I looked like I'd been rolling around in the woods, which I had. I yanked it out and finger combed my hair, but trashy was the look I was going for tonight.

"Where's Beau?" I'd asked them both to come in early.

"He's in the back room. Says he isn't coming out until the sun goes down." She snorted a laugh. "The idiot still thinks he's a vampire."

I went to have a word with him, but Dog came through the kitchen door as I was going down the hallway. "We need to talk."

"About what?"

Let the nagging begin.

He motioned to the kitchen. "In here."

"Yes sir." I followed him in and leaned against the sink. "If you're going to try to talk me out of going down to the Beast tonight, save your breath. You're not stopping me."

"I'm not even going to try. But I am going down there with you."

"You're serious?" I stared at him for a moment.

He pointed his finger at me. "That's the deal."

"You won't get past the bouncer at the front door, and you'll hose up the entire plan." Dog was usually rational, but this was an irrational idea.

"I'll get in there all right. I'm head of the local pack. If Steele wants to do business in this town, he's going to have to ante up. Cut the pack in."

"Are you suggesting we convince Steele that the pack is dirty?"

"Yes ma'am. The local wolves can make it real easy for him to do business up here. Having the pack in his pocket would be a smart business move. He wouldn't dare touch you with two of his allies in the room." His expression hardened. "And if he tries, I'll rip his head off before he sees me coming."

It wasn't a bad plan. I'd also feel a lot more secure walking in there with Dog. "We still have to convince Ian." There was a good chance he'd balk at the idea. "We'll discuss it when he gets here. Right now, I need to go check on Beau. He's having an existential crisis."

When I got to the back room, Beau was standing in the corner with his sunglasses on. I had to admit, he did look unusually pale. But that didn't mean he was a vampire.

I dropped my duffel bag on the floor and stared at him. "What are you doing?"

"Do you hear that?" He leaned closer to the wall, the glasses obscuring his eyes. They made him look like a highway patrol cop.

I listened for a second, but all I could hear was the sound of his heavy breathing. "I don't hear anything."

"You're going to think I'm crazy." He ran his hand over the wall. "I think I can hear the electricity running through the wires."

"You need to calm down, Beau. Patrick already told you you're fine. I think you're experiencing a touch of PTSD from what you went through in that jail cell." Being attacked by a vampire would be traumatic for anyone. I should know. But I handled it a whole lot better than he did.

"You're not listening to me, Charley. I'm telling you, I ain't right."

Maybe some logic would help. "Think about it, Beau. What do vampires avoid more than anything?"

His brow furrowed. "Sunlight?"

"Exactly. You've had plenty of it since you got out of jail, and you drove over here this afternoon. Would a vampire be able to do that?"

He thought about it for a second and then pulled off the sunglasses. "Then how do you explain this?"

I had to resist the urge to gasp. Beau's eyes were usually green, but today they were the color of bourbon. "Are those contacts?"

"No, they're not contacts!" He put the glasses back on and crossed his arms, hugging himself tightly. "I can barely see without the glasses when I walk outside, and my skin feels all creepy-crawly. I'm telling you, I'm turning into a vampire."

"Well, I've never heard of anyone turning at the rate of molasses, but something's definitely not right with you."

He cocked his head. "Really? You think?"

I needed to have Patrick take another look at him, and then we'd get a second opinion from Samuel just to be sure. But that would have to wait until morning.

"So much for covering the bar tonight," I said. "I can't have you out there looking like that, and Lucy can't handle it on her own."

"Where's Tucker?"

"She's gone. That vampire who paid you a visit in jail is her ex-boss from Atlanta. Mr. K. We think he took her last night." Or Mag did and delivered her to him.

His jaw went slack. "You're shitting me?"

"I wish I was. It's a long story, and I don't have time to get into it." I needed to make a decision about the bar tonight. With Beau in no shape to work and Dog going down to Reaperstown with us, there was no one to man the ship except for Lucy. And there wasn't a chance in hell I was leaving her here by herself. She'd probably throw a party.

Lucy stuck her head through the door, and she seemed nervous. "There's someone here to see you, Charley."

The first thing I noticed when I went back up front was how dusky it was getting outside. The second thing I saw was Ian Masterson sitting between two of my customers at the bar.

"I guess you're a dusk vampire." He seemed more like the dead-of-night type to me. "Do you garden at dawn too?"

He turned around and pulled his sunglasses off. "Only when I'm planting corpse lilies."

"What are you doing here?" We were supposed to be

meeting down in Reaperstown. Just outside of town to get our act together before heading over to the Beast.

"We have a date." He looked me up and down. "Is that what you're wearing?"

"I haven't changed yet."

He snapped his fingers at Lucy when she walked back behind the bar. "A double," he demanded, pointing to a bottle of bourbon on the shelf.

She looked like she wanted to break his fingers but wisely kept her cool—which was difficult for her—and poured him a glass. She set the drink down in front of him with a hostile glare. "That'll be sixteen bucks."

"Sixteen?" He glanced at the drink. "That's highway robbery."

"You ordered a double," she reminded him with a smug grin.

I let out a deep sigh. "It's on the house. Just drink it fast so we can get out of here." I kept glancing at the door, praying Samuel didn't walk in.

Dog came out of the kitchen and locked eyes with Ian. "I'm going down there with the two of you tonight."

"That's very amusing," Ian said with a chuckle.

"He's not kidding," I said. "He also made a good argument for it. The pack will offer their services in exchange for a cut in Steele's business up here in the northern region of the state."

The glass went still at Ian's lips. "That's not a bad idea. Some extra insurance that will allow us all to leave the Beast tonight in one piece."

My jaw dropped. "Did you doubt we would?" The bastard had me convinced it would be a piece of cake.

"I had a smidge of concern." He shot his bourbon back and set the glass on the bar. "Let's get this over with."

Lucy's eyes walked back and forth between me and Dog.

"You two are leaving me here alone with Beau?" Her frown suddenly turned up into a grin.

Dog glanced around the room. "Where is Beau?"

"Still having that crisis I mentioned. He won't be working tonight."

One of the customers at the bar swiveled on his stool to eavesdrop on the conversation.

I shot him a look. "Mind your own business, Mike. In fact, I'm shutting the place down for the night, so finish your drink." I glanced at his buddy. "You too."

"Don't bother, Mike," Candy said as she walked through the front door. "The bar isn't closing."

"What are you doing here?" I said.

She walked behind the bar and poured a beer from the tap and set it down in front of Mike. "Bartending."

Well, she was qualified. She had more experience mixing drinks than everyone in the room combined. She could probably whip up a Bloody Mary blindfolded.

Candy gave Lucy a dull look. "You got a problem with that?"

"Whatever," Lucy grumbled, brushing past her.

"Good." Her eyes landed on Ian. "If there's so much as a hair on Charley's head out of place when she comes home tonight, I'll hunt you down and make you regret the moment you popped out of your maker's ass."

Ian leaned over the bar with a wicked grin on his face. "I have a good mind to ruffle her hair myself and see your threat."

I was starting to get nervous about the time, so I broke up their foreplay. "We need to go."

Candy's phone rang a second later. She pulled it out and glanced at the number. "You better hurry. It's Samuel again."

"Samuel? Why is he calling you?"

"Because you're not answering your phone. He got my

number from somewhere and started calling as soon as you got into your truck."

My phone was dead when I pulled it out of my pocket. I guess I was still buzzing from that experience in the woods and probably drained the battery.

"I tried to ease his mind, but I guess it didn't work." Candy glanced outside at the fading light. "I'd say you have about ten minutes before he shows up."

She was right. As soon as the sky went dark, he'd be at that door. "Let's get out of here."

"Where's everyone going?" Lucy asked.

"On a fact-finding mission," I said. "Then tomorrow night we're going to clean house."

TWENTY-EIGHT

Not keen on the idea of cramming himself into the truck next to Dog again, Ian met us at an old gas station a mile outside of Reaperstown. The tanks had been dried up for decades, and the building was nothing but a set of unstable walls with windows.

Ian was sitting on the hood of an abandoned car when we pulled up. He hopped off and met us at the truck. "Steele isn't expecting the wolf." He glanced at Dog. "The bouncer will smell him before we reach the door, so let me do the talking."

"Just get us in and out of there as fast as possible," I said.

"Well, that depends on how good an actress you are." He looked me up and down. "You look sufficiently cheap."

He'd instructed me to wear something revealing. Something to wet Victor Steele's taste buds. Something that a vampire's *property* would wear. In other words, something trashy. It was the same outfit I'd worn the other night when I killed that vampire, and I'd broken a speed record changing into it back at the Stag before Samuel could show up.

"Thank God you approve," I said with mock relief.

"I have to convince him that you're mine." He came dangerously close, backing me against the truck. "So, lose the attitude and show some healthy fear when we get down there."

Dog stuck his hand between us and pushed Ian back. "Don't tempt me, vampire."

Ian looked down at his chest as Dog pulled his hand away. "Touch me again, wolf, and I'll make good on claiming her." His fangs descended. "The old-fashioned way. Then I'll kill you and stuff you into one of these rusty tanks."

Dog grinned and backed off with a growl. "Shall we?"

"See you down there." Ian was gone a second later.

We got back in the truck and drove the mile to Reaperstown where Ian was waiting for us in the parking lot behind the Beast. I swear that vampire moved faster than a stream of light.

"Don't do anything to get yourself killed tonight," I said to Dog before getting out. "I'm not as delicate as you think I am. If Steele puts his hands on me, I'll deal with him."

He chuckled. "Right."

Ian seemed a little jumpy when he walked up to the truck. "Don't do that," I said to him. "You don't get to be nervous tonight."

"I'd be a fool not to be, and you should be too." His eyes roamed around the parking lot. "I might have to get a little rough with you in there, so just play along."

Dog shook his head with a humorless laugh. "What the fuck are we getting ourselves into?" Ian opened his mouth to reply, but Dog cut him off. "That wasn't an actual question, asshole."

The love between them was palpable.

I sighed. "Let's get this over with before I puke."

Ian raised his wrist to his fangs and bit into his flesh, drawing a few drops of blood. It was thick and dark. Nearly black. "Help yourself."

"Don't you have a vial or something?"

He grinned. "Afraid not, darlin'."

With a groan, I pulled his wrist to my mouth and licked the wound. To my horror, I liked the taste. There was a sweetness to it, and it gave me instant energy, similar to my own adrenaline rushes.

"That's enough," Dog said, pulling Ian's wrist out of my grip when I pressed my lips to his skin and started to suck.

I shook off the euphoria and stepped back, steadying myself as I tried to hide the instant high it had given me so Ian would wipe that grin off his face. After a moment, I straightened my trashy skirt and took a deep breath. "Let's go."

Just as Ian had said, not one but three vampires blocked the entrance before we made it down the sidewalk to the front door. The one from the other night with the platinum-blond hair was standing in the middle.

Ian got right up in his face. "Victor is expecting us."

When the vampire's eyes shifted to me, his scowl turned into a grin. "Look who we have here. Mr. Steele will make you pay for what you did the other night."

I guess he remembered me.

Then he looked over Ian's shoulder. "The fleabag stays out here."

Dog growled, his fists tightening at his sides. Miraculously, he simmered down and just smiled at the vampire.

"Tell Mr. Steele that the wolf has come with an offer," Ian said. "The pack would like to provide their services." When the vampire wouldn't budge, Ian backed off. "Very well. Tell your boss the meeting is off. I'm sure he won't be too hard on you for blowing the deal."

"Wait." The vampire walked back inside while the other two continued to block the entrance. He came back out a moment later and motioned us in.

My eyes roamed around the club and landed on the bartender with the snake tattoo. When he saw me, his face turned to stone. I thought he was about to jump over the bar and come after me, but the bouncer gave him a look and shook his head.

I glanced at the stage, wondering if the girl dancing on it was doing so of her own free will, or if Steele had let her out of her cage for a few hours to earn her keep. There was no sign of Tucker, but I didn't expect to see her up here. If she was in the place, she was somewhere below the floor we were standing on.

Ian pointed to a hallway on the other side of the club and nudged me to keep moving. At the end of it was a door leading to a set of stairs. It was dark down there, with barely enough light to see the bottom step.

He motioned me through it. "Ladies first."

"I'll go first." Dog muscled past him and descended the stairs.

I followed him down. With each step, the music from the club got quieter while a hard-driving beat came from the basement below. It was coming from a long corridor.

Ian followed us, shutting out the world above as he closed the door behind him. His eyes kept darting around the dim space as his jaw clenched tight, which did nothing to ease my own nerves.

There were doors up and down the hall. Some were shut, but others were wide open. I looked inside the first one and spotted a cage in the corner. It was only about five feet tall and wide. Like some kind of animal crate. I was relieved that it was empty, but halfway down the corridor, I glanced inside a room and spotted a cage that wasn't.

The woman saw me and pressed her face to the bars as she tried to speak around a ball gag in her mouth. Her hands were bound by cord behind her back. It might have been the vampire Tucker had seen in her vision.

Ian pushed me forward. "Keep moving."

Her cries were drowned out by the sound of the music getting louder. There were a lot of empty cages in the rooms as we continued toward the end, but there was no sign of Tucker or Irina. But some of the doors were shut. When I looked in another room, I saw a man sitting in a chair against the wall. He had tubes connected to both arms, and there was blood flowing through them into bags.

He flashed a set of fangs when he saw me looking at him, and his eyes looked hollow. Another man stepped out from behind the door and shut it in my face.

"What the hell is going on in there?" I said to Ian.

"He's a donor."

It shouldn't have surprised me. Victor Steele sold vampire blood, just like the co-op did, only we didn't shove our donors into dingy rooms to siphon them. And it looked like that vampire was about to be bled dry.

We continued down the corridor and stopped when we came to a door at the end. Ian just stood there staring at it.

"Are you going to open it?" Dog said.

Ian shifted his eyes to Dog. "Not unless I want to get my head chewed off. Literally."

The music was loud enough to give me a headache, but I could still hear huffing and grunting noises coming from the other side. "What is that?"

"It's the devil." Ian took a step back. "I'd suggest you move away from that door."

It swung open before I could take his advice. I stumbled when a giant beast came flying out. Dog shoved me out of the way and stepped in its path, growling back with his wolf eyes flickering. The canine stopped but held Dog's gaze with raised hackles.

"Sit!" The booming voice belonged to a vampire standing in the doorway. The dog stopped instantly and planted its rear end on the floor. It was solid black and looked like a cross between a mastiff and a Cane Corso. It might have had a little hellhound mixed in too, because it didn't have eyes like any dog I'd ever seen. They were ruby red, not unlike a vampire's.

The man sneered at Dog and then motioned us inside. Ian went first, grabbing me by my arm on his way in so he could manhandle me across the room. There were at least half a dozen more vampires inside, standing like sentinels around a man who had his back to us in the shadows of the dim room. I assumed it was Victor Steele because of the way the others flanked him. He was bent over slightly with something in his grip. A moan filled the room as he dropped it to the floor. A woman lay sprawled at his feet as he turned around, his tongue flicking at a drop of blood at the edge of his mouth.

My gut instinct was to ask if she was okay, but it was kind of hard to talk over the loud music, and I knew better than to speak unless spoken to. I was Ian's property for the night, so I needed to know my place. I was relieved when her eyes fluttered open and a satisfied sigh escaped her lips. A moment later, one of the vampires lifted her off the floor and carried her through a door at the back of the room.

Steele snapped his fingers, and the music stopped. The huge dog trotted over to him and obediently sat. "You'll have to excuse Diablo. He's very protective." His voice was cavernous.

When I got a good look at Steele, I nearly gasped. He resembled Samuel. Or Samuel resembled him. It was the eyes. He had the same striking blue eyes. It shouldn't have surprised me. He was Samuel's maker, and like any procreator, some physical traits were passed on to offspring. To progeny. He was older, though. Probably turned in his mid-forties. Tall and handsome, he was impeccably dressed in a suit that probably cost as much as a used car. But there was a cruelness in his eyes that Samuel hadn't inherited. And after what I'd just seen down that corridor, there was no hiding the monster beneath the facade.

He strolled over to an ornately carved chair and took a seat.

Crossing his legs, his gaze settled on Dog as he spoke to Ian. "You brought me gifts. I'll get back to the wolf in a moment." Then he turned his attention to me. "Charlotte Underwood, but I believe you prefer Charley. Daughter of Delia Underwood." A smile slid up his face. "My progeny's lover."

Ian twisted his head to look at me with arched brows.

So Samuel was right. His maker could still sense him. He'd sensed him in my bed, which made me even more uncomfortable with the way he was looking at me. I didn't waver as I glared back at him, but I was smart enough not to remind him that he'd abandoned his progeny. Who Samuel slept with was none of his business.

"You're a very bold woman, Charley. Not many would defy me." His smile slowly flattened. "Or have the guts to lie to me."

In my defense, I didn't know who or what he was when his men walked into my bar looking for Tucker. But even if I did, I still would have lied to protect her.

"I've enjoyed our game. Have you?"

I doubted it was an actual question, so I chose not to answer.

He turned back to Dog. "You have two minutes to convince me not to kill you. Go."

"Now, why would you do something that foolish?" Dog said.

I detected a slight twitch at the edge of Victor Steele's tight lips. "Your two minutes are ticking by fast."

"Because you need me. I don't know how you do business down in Atlanta, but up here it takes connections. We don't trust outsiders. In other words, the pack wants a cut in exchange for letting you go about your business in North Georgia."

He was doing an awfully good job of sounding like a corrupt wolf.

Steele glanced at the vampire standing next to him. Before Dog could react, two of the henchmen had him in a firm hold.

Victor Steele's fangs clicked into place. "Bring him here."

They started to muscle Dog across the room. He dropped down on all fours, slipping through their hands. The wolf turned and lunged at the one on his right, locking his jaws around the vampire's neck. The other one backed off when he clamped down harder. Then Dog trained his amber eyes on Victor Steele while slowly crushing the vampire's neck.

"Enough!" Steele stood up and nodded to the others. Every vampire in the room backed up to the wall. "Let him go, and you have my word I won't kill you."

Hesitating, Dog finally dropped the vampire and shifted. Then he stepped back toward us.

The vampire rolled away, gripping his mauled neck as he climbed to his feet. "We'll be meeting in an alley real soon, wolf. You better watch your back."

As the vampire was turning around to join the others against the wall, Steele grabbed him and sank his fangs into his neck. He tore at his guard's flesh and then placed a dagger at his throat, slicing it deeply until his head wobbled and flipped backward. A second swipe with the blade severed it, sending the vampire's head tumbling to the floor. Diablo eyed it and licked his chops, but he didn't dare move from his spot.

Steele dropped the vampire and stepped over the body, pulling a handkerchief from his fancy jacket to wipe the blood from his mouth. "Continue."

"Kill me and you'll have the pack to reckon with," Dog warned. "But my wolves aren't the only ones you'll have to deal with."

Steele narrowed his eyes. "Such as?"

"Folks do things differently up here in the mountains. There are all kinds of packs in these parts, moonshiners being the most volatile." Dog raised a brow. "Now those are some batshit-crazy wolves."

Steele was getting impatient. "Make your point."

Dog grinned. "There are packs that don't take kindly to those who try to set up shop up here in the woods. Without a proper introduction and their blessing, that is. You'll have to pay for the privilege."

"That's your problem," Steele said. "Pay them out of your cut."

Dog nodded. "Sounds like we have a deal."

The vampire sat back down and shifted his eyes to me. Then he looked at Ian. "Now that we have that settled, let's move on to other business. You say Charley is yours?"

"That's right," Ian replied. "I've claimed her."

A cold smile slid up Steele's face. "I believe you're too late for that. *Samuel* has already claimed her, and my progeny's property is technically mine."

So much for Ian's bright idea to give me his blood. But it was utter bullshit for Victor Steele to try to assert maker's rights. He'd given up those rights when he abandoned Samuel. But how was I going to argue the case without infuriating the vampire? He didn't seem like the type to tolerate a woman mouthing off to him.

Despite the revelation about me and Samuel, Ian managed to come up with a save. "She doesn't belong to Samuel anymore. He offered her to me in exchange for something younger."

Younger?

I kept my cool, reminding myself of why we were here. We still needed to find out if Tucker and Irina were somewhere in the basement.

"She's all mine now."

Steele's voice dropped an octave. "But I want her."

"And you have something I want." Ian stepped behind me and ran his hands over my shoulders and down my arms, bringing his lips dangerously close to my neck. His breath walked all over my skin as he spoke. "As much as I'll hate to give her up, I'm open to an equal exchange."

"You mean Irina? I have an interested buyer, so she's worth a lot of money to me." He drummed his fingers against the armrest of the chair. "I'll have to think about it."

Ian patted me on the ass. "Let me remind you. Vampires are a dime a dozen, but Charley is a witch. You won't find many of those for sale." After allowing his words to sink in, he shoved me toward Steele. "Get a whiff of this. I wouldn't think about it for long, if I were you."

I shot Ian a hostile glare over my shoulder. I owed him a punch in the face, and I intended to make good on that debt. As I was turning back to Victor Steele, he grabbed me and pulled me into his lap. I cringed from the feel of him underneath me.

"Yes, I think you're right." He flicked his hand at one of his guards. "Bring the one with the pink hair."

"Wait," Ian said. "I still have my own unfinished business with Charley." A salacious grin appeared on his face. "You're not the only one she's disrespected."

"What are you saying?" Steele asked.

"I need one more night with her. To teach the woman a lesson in respect. After that, she's all yours. As long as you turn over Irina, of course."

The vampire gripped me tighter. "I could take her right now and give you nothing. Keep them both."

"But you won't," Dog said. "You need the cooperation of my pack and you need Masterson, or your budding business venture will turn into a train wreck. I'll personally see to that."

The two of them glared at each other for a moment, and then Steele shoved me off his lap. "I want her intact," he said to Ian. "Is that clear?"

He grinned. "Of course."

Steele snapped his fingers and two of his men came across the room to see us out.

"Before we go," Ian said. "I want to see Irina."

The vampire squinted. "Why? Don't you trust me to hand her over?"

"I have no doubt you will. I just want to see what condition she's in." He narrowed his eyes back at Steele. "Is there a problem?"

Steele gave a nod, and one of the vampires slipped through the door at the back of the room and returned a few minutes later with Irina. When we first met, she was a feisty thing. All vim and vigor and ready to choke me out. But now she was nothing but an empty shell. Her bright eyes had dulled, and her skin was shockingly pale.

Ian strode toward her but was cut off by Steele's guards. Diablo snapped at him, keeping him at bay. "What have you done to her?" he growled.

Victor smiled. "Nothing that a good feeding won't cure. Starvation is a very effective way to control troublesome vampires. Although most of them are more than happy to cooperate once they realize I'm the key to their survival." He gave her a quick glance. "Irina was not."

Ian looked like he was about to do something that would blow the deal, but he managed to rein himself in. "I expect her to be fed before we make the exchange tomorrow night." It was killing him. I could see it in his eyes. The heartless Ian Masterson actually cared about someone other than himself. I'd go as far as to say he loved her.

A smile slowly spread across Victor Steele's face. "Of course." Then it vanished. "But if you fail to show up with Charley in exactly twenty-four hours, I'll throw Irina in a cage and let her waste away until she's nothing but a pile of ash."

The vampire led Irina back out of the room. A moment later, Victor Steele was on his feet and heading for the same door with his hellhound at his side. "Where's Tucker?" I asked before he could walk through it.

He stopped but didn't turn. "She's around here somewhere.

I'll reunite the two of you tomorrow night. In fact, you can share a cage. I intend to keep you both for a very long time."

The words made my blood run cold as he disappeared from the room, leaving me to imagine the fate waiting for me if tomorrow night was an epic failure. I doubted even the pack would be able to save me then.

TWENTY-NINE

I couldn't get out of the Beast fast enough. I kept looking over my shoulder on the way to the parking lot thinking Diablo was about to come around the corner and take us down. After climbing into the truck, I pulled out of the lot and took the turn so fast that Dog's knees slammed into the dashboard.

"Take it easy, Charley. I only have two of these."

"Hold on tight. We're almost out of this godforsaken hellhole of a town."

We drove the short distance to Ian's house to debrief. Seeing the place again made me shudder because, the last time I was there, my best friend was being tortured in the basement. It was a creepy old place that screamed vampire.

"Do you own this house, or are you just borrowing it?" I asked Ian when he opened the front door. It made me wonder if the owners were tied up somewhere on the second floor. Or dead.

"Of course it's mine. I bought it during the Great Depression for a steal."

"Why doesn't that surprise me?" The vampire was a real opportunist.

"Let's get on with it," Dog said. "We need a plan to kill that son of a bitch."

I recalled the conversation between him and Victor Steele. "Moonshining wolf shifters?"

He chuckled. "You'd be surprised at what's up in those hills."

"And what was with that guy giving blood?" I asked Ian, recalling the man with tubes sticking out of his arms.

Dog snickered. "Said the woman who runs a vampire blood co-op out of her bar."

"Only we don't bleed our donors to death. They bring their blood to us voluntarily. That man looked half dead, for God's sake."

"Not quite," Ian said. "He was donating his blood in exchange for his life. Why would Steele pay wholesale for something he can simply take?" He chuckled quietly. "What that poor sap doesn't realize is that eventually Steele *will* drain him dry."

Which made me wonder about Ian's hustle. "How about you? Is your business model the same as Victor Steele's?"

"Don't insult me, Charley. I pay my suppliers."

I bet he nickeled and dimed them to death, and then he supplemented his profits through extortion, like he tried to do to me. There were moments when I thought Ian Masterson might actually be a decent vampire, but then things always seemed to creep in and change my opinion of him.

"There were a lot of empty cages in the rooms down that corridor," I said.

Ian shrugged. "And that's just a taste of things to come. Victor Steele intends to fill them all. He'll exploit Crimson for every vampire he can get his hands on before moving on to the next unfortunate town."

A growl came from Dog's mouth. "That'll never happen. That vampire dies tomorrow night."

"You're right about that," Ian said as his lips curled into a snarl. "But you're wrong about tomorrow night. Irina is dying. I can feel it. She won't last another twenty-four hours, so we're going in there tonight."

It took me a second to comprehend what he'd just said. "We don't even have a plan yet." The vampire had clearly lost his mind. "I think your judgment is clouded."

His eyes bored into mine. "Plan? I'll give you a plan. We're going to rip their heads off!"

"I hate to say it, but I think Ian's right," Dog said.

"Then you've both lost your minds."

"Think about it, Charley. Victor Steele is expecting Ian to walk in there tomorrow night to hand you over. He'll have every one of his vampires at the ready. If we go in there tonight, they won't see us coming. It's the only way to take them off guard."

"There are more of them than you think," Ian said. "That door Victor left through at the back of the room leads to the second half of the basement. To a much larger area. There's another corridor with rooms where they're keeping Irina and your bartender." The anger in his eyes flared. "I haven't been down there since he bought the place, but I suspect it's where they store and package their product."

I huffed. "You mean the blood they've been siphoning from those vampires down there."

"Among other things. You can bet the operation is heavily guarded in that room, so you can double however many vampires you saw tonight. Like Dog said, it's in our best interest to go in there now and take them by surprise."

"Where's the entrance to that tunnel?" Dog asked.

"At the end of the corridor on the other side. It's far enough away from the main room to buffer some of the noise we'll have to make to get in. That obnoxious music will buffer the rest."

"How many vampires do you have to take with us?" Dog asked.

Ian shrugged. "Seven. Maybe eight."

"With the pack, we have six more," said Dog.

Ian scoffed. "That's pathetic."

The extended pack was significantly larger than that, but I suspected Dog was only bringing in his top wolves.

Dog looked him in the eye. "Unlike you, I'm not risking anyone unless I know they'll come out of that basement alive." Then he smiled. "Besides, one wolf equals two vampires."

"Enough with the testosterone contest," I said. "Let's focus here."

Dog got back to the non-existent plan. "There's one thing I know without a doubt. We'll need to get some of those vampires out of that basement before we break through the tunnel door. We're going to need a distraction."

* * *

"Who's your decorator?" Candy asked as Ian led her into his office.

"Why, do you want a referral?"

She let out a laugh. "I want to fire him or her personally."

I eyed her getup. "You look… nice." She was wearing a trench coat that only came halfway down her thighs.

"Nice isn't what I was going for."

"I was being polite. You look like a stripper on your way to a bachelor party."

She pulled the coat down an inch or two over her legs. "That's more like it. Let's just get this show on the road before I change my mind."

Dog walked into the room and got a look at her. "That'll work."

She smiled at him. "I'm just aging like a fine wine."

Candy didn't age, she ripened to perfection. I just hoped

her knees were up to the task. Not to mention her legs if we had to make a run for it.

"What do you make of it?" Ian asked Dog.

The vampires and the pack were already in the tunnel inspecting the obstacle between them and the basement. The door leading to it that had been sealed from the inside.

"Easy. We just have to time it right."

The plan was for Candy and me to walk into the Beast and create enough of a distraction to bring half that basement upstairs to investigate. That would level the playing field down there. When enough of them came rushing down that hallway into the club, that was my cue to text one of Ian's vampires back at the house, to deliver the command to break down the door in that tunnel. After that, it was up to us to get out of there and wait back here until it was over.

I took a deep breath and straightened my tight skirt. "Then I guess it's time."

"Charley," Dog said as I followed Candy out of the office. "You be careful in there."

"You too. Don't get yourself killed trying to be a hero." He was smiling at me, but I could see the worry on his face. The uncertainty. The way I saw it, we had a fifty-fifty chance of killing Victor Steele and getting Tucker out of that basement. But in my eyes, Dog came first. Always did and always would. If it came down to saving himself or finishing the job, God help me, but he needed to leave her behind. But enough of thinking like that. Come hell or high water, I was going to make sure we all came out there alive.

THIRTY

"How do I look?" Candy asked.

I turned her around and brushed some lint from the back of her coat. Not that it would matter to any of those letches inside. "Like a hot mess, but in a good way."

She smiled nervously. "Then let's do this."

"Okay. I'm ready."

As soon as we walked inside the Beast, we were met by that platinum-blond vampire. He tried to grab me when he recognized me, but Candy stepped in his way.

"She belongs to Ian Masterson. Touch her, and you'll be a pile of ash when the sun comes up." Victor Steele may have purchased the Beast, but Ian was still a heavyweight in Reaperstown.

He smiled, revealing his fangs. "Then why is she here without him?"

After I killed that vampire, I guess I wasn't welcome. At least not without an escort.

I figured boldness would get me more respect than hiding behind Candy's back, so I spoke up. "Ian gave me permission to go out." God, I hated saying that. I almost added *until he turns me over to your boss tomorrow night*, but for all I knew, this vampire was unaware of the pending exchange. He was just the bouncer. "He's meeting me here later," I said when he seemed unconvinced. I reached into my pocket. "But I can call Ian and tell him you won't let us in?"

There was a tinge of fear in the vampire's eyes. He stepped aside without another word and motioned to the bartender to back off.

"The floor is yours," I said to Candy as soon as he walked away. "We need to move fast."

"I'm going to need a stiff drink first." She went to the bar and ordered a double bourbon.

The bartender glared at me with a thirsty look in his eyes as he poured her a drink. I got the distinct feeling he wanted to eat me. It's a strange feeling knowing you're prey. Just one wrong move away from becoming someone's dinner.

Candy downed her bourbon and looked at the stage across the room. "Okay. It's time. I'm a little rusty, so wish me luck."

On her way over to the guy controlling the music in the corner, she stripped off her trench coat and tossed it on a chair, revealing a fifty-seven-going-on-thirty-five body adorned with nothing but a pair of pasties, a G-string, and the amulet around her neck. She looked hotter than me.

After making a request, she walked across the room like a boss, her mane of auburn hair swaying with her stride. The woman was pure confidence, or maybe it was the bourbon. Then the deep bass of a song came over the speakers as she stepped up on the stage and shooed the dancer off. Every eye in the place turned when she grabbed the pole and climbed it with nothing but her hands, her legs extended straight out in a V.

"Rusty?" I said to myself.

She wrapped her legs around the pole and twirled her way down, going into a one-handed spin as she landed on her four-inch stilettos. Then she leaned against it and arched her back, slithering down the length of it like a snake.

The music turned hypnotic as Candy reached for her amulet and stroked it to the rhythm. The chatter in the club ceased as everyone focused on the stage. I could feel the atmosphere in the room change as Candy continued to stroke the sapphire, releasing magic into the air. People kept moving closer, gyrating with her movements. Hell, I started to move my own hips but shook it off before I lost sight of why we were there.

A vampire at the back of the room walked toward her. He finished his beer and set the empty bottle on the stage, grabbing for Candy's G-string.

She stepped out of his reach, with her long legs planted wide, and gave him a warning look. When he ignored it and climbed up on the stage, she kneed him in the groin, sending him tumbling off.

The music abruptly stopped. Candy clutched her amulet as her eyes scanned the room, daring anyone else to make a move.

"Keep dancing, grandma!" someone shouted from the back.

"Here we go," I muttered, feeling a bar fight coming on, which was exactly what we wanted. We just needed to make it count.

A grin slowly spread across Candy's face as she crooked her finger at the heckler. When he strolled up to the stage, she grabbed the empty beer bottle next to her feet and smashed it over his head. "I'll give you grandma, junior." As he tried to shake off the blow, she kicked out and drove her stiletto heel into his chest.

The vampire fell to the floor and glanced down at the hole in his ribcage, his fangs descending as he looked back up at her. "I'm gonna to take my time with you, bitch!" As he was climbing to his feet, his face froze. He looked back down at the wound, dead center over his black heart, and started to tremble.

Candy walked up to the edge of the stage and peered down at him. "Vintage wooden stilettos, baby. This *bitch* comes prepared."

His body started to shake violently, and suddenly he was crumbling like a wall of dirt. When it was over, he was nothing but a pile of ash on the floor.

The spell broke, and every vampire in the room was snarling at Candy.

She jumped off the stage and ran toward me. "It's time to accelerate the plan."

The objective wasn't for me and Candy to have to kill a bunch of vampires. We just needed to get Victor Steele's men out of that basement. Then it was time for the two of us to leave before the real fireworks began. But if there were a few casualties while we created the distraction, so be it.

"Just remember what happened out in those woods," she said.

"I thought you didn't know what happened out there?"

"I don't, but I've got a good idea."

The vampires in the room were looking hungry. In a matter of seconds, we'd be lunch if we didn't do something fast.

Candy looked across the room at the stage. "Focus on that thing."

I followed her gaze. "Then what?"

"Then give it all you've got."

The crowd started to move toward us, and the ring on my finger lit up in a blaze. Candy looked at it and then gripped her amulet tightly, holding it out in front of her. A stream of light shot from it and hit the stage.

"Focus, Charley!"

I held my arms up when they started to tremble. Light traveled across them and into my hands, creating the same blue mist I'd seen out in the woods. When it pooled in my palms, I brought them together to create a sphere. Then I spread my fingers, releasing it. A wave of energy flowed through me as the magic shot across the room, intersecting with the light coming from the amulet. The round stage lit up in a glow and flipped on its side, spinning like a coin before slamming into the crowd.

For a moment, I was blinded by the brilliance of the light. When it faded, I saw that a fight had broken out. Furniture was flying.

Never underestimate the predictability of a bunch of drunk vampires.

My eyes shot to the bartender across the room. His phone was pressed to his ear. "Vampires should be coming up from that basement any second now," I said to Candy.

"Then it's time for us to leave while we still can." She nodded at the bouncer. He was in the thick of it across the room, leaving the entrance wide open.

We stayed near to the wall and worked our way around the ruckus toward the front door. Halfway to freedom, all hell broke loose as Steele's vampires came rushing down the hallway. I counted at least a dozen, which I prayed was enough to thin out the competition below, and sent the text message for Ian and the pack to go in.

Candy slipped out the door, but as I was about to follow her, someone grabbed me from behind and threw me into the mob. I hit the floor hard. The bartender was grinning down at me when I looked up. He reached for my ankle and started to drag me toward him, but another vampire slammed into him and drove him into the wall.

I scrambled to my feet, dodging fists, only to take a kick to the gut. With the wind knocked out of me, I fell to the floor, struggling to breathe. A vampire was standing over me, straddling me with his heavy boots and licking his fangs. And then I felt it. That sickening feeling of something crawling inside me. I lurched, and a stream of blue light floated from my mouth like smoke. It snaked around his legs, growing darker as it continued up his body and wrapped around his torso.

He stumbled back, clawing at the black mist. "Get it off me!"

I blinked a few times to check my vision, but I wasn't seeing things. The mist had solidified, replaced by the spider. It crawled up to his head and engulfed his face, giving me a chance to get away.

After climbing to my feet, I looked at the exit, but it was blocked. The hallway was the only way out. It was clear, so I ran to the end and opened the basement door, looking back to make sure no one was behind me. That same intense music was coming from below as I went down the steps, and I could hear the battle taking place at the end of the long corridor.

I slowly worked my way down the long stretch of rooms, clueless about what I was going to do when I got to the end. To my right, I heard that same crying from earlier that night. I walked into the room and saw the female vampire still locked in that cage. She'd managed to work her hands free and had taken the ball gag out of her mouth. When she started to rattle the bars and plead for help, I placed my finger to my lips to quiet her.

After shutting the door behind me, I walked up to the cage, careful not to get within reach until we'd established some ground rules. "I'm going to get you out of there, but you have to listen to me."

There was caution in her eyes. "Okay."

"What's your name?"

"Maggie."

"Well, Maggie, you hear that noise?"

She listened for a moment. "Yeah?"

"There's a siege taking place in the next room." I couldn't think of another word to describe it. "Friends of mine are about to kill the vampire who put you in that cage."

Her face went cold as her fangs popped in and out. "Good! But I want a bite of him first!"

"You'll have to get in line for that." I could name at least three or four people ahead of her who wanted a shot at Victor Steele, including me. "What I'm saying is, you need to lie low until it's over. I'll let you out, but you need to stay in this room until I come back for you."

Her eyes filled with panic. "No!"

"You don't have a choice." I looked at the lock on the cage. "I don't suppose you know where the key is?"

She pointed to the door. "Over there."

The key was hanging from a hook next to it. After retrieving it, I unlocked the cage and pulled the door open. "You can take your chances and try to go out through the club upstairs. I wouldn't advise it, but it's your neck."

I went back into the hallway, checking the other rooms on my way down the corridor. I found two more women locked in cages, and like with the first room, the cage keys were hanging next to the doors.

There was one more room on the left before the door to the main basement where we'd come face-to-face with Victor Steele. I hadn't looked inside earlier that night because the door was shut. When I opened it, it was pitch-black inside. But I heard something and felt for the light switch. I had to muffle a gasp when the room lit up. There was a man chained to the wall, with heavy steel shackles around his wrists and ankles. His head hung like dead weight as his chin pressed to his chest, and I could see blood on his forehead.

He stirred and lifted his head slightly as his eyes opened. "Charley?"

"Mag? What happened to you?" I looked back at the door to see if the key to the shackles was hanging on a hook, but it wasn't.

He spat blood from his mouth and yanked at the restraints.

"You've got to get these off me." When he yanked at them again, they cut into his wrists. "She's on the other side of the basement. Beyond that door at the end of the hall."

"Who?"

"Tucker!"

Well, that blew our theory to hell. "So I guess you're not working for Victor Steele."

He cocked his head. "Does it look like it? His vampires broke into her apartment and took us both."

Dog was right. Mag was with her when she disappeared. It just wasn't for the reasons we thought. "Can't you just shift out of those shackles?"

He shook his head. "You see this thing around my neck?"

"The necklace?" Mag didn't seem like the jewelry-wearing type, but that's what it looked like.

"It's a lycan repellent. Dirty magic." He laughed bitterly. "I can't even summon my own wolf."

I'd never heard of such a thing, but I was going to get it off him.

"Don't!" he growled when I reached for the chain, but it was too late. I got a wicked jolt, sending me flying back against the wall.

"Motherf—!" I slid to the floor, wincing from the pain. But as I pumped my fist it subsided, and light glowed from my palm.

"I warned you." He yanked at one of the shackles again. "I'll have to do it myself, but I need to free a hand."

I climbed to my feet and walked back over to examine the restraints. The chains connecting them to the wall were only a few inches long, so there was little room for error. "How much pain can you tolerate?" I was pretty sure I could break one of the wrist shackles, but it was going to hurt.

He looked down at my glowing hand. "You really are just like Delia." Then he brought his eyes back up to mine. "Do it, but try not to kill me."

I'd do my best. And as soon as he shifted I figured that hand would be good as new.

"You might want to turn your head the other way." No sense blinding him if it backfired.

He braced himself as the ring lit up. The glow intensified, but this time it only flowed to my right hand. The left one was a dud. "I'm going to have to improvise here."

"Just do it!"

I reached for the shackle but stopped short of touching it. The blue light stretched toward the metal, causing it to heat up until it was red-hot molten steel.

Mag gritted his teeth as the shackle began to melt, fighting back a scream when his wrist ignited. His arm fell away from the wall a moment later, allowing him to rip the chain off his neck.

A howl filled the room as he shifted into the wolf and ran out.

"Wait!" I yelled.

The wolf slammed into the door at the end of the corridor. It held, so he came at it again. This time it cracked. He backed up halfway down the long hallway and charged, hitting the door a third time with all his strength, knocking it off its hinges.

I ran into the room after him, stepping over a body that was still moving. A vampire. I stumbled away when he grabbed at my legs.

Mag disappeared through the second door as I spotted another wolf fighting with a vampire at the back of the room. It was Dog. He looked up when he saw me, and the vampire dug his fangs into his leg. Dog howled and grabbed him by the neck, shaking him as he squeezed his jaws tighter. The vampire's head twisted grotesquely, eventually severing.

Dog shifted and growled, "Get out of here, Charley!" The wolf reappeared a moment later when another vampire lunged at him.

I turned to run back out but stopped when the bartender came through the door. He took his time stalking toward me, the jaws of his snake tattoo seeming to close in around his face as he smiled.

When he picked up the pace, I hurled a ball of energy at him. I didn't even have to think about it. It was just a reflex. It hit him square in the chest, his body absorbing the light. A moment later, his torso lit up. The bastard convulsed as the light crawled along his limbs. When it reached his head, he began to crumble like an after-dinner mint.

I was about to turn around and get into the fight when someone grabbed me from behind, pulling me into a tight grip with my arms pinned at my sides. The cold feel of a blade pressed to my throat as a voice whispered in my ear, "I've enjoyed our game, Charley. It would pain me to kill you." Victor Steele brushed his cheek against mine, taking in my scent. "I had such interesting plans for us."

Dog shifted and came toward us, glaring at the vampire like he wanted to rip his head off.

"But I'll slit your throat if your wolf takes another step." The knife pressed deeper into my skin, just enough to up the stakes.

I winced but didn't dare struggle.

The fighting stopped, and the room fell silent. Steele's vampires stepped forward and formed a line in front of him.

Ian emerged from the adjoining room and stood next to Dog. The two of them had a silent conversation, and then Ian fixed his eyes on mine for a moment before addressing Steele. "So, how do we end this?"

I heard footsteps coming from the doorway behind us and the distinct sound of a click. The cocking of a gun. My heart started to beat faster as the vampire slowly turned me around with him.

Steele let out a low laugh. "I thought I smelled something rotten."

Samuel's revolver was inches from his maker's face. "Garbage like you should know." His eyes shifted to mine briefly before landing back on Steele's. "Let her go and I'll kill you quickly."

"A hunter hunting his own maker. How amusing."

Samuel's eyes were nearly black. Filled with loathing. Hatred.

"You know you can't kill me with or without a gun," Steele said. "So join me. Since you've become so fond of Charley, I'm happy to share her with you."

A smile barely lifted the edges of Samuel's mouth. "I am fond of Charley. Very. But you're wrong about my ability to kill you. In fact, I've dreamed about it since the night you took my mortality and left me for dead, which is why I can indeed kill you. You relinquished your control over me." His smile vanished. "I've fantasized about seeing your head explode every night since."

"Right. I shouldn't have just left you to die." Steele dug the blade deeper into my neck, causing me to wince again. "I should have ripped your heart out and eaten it!"

Samuel raised his brows. "Yes, you should have."

The gun fired, sending a bullet between Victor Steele's eyes. He dropped the knife and released me, his face a canvas of shock as he stepped back and looked down. His skin turned translucent as a flare of light emitted from the center of his chest. It radiated from his pores and shot from every orifice of his body. Like a sunburst.

Samuel took my hand. "We should back up."

A moment later, Victor Steele exploded. I turned and covered my face, hoping I wouldn't spend the next week pulling pieces of vampire guts out of my hair. Then I looked back at Samuel. "The sunlight bullet?"

There was no satisfaction on his face. Just an air of finality. "I was saving it for him."

I turned when I heard something hit the floor. Half the vampires in the room were dropping like flies. Crumbling and turning to ash. Victor Steele's progeny were dying. He'd never released them, sealing their fate. But it didn't surprise me. A vampire like Steele thrived on controlling people.

Tucker came running through the door at the back of the room and looked down at the mess on the floor. "Is he dead?"

"He's deader than dead," I said. "You don't have to worry about the King anymore."

Dog saw Mag standing by the door watching her. "We need to talk."

Mag nodded. "Tomorrow. I need to get Tucker home."

I glanced around the room. "Where did Ian go?"

Right as I said it, he came from the other room with Irina and walked straight toward the door leading to the corridor.

"Where are you going?" I asked him.

"To make it clear who the boss is in Reaperstown."

Something told me the Beast would be under new ownership by the end of the week.

We were about to leave when I heard sounds coming from somewhere in the room. Whining. "What is that?"

Loki nodded to the corner. "It's that mongrel over there."

Diablo was cowering under a table, his massive paws shaking when I walked toward him. "What did you do to him?"

Loki shrugged. "Nothing." He flashed his wolf eyes at the dog and growled. "I guess he's not as vicious as he looks."

I bent down and slowly stuck my hand out toward the dog, hoping I didn't regret it. The poor thing flinched, his ruby eyes dulling to black. He finally got up the nerve to sniff it and then licked my fingers. I wasn't exactly sure what to do with him, but I'd figure it out. "We can't just leave him here. Those vampires will probably eat him."

Dog shook his head and groaned. "Fuck. Anyone got a leash?"

THIRTY-ONE

I woke up and reached for Samuel, feeling his slightly cool skin against my hand. He was still there. It hadn't all been a dream.

He rolled over and gazed down at me. "Good morning." When he kissed me, I melted into the mattress as the nightmare of the past few days faded away.

I never thought I'd hear him say those words to me. "I like waking up with you."

But it wasn't actually morning. We'd stayed in bed all day. I was exhausted and needed some time off, and Samuel was more than happy to spend it with me. We just needed to make a few adjustments.

The room was dark. We'd closed every curtain and blind in the house. I even pinned a blanket over the bedroom window to make sure not a single ray of sunlight got through. Several pairs of blackout curtains were on my shopping list.

I turned to face him when he rolled onto his back. "Will you be in trouble with your employer when he finds out you killed Victor Steele?" He was supposed to deliver the vampire to the man who hired him, not kill him. "He'll probably want the bounty money back."

Samuel tucked his hand behind his head and stroked my cheek with the other. "He can have it. This was never about the money anyway."

I was curious about something else. "How did you know where to find me last night?" I was long gone by the time it was dark enough for him to venture outside, and it wasn't like I'd left a trail of breadcrumbs.

His hand wandered down to my thigh, stroking the spot where he'd bitten me. "My blood is inside you, Charley, and yours is inside me. I can sense you."

I squinted at him. "Then why can't I sense you?"

"Because you're not a vampire."

"True."

When my brow furrowed and I looked away, he reached for my chin to turn my face back to his. "What's wrong?"

"Will Ian be able to sense me?" I'd only swallowed a small amount of his blood, but it made me nervous to even think about that vampire being able to track me.

"Possibly, but with my blood inside you, his will quickly run its course." His blue eyes darkened. "I'll make sure of that. In fact, I should probably give you more."

"Uh... maybe later." I still had to work tonight, and Samuel's blood was intoxicating.

I liked the idea of Samuel being able to feel me inside of him, but I also liked my independence. Maybe I didn't always want to be found. Especially by Ian Masterson.

Seeing the look on my face, he propped himself up. "I can't ignore it, Charley, but I promise not to intrude on your life unless you need me." His relaxed eyes grew more intense. "Like yesterday afternoon. What was going on with you? I was getting some seriously strange vibes."

So that's why he was blowing up my phone. I guess even a vampire couldn't see inside the Squad's warped world. And that was a good thing. I shuddered to think of what would have happened if Samuel had seen that creature attacking me. He might have gotten himself killed trying to find me in broad daylight.

"I'll tell you about it later. What time is it?"

He checked his phone. "Almost seven thirty."

"Seven thirty!" I glanced at the window. The faint glow of the sun around the edges of the blanket had faded away. It was dark outside. "I need to get to the Stag." I was surprised Dog hadn't called me by now. He knew I was with Samuel and was probably hoping I'd stay home for a well-needed night off. But I'd been in bed long enough.

As I was getting up, I tripped over something on the floor. Diablo yipped and jumped. I'd left him in the living room after feeding him some bacon and eggs that morning, but I guess he preferred my bedroom where he could smell me. I couldn't blame the poor thing. His world had just been turned upside down, and I was the only thing he had left. He'd stuck to me like glue half the night until Samuel and I retired to the bedroom.

"You might want to let him outside," Samuel said.

I hadn't walked him since morning, and I was hoping I wouldn't find a present on the living room floor when I went out there.

"You want to go for a walk?" His ears perked up. "Well, let's go." After seeing Diablo jump out of my truck last night, Rex was probably gone for good.

As Samuel climbed off the bed and came toward me, the dog growled. "I don't think he likes me."

I shrugged. "I think he's just being protective." I was his savior after all. "Don't worry. He's not staying for long." The last thing I needed was a dog, and Beau had been talking about getting one for ages. And he wanted a big one. Well, I had a big one for him. "I'm going to talk Beau into taking him."

Samuel scoffed. "Beau? The man is a child. How's he going

to take care of that?" He nodded to the massive canine standing next to me. "We're not even sure what that thing is."

Beau was immature at times, but he was responsible enough to pay his rent and do his own laundry. And he had a big yard. "He might be a little unusual, but he's still a dog. I think it's a perfect match."

I didn't have to ask the dog to follow me when I walked out of the bedroom. He was glued to me again. But when I stepped out on the porch, I took just as much comfort from that "vicious" dog at my side as he took from me. It was dark outside, and the mild anxiety was still present. Victor Steele was dead, but I imagined it would take a while to shake the feeling that a threat was looming over me whenever I walked out of my house.

When we went back inside a few minutes later, Samuel was putting on his jacket.

"Are you leaving?"

"I need to take care of a few things."

Meaning he needed to make that call to his employer, I assumed. "Will you drop by the Stag when you're done?"

He kissed me on his way out. "Try to stop me."

After Samuel left, I went into the kitchen to quickly cook something up for Diablo and refill his water bowl. Instead of springing the dog on Beau at the bar, I intended to ease into the subject of adopting him first. I'd pick up some dog food on my way home.

"Don't get used to it," I said, pulling a carton of eggs from the refrigerator to whip up an omelet for him before leaving for the Stag. "This isn't Club Med."

* * *

Dog glanced at me through the order window with a grin when I walked into the Stag.

"Don't look at me like that," I said to him as I walked up to the bar.

He grinned wider. "How's that vampire of yours?"

I couldn't contain my own smile from the memory of the last twenty-four hours. Most of which had been spent in bed. "Who? Samuel?" Even Lucy was giving me a look.

On our way out of the Beast last night, I'd told Tucker to take tonight off. After what she'd been through, she needed some recovery time. I was sure Mag was helping her.

Speaking of which.

I looked back at Dog through the window. "Did you settle things with Mag?"

He grunted. "We're talking."

That was good to hear because wolves were notorious for their mating habits. I had a feeling Magnus Ryan wasn't going anywhere. The way he was looking at Tucker last night, you'd have thought she walked on water. He was eyeing her like she was his.

Candy walked into the Stag with a grin on her face and took a seat at the bar. "Did you have a good rest?" She pointed to a bottle of scotch. "I'll have a glass of that."

Lucy poured her a drink and set the bottle down in front of her. She lingered, despite the fact that a customer was waving at her from the other end.

"Why is everyone so interested in my love life?" Though it was nice that I actually had one for a change.

When Samuel came strolling through the front door a moment later, I felt a flutter.

"That was fast," I said when he walked up to us.

"It was just a phone call I needed to make." He nodded to the bottle of scotch. "I'll have one of those, please."

I grabbed the bottle before Lucy could. "Go take care of your customer. And where's Beau?" I said as she was walking away.

"In the back. He's been there for a while."

It was Friday night, so he needed to be behind the bar.

After pouring Candy her drink, I went to find him. Not only to tell him to get back up front but also to mention the dog. When I got to the back room, he was sitting on the floor in the dark.

"What in the world?" I flipped the lights on, getting a look at his eyes. "Jesus, Beau!"

He backpedaled and hit the wall, throwing his hands up to stop me when I walked toward him. "Stay back, Charley. I'm dangerous."

His pupils had narrowed into slits. Like a cat's eyes. And they were that shade of bourbon again. But what really had the hair on the back of my neck standing on end was the color of his skin. He was shockingly pale.

I grabbed his hand before he could pull it away. His skin was warm, but it felt thin and fragile. "What happened, Beau?"

His face twisted. "I told you! I'm a vampire!"

The hinges on the door squeaked as Samuel slowly pushed it open and came into the room. He walked over to Beau and dropped down on his haunches, cocking his head to examine his eyes. "Have you been bitten?"

I hadn't told Samuel about what had happened to Beau in that jail cell.

Beau looked up at him with a nervous smile. "Can you help? I don't know what to do."

Samuel straightened back up. It was hard to tell if the look on his face was one of concern or confusion. "Who did this to you?"

"It was Victor Steele," I said.

"Steele? When did it happen?"

"A few nights ago. He broke into Beau's jail cell and attacked him. It was meant as a warning for me."

"Why didn't you tell me?" There was slight anger in Samuel's voice.

I took a step back. "I didn't think I needed to." Vampires bit people all the time and nothing happened. For different reasons. Sometimes to turn them, but more often for pleasure. "You bit me the other night, and I'm not a vampire."

Beau looked horrified. "You let Samuel bite you?"

"Never mind," I said to him without taking my eyes off Samuel's. I was starting to get a little angry myself, with his accusatory tone. "I took him to see Patrick right after it happened, and he didn't think anything was wrong with Beau either. And sunlight doesn't seem to affect him." Although he was sensitive to it lately.

Samuel stroked his chin thoughtfully. "You're sure it was Victor Steele?"

"Of course I'm sure. Why?" Then a terrifying thought occurred to me. "All of Victor Steele's progeny are dead. They started dying right after we killed him."

Beau gasped. "Dead? What are you talking about?"

"The change should have happened by now." Samuel looked back at Beau. "And he should be dead."

"Wait. Are you saying that Beau *is* a vampire?"

"I'm saying he appears to be stuck somewhere in the middle." He gave Beau a commiserative smile. "I think Beau is a halfling."

"What's a halfling?" I wasn't sure I wanted to know.

"Half vampire and half... something else."

My head shook with confusion. "Something else what?"

Samuel's brow furrowed. "I don't know, but it's the only reason he's still breathing."

Dog walked into the room with a bag of garbage in his hand. "Sorry to interrupt your vampire intervention. I need to take this out." He looked down at Beau on his way to the back door. "What the hell happened to you?"

I sighed. "I'll tell you after you take that out to the dumpster." The bag was starting to stink.

When Dog walked back inside, he had a box in his hands.

"What's that?" I said.

He tossed it on the desk. "I don't know. It was on the bottom step."

A strange feeling came over me as I picked it up. It was sealed with packing tape, but it didn't have a label on it. "Well, it's my bar, so I guess it's for me." I grabbed a knife from the drawer and cut the tape. When I pulled the flap open, I stumbled back and nearly fell over a chair.

Dog grabbed the box from the desk to take a look. For a moment he just stood there without moving. Then he stuck his hand inside.

When he finally pulled it out, I wanted to gag. "Is that what I think it is?"

"It's a heart," Samuel said, taking a closer look at the organ resting in Dog's hand. "And it came from a human."

A LETTER FROM LUANNE

Thank you for reading *Bloodlust Bites*. Charley's journey is just beginning, and I can't wait for you to see where she and the rest of Crimson's strange and unusual residents take you as their stories continue. Never a dull moment. I promise!

Stay up to date with my latest releases by signing up at the link below. Your email address will never be shared and you can unsubscribe at any time.

www.secondskybooks.com/luanne_bennett

The best way to support an author is to spread the word and leave a brief review. It really does make a difference, and I appreciate every one of them. Just a sentence or two is all it takes.

I love hearing from readers. Get in touch on my social media or website. And don't forget to follow me!

www.luannebennett.com

facebook.com/LuanneBennettBooks
instagram.com/luannebennettbooks
bookbub.com/authors/luanne-bennett
goodreads.com/lbennett14

ACKNOWLEDGMENTS

As always, a big thank you to the team at Second Sky and Bookouture for making things run so smoothly. Jack Renninson, you're a patient editor. Thank you for all the saves and for putting up with my stubbornness on certain points. Writing a book requires some give-and-take, and I think we found our middle ground with this book. And thank you to Noelle Holten for spreading the word about the Charley Underwood series. Your help has been greatly appreciated.

To my friends and family for their support. In particular, Sharon Marden, who has stuck around since high school. Vampires and witches aren't her thing, but she patiently nods her head and cheers me on, even when some of my ideas are a little off the wall. But I write fantasy. Anything less would be boring.

And to Bear and the rest of the four-legged bunch for being the best writing buddies a person could have. Those crack-of-dawn sessions would be terribly lonely without them.

PUBLISHING TEAM

Turning a manuscript into a book requires the efforts of many people. The publishing team at Bookouture would like to acknowledge everyone who contributed to this publication.

Audio
Alba Proko
Melissa Tran
Sinead O'Connor

Commercial
Lauren Morrissette
Hannah Richmond
Imogen Allport

Cover design
Damonza.com

Data and analysis
Mark Alder
Mohamed Bussuri

Editorial
Jack Renninson
Melissa Tran

Copyeditor
Rhian McKay

Proofreader
Maddy Newquist

Marketing
Alex Crow
Melanie Price
Occy Carr
Cíara Rosney
Martyna Młynarska

Operations and distribution
Marina Valles
Stephanie Straub

Production
Hannah Snetsinger
Mandy Kullar
Jen Shannon
Ria Clare

Publicity
Kim Nash
Noelle Holten
Jess Readett
Sarah Hardy

Rights and contracts
Peta Nightingale
Richard King
Saidah Graham

Milton Keynes UK
Ingram Content Group UK Ltd.
UKHW030623250924
448780UK00004B/55